# THEIR VIRGIN'S
# SECRET

THEIR VIRGIN'S SECRET, Masters of Ménage, Book 2
Shayla Black and Lexi Blake

Published by Shayla Black and Lexi Blake
Copyright 2011 Black Oak Books
Edited by Chloe Vale and Shayla Black
Print ISBN: 978-1936596-07-2

# THEIR VIRGIN'S SECRET

## Masters of Ménage
## Book 2

## Shayla Black and Lexi Blake

Enjoy exclusive excerpts from Shayla Black, Lexi Blake,
and Eliza Gayle at the conclusion of this book.

# Chapter One

*Present Day – Virginia*

Burke Lennox stood outside the two story house, his eyes narrowed in study. The gorgeous Victorian practically glowed, a warm welcoming sight in contrast to the frigid wonderland surrounding it. It was a huge damn disparity to the distress signal they'd received earlier. Right now, everything about this place looked perfect and cheerful. Beautiful—a lot like the woman who lived here.

Looks, Burke had learned over the years, could be very deceiving.

"She's still not answering her phone." His brother's voice cracked harshly through the chilled air as he tucked his phone in his pocket.

Cole was bone-deep tired. Burke could feel the weariness coming off his brother in waves. He was certain he reflected the same back, and that Cole felt it, too. Their mother had termed their odd, silent communication "Wonder Twins" powers. Burke didn't need to ask Cole how he felt. He simply knew. And they shared other feelings tonight. Desperation. Edginess. They both shook a little like an addict who'd been on the wagon for a long time and realized that he might just get one more coveted taste.

No doubt about it, they were both addicted to Jessa Wade.

"Should we knock?" Cole asked, sounding more uncertain than Burke could ever remember.

Cole was the darker one. He usually plowed through any given mission without ever letting on that he wasn't one hundred percent confident. But Jessa had knocked him on his ass, and just over a year later, Cole hadn't quite recovered.

It had been that long since either of them had laid eyes on the lovely girl. Burke still remembered the last time he'd seen her, naked in a hotel room bed, rumpled sheets around her. Her auburn hair had been a sensual contrast to the white pillow. She'd looked like an angel.

When he closed his eyes, he could still remember the scent of that room. Jessa always smelled like citrus, sweet and sharp. And that night she'd smelled like sex, like him and his brother because they had spent the whole evening inside her. In her pussy, her mouth, her ass. They had taken her over and over again, as though they could imprint themselves on her.

She'd been the most gorgeous thing he'd ever seen, ever touched.

He'd left her there with a promise that he'd be back. Cole had made the same promise, kissing her deeply before they'd gone.

In the last year, everything had gone to shit. God,

sometimes that amazing night felt like a fucking lifetime ago.

"Why would she leave us a distress message then not answer our calls? Shit. What if she can't answer the phone because that fucker she married is stopping her?" Cole asked as they walked across the yard.

Yeah. The fucker she'd married. Angus.

According to the reports they'd received from the investigator they'd hired to keep tabs on Jessa, she hadn't let the grass grow under her feet before moving on. Less than three months after they'd left, she'd traveled to Scotland, apparently met and married some guy named Angus, then returned to the States with him in tow.

Burke could still remember the day their fantasy of Jessa waiting for him and Cole had come crashing down. Their dutiful personal assistant of five years, Hilary, had kept Lennox Investigations running during their long operation in South America. They'd returned home, ready to hop a plane to New York and claim Jessa for good, but their assistant had delivered the terrible news their private investigator had dug up: Jessa was married. He winced at the memory and tried to console himself with the knowledge that he'd given Hilary an extra holiday bonus to atone for their bad behavior that day.

"He doesn't take good care of her," Burke muttered, wishing he could take something apart with his bare hands. God, he knew he had no right to be, but he was really fucking bitter that she'd married someone else. "He doesn't even shovel the damn walkway. She could break her leg just trying to get her mail."

"Which she clearly retrieved as soon as the storm let up."

Burke's gaze tracked the dainty footsteps in the snow directly to the mailbox, then back to the front door. It was so damn cold those footprints had frozen in the powder.

It hadn't been cold in South America. The weather had been hot, so humid he could still feel the thick air clogging in his lungs. The chill of the Virginia night should have been a welcome change, but it only brought home the fact that he'd spent the worst year of his life in a tropical hellhole doing a job that had cost him and Cole the only woman they would likely ever love.

But when they'd gotten the urgent call twenty-four hours ago, they'd come running for Jessa, anyway.

Last winter, as their case had led them to South America and they'd realized just how deep undercover they would have to go, they had left behind a phone number for Jessa to contact them in case she needed anything. While abroad, they'd left that phone with their friend and sometimes employer, Dex James of Black Oak Oil, along with instructions to keep it charged and to contact them immediately if Jessa called. Dex owed them a couple of big-time favors, and it seemed more appropriate to task the man experienced with security— and ménage relationships—than their assistant. That poor woman had enough to keep up with in their absence.

God, he hadn't expected to survive the op in South America. In fact, neither one of them really had thought they would make it. In the back of his head, Burke had hoped that Jessa would reach out to them. But she hadn't called. Finally, nearly a year after they'd last seen her, she'd sent a simple text, which Dex had relayed.

*Please. I need to see you. As soon as possible.*

Burke had instructed Dex to call and find out what

she needed, but she hadn't answered. She hadn't replied to a text back, either. Three planes, thousands of miles, and not a wink of sleep later, they stood outside her house, wondering what the hell was going on. If she needed help, why wasn't she turning to her husband?

Unless he was the problem... Had Jessa brought home a man who hurt her, who scared her so much she would reach out to two men who had left her so abruptly after a few brief days of heaven?

"There's no way to know until we find her and ask." God, he'd faced down some of the most dangerous men in the world, but one sweet-faced five foot three inch woman had him trembling.

Perhaps because that sweet-faced woman held way more in her hands than his life. She still held his goddamned heart.

He stared at the front door, his breath puffing out in little clouds. Jessa was behind that door. She'd built a whole new life for herself while they'd worked that op. She'd left New York and her school, found someone new. Jessa had utterly moved on, while he and Cole hadn't even begun to try yet.

The wrongness of the situation hit him. It felt like a blow to the chest. Jessa hadn't just moved down the road, but from one state to another, from one relationship to another. From one life to another.

"According to Dex, she didn't give us her new address. How did she expect us to find her?" How had he missed that? His brain was overloaded with possibilities.

Cole turned to him with troubled blue eyes. "She can't possibly have a clue that we know where she lives because we've kept tabs on her. Was she trying to get us to New York? Is this some kind of fucking game? It feels all wrong."

Burke was about to agree. Then the lights went out, all at once. Every last one of them.

"What the hell?" Cole tensed.

Burke could feel him shift. One moment Cole teetered on the edge. The next, his brother was a predator, his every muscle tense and every sense on high alert.

Scanning the area, Burke focused on small clues. Despite the fact that the house had suddenly gone black, the snow and the moon worked in tandem to illuminate the yard. He could see his and Cole's boot prints. They had already noted the line of smaller prints that ran from the front door to the mailbox and back. He would bet his life they were Jessa's.

But he saw another larger set that led from the side yard, then around the porch. The husband's? Why would he be creeping around the house and onto the outdoor space in January after a fucking snow storm? Keeping as silent as possible, he pointed them out to his brother.

Cole nodded, already on it. His stare followed the line of prints. Thick, heavy. They were made by boots Burke estimated were somewhere around size twelve, maybe bigger. Definitely not Jessa's. Probably not Angus's, given the location. Then who?

They followed the footprints and found something that scared Burke even more. Someone had stood by her big elm tree. From the number of cigarettes dotting the snow like nasty little scars on a blanket of white, that someone had been there for a while. Five butts. One still spiraled smoke into the frigid air.

"We need to get inside," Cole whispered. "Now."

Burke knew it, too, felt the wrongness. Something nasty was about to happen. The world seemed too quiet, as though simply holding its breath and waiting.

And then he heard the sharp female scream.

Burke took off, Cole right beside him. He hit the porch at a run and tried the door. Locked.

Another scream, high-pitched and primal. Jessa. Sweet Jessa, who wouldn't hurt a fly, was screaming. No words, just screams, as though the horror could only be conveyed by yelling.

Cole hit the door with his full force. It held strong. The door looked solid, and the glass in the middle was a thick stained glass. But the windows nearby looked to be regular glass.

There was a heavy potted plant sitting at the doorstep. With a grunt, he hoisted it up and tossed it through the big bay window. The glass shattered, the sound splitting the air. He hated making their entrance obvious, but he didn't see another quick way in.

Cole followed his lead, using his foot to shove glass free. He kicked at it, trying to make a man-sized hole. This maneuver had the potential to slice him wide open. Not getting to Jessa was far worse. Her screams echoed through the house now, followed by a loud thud. Burke leapt through the window, wincing as protruding glass cut him. The thick coat he'd bought for way too much money at Dulles protected most of his torso, but his knuckles burned with pain. He ignored it.

There was a loud hissing sound, and then Burke was assaulted by a ball of fur and rage. Big green eyes. Claws. He couldn't see it as more than a blur of moving animal parts, but that hiss registered as cat. Again, he was deeply grateful for the parka as the big feline clawed the Goretex, trying to climb Burke like a tree. Wishing he'd bought gloves, he reached for the animal. The cat scratched at him, but Burke took it by the back of the neck and tossed it across the room. It fell on the floor with a thud.

"Is that loud fucker a…cat?" Cole asked, SIG Sauer in hand, pointed at the animal who snarled and shook.

"Yeah. Probably Jessa's." She'd talked about buying a house in the country and getting a kitten. Apparently she'd done just that after meeting Mr. Fucking Right.

The furball whined, assuring Burke that it was still alive. He reached into his holster and pulled his own gun. The weight was reassuring in his hand. He flicked off the safety. "Where is she?"

Cole pointed toward the back of the house. "The scream came from the back, but not the second floor."

They ran together on nearly silent feet. It was difficult to see in the darkened house. The only light came from the windows of Jessa's kitchen, casting ominous shadows.

"Basement." Cole pointed down the hall.

Another scream had Burke running down the hall. His brain assessed the situation, asking all the questions. Was this a domestic situation? If so, how many pieces could he reasonably get Angus's body into with his bare hands? Or was it an intruder? If so, one or more? What did they want?

Was Jessa still alive? God, please let her be alive.

Cole kicked in the basement door. It was dark down there, too. The sharp scent of chemicals assaulted Burke.

Jessa screamed again, the sound so much louder as

they closed in. He charged down the shadowy stairs, his feet taking each step with a short jerk, his hand holding the railing. Cole was hard behind him. No damn way to be quiet now. Whoever was here could hear that they were coming.

What was that awful smell? Turpentine? Yeah, and a lot of it. He felt the moment his feet hit the bottom, his body jerking to stay balanced. A thin stream of light whirled around, seeking. Burke couldn't duck fast enough and was nearly blinded when it hit him, his eyes accustomed to the dark. He threw his arms over his face and pressed forward, nearly tripping over something that lay squarely in his path. A body. There was no way to mistake it for anything else.

"Get out! Get out! I already called the cops!" Jessa's voice sounded hoarse and shaky.

"Sweetheart, it's us." Burke took a step toward her.

"Get out! I have a gun." She wasn't listening. He couldn't see her eyes, but he could practically feel the panic screaming off her. And she was lying. He hadn't heard a shot, and Jessa didn't know shit about guns.

"Jessa," Cole barked in that voice that always let Burke know he was taking control and wouldn't tolerate an argument. "Stand down. You're safe, baby."

"Cole?" Her voice suddenly sounded so small. "Burke?"

"Yes." Burke breathed a sigh of relief. "Yes, sweetheart, it's us. You're safe. We won't let anything happen to you."

There was an ugly laugh from behind him. "Shows what you know, Lennox."

The voice made his blood freeze instantly. Who the

fuck would know his name without seeing his face? Unless this someone else had sent the text, not Jessa. And this someone had expected them to come running. Had they walked into a death trap?

"Give me some light on him, Jessa." Burke thought his heart rate would slow once he knew Jessa was alive, but now his pulse jacked up all over again.

The light shifted and illuminated the man lying on the floor. There was an enormous gash on his head, blood dripping everywhere, and he held his hands over his eyes.

"Who the fuck are you?" Cole asked.

"I'm no one. I'm nothing now that this bitch beat me in the head and caught me. Doesn't matter. I already planted the charges. This whole place is going to blow, and there's not a damn thing you can do. I didn't mean to go down with her. Fucking bitch."

"Charges?" Jessa's hand began to shake, the light bouncing.

"I recognize that asshole," Cole snapped. "He worked for Ricardo Delgado. What the fuck is going on? Delgado died almost a year ago in prison."

Burke's stomach turned. He'd assumed the world would be a safer place without Ricardo Delgado. How was the asshole reaching out with his violent fist from beyond the grave?

"Later," he snapped. "We need to leave before this house blows!"

The flashlight dropped, and Burke felt something whiz by him.

He picked it up and aimed the stream of light up the stairs. *Fuck.* Jessa was running. He didn't know where she was headed, but they had to get her out of the house damn quick.

Cole turned, his body a ghostly shadow in the darkened room. "Who the hell sent you?"

"Don't, Cole," Burke snapped. He had no idea when the charges were set to go off. It could be right fucking now. He didn't know if they were on a timer or a remote. The whole house could explode at any minute, and Jessa was running to god knew where. "As much as I'd love to interrogate this asshole, we don't have time. We have to get Jessa out of here."

"You'll never make it." The man on the floor groaned. "Bitch is going to get what's coming to her. Well, what's coming to you. Did you think you could fool anyone? You better pray my bombs kill her. If my boss catches her instead, he's gonna have a real good time with her."

*Boss?* His stomach turned. If this guy had been working for Delgado and was talking about a new boss… Fuck, this organization hadn't died. It had more lives than a fucking cat. Was there a new boss out for revenge? How could the bastard know about Jessa and the few precious days they'd spent with her?

He had a million questions, but no time to ask. They had to get Jessa out. If the man on the floor wasn't lying, they were all in grave danger. With a deep and angry regret, he turned and darted up the stairs just behind Cole, locking the fucker in the basement.

"Jessa!" Burke shouted.

"I can hear her going to the second story." Cole took off after her.

The light was better upstairs. Jessa had left the drapes open, and moonlight drenched the hallway in an eerie silvery glow. Burke ran beside his brother. They caught Jessa at the top of the stairs, Burke's arm going around her waist.

He'd dreamed of holding her again, touching her. Not once in those dreams did she kick and scream and fight like hell.

"No! Let me go, damn it."

"Jessa, calm down." Burke demanded.

"Let me go. I have to get him!" Jessa's voice sounded strangled in her throat. He could feel her hot tears hit his hand.

Her husband. She was fighting for him. She was clawing at Burke, scratching and fighting to get to another man. His chest buckled. His heart fucking ached. Jessa was in love with someone else and willing to die to save this douche she'd married who'd left her alone to fend off an intruder in the basement by herself.

"I'll get Angus, Jessa," Cole growled. "Where is he? You let Burke get you the hell out of here."

"Angus? Oh, god. He was in the living room sleeping earlier."

"On it." Cole turned and ran down the stairs.

"Oh, god. Please. Let me go. I have to get Caleb!" Jessa fought again, bringing her foot forward, knee up to her waist, and kicked back with all her might.

*Caleb?* Burke groaned as her heel met his cock with surprising force. He released Jessa and dropped to his knees.

She wasted not a minute. As Burke strained to get to his feet, she disappeared around the corner.

Goddamn it. Burke forced himself up. From downstairs, he heard a loud hissing and Cole swearing.

Apparently his brother had found the damn cat again instead of Jessa's husband. He let it go. If Cole couldn't handle a kitty cat by himself, then all those years as a SEAL had been for nothing. Ignoring the pain, he ran after Jessa.

Who the fuck was Caleb? Another lover? Why hadn't the investigator's report mentioned him? And why did Jessa think he was worth dying over?

He lurched down the hall. There was no question where she had gone. Only one door was open at the end of the corridor.

Rage churned in his gut. She'd obviously never loved him or Cole. He'd tortured himself nightly with visions of her, sweet and warm and loving, while she'd run happily off and apparently found not one but two men. Well, he and Cole had shown her the pleasures of ménage. He guessed it was all their fault. She'd taken to it beautifully even though she'd been a virgin at the time.

Yet he couldn't walk away. He was going to get Jessa, Angus, and this Caleb person out of here if it was the last fucking thing he did. Then he was going to find some way to get on with his life.

He stalked into the room, unwilling to take no for an answer. This time he would be ready for her struggles. He would drag her out, kicking and screaming if he had to. He opened his mouth to explain to her just how this was going to go. Then he stopped dead in his tracks. He'd expected to be in her bedroom. This room was filled with stuffed toy puppy dogs and smiling lions. And a crib.

Jessa stood, tears coursing down her face as she grabbed a swaddled, slightly fussing baby to her chest. She'd slung a big tote bag over her shoulder.

"I'm ready. We can go," she headed for the door. "As soon as Cole gets Angus. You should warn him. Angus gets twitchy around new people. He scratches. Uhm, and he throws up. He's really a terrible cat."

*Cat?* Angus wasn't her husband, but a cat. And Caleb was… Even in the dark, he could tell the baby was small and very young. He came to one stunning, jaw-dropping conclusion.

Caleb was their son.

\* \* \* \*

*One year earlier, Christmas Eve – New York City*

Jessa Wade eyed the ladder.

"Ah, my nemesis. We meet again. Don't think you'll best me tonight. This time, I will use you and put you away and come out of the experience unscathed."

Fat chance of that happening. And, awesome, she was all alone on Christmas Eve, talking to a ladder. Nothing said "pathetic" quite like that.

She glanced around the bar of the Hotel DuMonde. Her aunt owned the place, but she was off in Barbados, her usual holiday haunt. Jessa had been invited to go, but she'd had the ridiculous dream that her parents would get into the Christmas spirit and call her home.

Clearly, that wasn't happening. So she was alone in the hotel bar, cleaning up and doing inventory. And dealing with a ladder that had it in for her.

She picked up the martini glasses. They belonged on the highest shelf. The DuMonde's bar was a magnificent concoction of glass and silver and mirrors that reached to the top of the twelve-foot ceiling. On a normal night, she wouldn't have to climb up there. Those glasses on the highest level were almost decorative, but the night before had been a blowout of the highest order. Some corporate party. Every damn glass in the place had been used, and the cleaning crew had only just finished with the dishes.

She sighed. She'd sent the bartender and the waitress home. She'd always heard that Christmas Eve was a big night for bars, but she didn't have any customers. It hadn't seemed right to keep those two away from their families when the money would be crap.

"Miss, a Scotch, please? Single malt."

She nodded, grateful for the distraction. Working would keep her mind off the fact that her mother and father had turned her out, and the only relative still speaking to her in the world was currently windsurfing in the Caribbean. She turned to look at her new customer and practically forgot to breathe.

He stood at the bar, six feet four inches of pure sex. Dark hair, vibrant blue eyes, shoulders that seemed to go on forever.

"Miss?" He stood there with a knowing smile on his sensual mouth.

Jessa forced herself back to reality with an inward sigh. He knew how ridiculously hot he was. And she knew she was a waitress who needed to lose a couple of pounds. Her mother's admonitions came back to haunt her. She would never land a man at a size 12. Her mother, the bulimic. She viewed throwing up as a socially polite way to stay thin. Why had she wanted to go home for the holidays?

Jessa turned on her best sassy-girl smile. "There's no

poor single malt. So you get your choice of expensive or even more expensive."

"Oh, a sarcastic one. Cole, we hit the jackpot."

There were two of them? A second wretchedly hot man walked up to the bar, identical to the first. This one shrugged out of his coat. It took all Jessa had to not fan herself despite the cold.

Cool blue eyes assessed her. She stared back. The two brothers weren't totally identical now that she really looked. There was something more reserved about this twin. The first had a sensual ease about him. She found nothing gentle in Cole. He was pure predator.

So why didn't she want to run? Why was she wondering what it would be like to be caught by him?

"Saucy, huh? Well, I know how to fix that." His smile was razor sharp, dangerous. "Now, we'll both take two fingers of the Glenlivet, fifteen year."

So richer. Even more expensive. She reached for the bottle, catching two of the heavy crystal glasses the bar reserved for premium beverages. She poured the Scotch out, measuring carefully before sliding them toward the men.

"Here you go. Feel free to sit anywhere. It looks like you're my only customers tonight." She tried to give them a friendly but dismissive nod. She might be inexperienced, but she wasn't an idiot. If they weren't with family, one or both of them might be looking for a lonely heart to share the sheets with tonight. If so, they would hit on her because she was the only woman available here. Best to sidle away now. "Just yell if you need a refill."

The first man leaned forward, smiling. "Why should

we yell when we could sit right here and talk to you?"

Yep, they were definitely going to hit on her. She opened her mouth to shut them down, but Cole put out a hand to stop her. He looked at his brother, and she could see them having a whole conversation with small facial tics and raised eyebrows. She stared in fascination.

Finally, they looked back at her. Cole seemed to have won the silent argument. He nodded her way, his hand on his glass. "Thank you, Miss. We'll let you know when we're ready."

She watched as they walked to the corner of the bar. Damn, their back sides were just as nice as their fronts. Each man wore tight jeans that molded to perfectly formed butts.

She sighed. They were way, way out of her league. She didn't even have a league anymore. Once it had been the debutante circle, but she'd hated the wealthy social whirl she'd been brought up in. She'd hated it so much that she'd turned down a job with her father after the prescribed years at Wharton Business School. She'd played the dutiful daughter, but she couldn't stomach the idea of working in big business. She'd just wanted to paint.

And her parents didn't want an artist for a daughter. They had cut her off with the ruthless precision that had gotten her father to the top. They wouldn't take her calls or allow her on the grounds of their estate until she came around and accepted a job with the corporation. They had thought she wouldn't last two weeks on her own, but a year later, she could see the end of the tunnel.

In a few months she would turn twenty-three, and her trust fund would kick in. Her parents couldn't stop it, couldn't touch it. *Thank you, Grandmere.*

Jessa turned away from the hotties. They weren't for her. She had a job and a life. That would have to be enough. Well, she had a job anyway, and right now it involved the hated ladder. She could see herself grimacing in the mirror. Yeah, that was attractive. She grabbed the last of the martini glasses and prayed for grace.

She started up the ladder, every step a careful move. She passed the rows of vodka and whiskey, rose above the gin and tequila. She stole a look toward the bar. The men sat there, leaning toward each other, speaking in whispers, in their own world. She wished she had a sister or someone to talk to. Despite the heady freedom of the last year, she had to admit she was lonely. She'd pulled into herself and her work, shutting out everyone.

Would it be so bad to get hit on? Would it be so horrible to finally give in to a man? She was twenty-two years old and out on her own. There hadn't been time for a relationship, and she'd clung to the idea of true love. Well, that wasn't anywhere on the horizon. Did she really want to turn another year older without knowing what a man's touch felt like? No. Ugh, she sounded pathetic. She felt pathetic, too.

And clumsy. Her foot slipped on a rung. She hadn't been paying attention. The glasses fell out of her hand, crashing to the floor. The ladder teetered and she began to lose her balance. She groped but had nothing to hang onto. She began to fall.

*Crap.* She didn't have the money to pay for an ambulance, and she'd need one for sure after she fell ten feet. She shrieked and braced herself for impact. She was going to land on shattered glass, cut herself wide open, and break something vital. It was going to hurt so freaking much.

She woofed, the air thudding from her lungs as she landed not on hard tile, but in two strong arms. She looked up into Cole's eyes, her heart racing. He was the most beautiful man she'd ever seen, even more so up close. The only one who matched him was his twin, who stood behind him, a slight smile on his gorgeous face.

"What's your name, baby?"

"Jessa," she breathed. The way he'd called her baby made her shiver.

"Well, Jessa. You should be more careful," Cole said.

Yep, she should definitely be more careful because right now, it felt like she was in big trouble.

\* \* \* \*

The woman was serious trouble. Cole knew it the second he laid eyes on her. He'd been a man who cleaned up messes for too long to not be able to recognize that a mile away. He'd done it first for the Navy, then with his brother privately for a lovely fee. This little waitress was the softest, sweetest mess he'd ever had the pleasure to hold.

Pure, gorgeous trouble.

The firelight illuminated Jessa's soft features, making her creamy skin look warm and inviting. She took the drink in her hands, still shaking a bit.

"Thanks. I shouldn't be drinking." She took a little sip anyway. Her face twisted up in the most adorable grimace. "Ugh. People pay top dollar for this?"

"Scotch is an acquired taste, but it'll get rid of the shakes. Sip a little."

Burke sank into the couch opposite from Cole and Jessa, a knowing smirk on his face. His little brother was just loving this, Cole knew. Burke had wanted to pounce on the redhead the minute he'd laid eyes on her. Sometimes his brother thought with his cock. But they were too close to Delgado right now. Six months on the case and they were finally going to meet the man who had taken their clients' cousin. They couldn't get involved with any woman, no matter how beautiful or sweet. No matter how her big green eyes pulled at him or how sexy her curves were. They couldn't.

"I swept away the broken glass. Everything is fine now." Burke grabbed his own drink. He didn't struggle with the liquor the way Jessa did. Burke could imbibe it all night and never notice the effects.

Thanks," Jessa said quietly. Her attention moved between them as though trying to pick apart their differences. "I still shouldn't be dipping into the stock."

"Don't worry. We won't tell," Burke said with a wink.

Cole had to stop himself from rolling his eyes. Burke was using his seductive voice. He wanted this girl bad.

"Tell me something, sweetheart. Why aren't you at home with your husband?"

"Smooth," Cole said under his breath. One of Burke's shoulders came up in a negligent shrug.

Jessa's lips curved up in a smile. She held up her left hand. "No husband. And before you come up with a subtle way of asking, no boyfriend either. I'm on my own this Christmas. My family, well, let's just say they aren't exactly in the picture."

Cole didn't like the sound of that. She didn't look like she could be much over twenty-two or twenty-three. She was living in midtown Manhattan on her own? "Are your parents gone?"

She shook her head. "No. They don't approve of my choices. I decided to pursue art instead of big business. So they cut me off. Luckily, my aunt runs this place. She gave me a room and a job."

"So you live here?" Cole heard himself asking. He needed to make sure she was okay, then haul his brother upstairs to their room so they weren't tempted to linger all night and work their way inside her. Yeah, that was a solid plan. Instead, he found himself settling into the comfy sofa and inching closer to her delectable body. She would be small in between them. She could nestle in the middle, her breasts against his chest, her ass cradled against Burke.

He glanced at his brother as Jessa talked about her room and the view of Central Park. Burke arched a brow. *Come on, brother. She's right here. She's gorgeous and she's alone. We can take care of her. We can make her feel good tonight.*

*And what about tomorrow?* They'd had the argument moments before Jessa had taken a header off that rickety ladder and almost broken her neck. Cole had just finished his "we're-undercover-and-things-could-get-dangerous" spiel when he'd seen her begin to fall. He'd moved faster than he had in forever, getting there just in time to catch her.

Not that Jessa Wade wasn't tempting. And so

fucking luscious she made his mouth water. She was attractive in a way no woman had been to him before. She also wasn't a good-time girl. That fact was stamped all over her face. She was the kind of girl a man dated and cared for. Eventually married. She absolutely wasn't the kind of girl a man shared with his twin brother for the night. She looked so innocent. Hell, she would probably run from a ménage if he even suggested it. Not that many women truly wanted one. Sure they fantasized, but when push came to shove…not so much. Then when he added his other proclivities on top of it… Cole winced. Definitely not.

Of course, he mused as she and Burke chatted, his friend Dex had found a woman to share with his two brothers. And they all topped her. Hell, he and Burke were practically normal compared to the James gang.

But that wasn't the real issue. He and his brother were knee-deep in a case involving missing girls being sold into sexual slavery.

At the mental reminder, he sat back up. Jessa didn't need to get involved in that. God, she really didn't need to get involved with them, but fuck if he wasn't salivating over her. He'd met her thirty minutes ago, and he already wanted to know about her childhood, her favorite foods, and how she'd feel around his cock. *Too damn dangerous.*

"Gosh, that's enough about me. I'm going on and on." She blushed, the color invading her skin like a rosy blanket. He'd been surrounded by tough women for too long. Jessa's softness was getting to him.

"We don't mind, do we, Cole?" Burke's question was pointed like a dagger. *Don't fuck this up. I want her.*

26

Cole wanted her, too, but he was more realistic. Burke was an optimist who thought the world crapped rainbows and that the sun really fucking would come out tomorrow. Cole refused to believe that shit until he saw it. Burke seemed to have gotten all the positive DNA their parents had to give, leaving Cole the broody realist. Still, his mouth moved as though it agreed fully with his cock, rather than his wholly sensible brain. "No, we don't mind, baby."

She shook her head. Her gorgeous hair was a deep, burnished auburn. It would look beautiful spread across his pillow while she took his cock. "I'm boring. Poor little rich girl. Not so rich anymore, but that's okay. Where are you two from?"

"Dallas," Burke replied. "We grew up in the suburbs, but we live in the city now."

They had a very nice condo with a great view. It had three bedrooms. One for Cole. One for Burke. And one ridiculously oversized master bedroom for the women they shared. They hadn't shared in a while beyond the occasional one-night stand. Cole was sick of them. He wanted more. But now wasn't the right time. Jessa wasn't the right girl, as much as he wished otherwise.

The conversation flowed, more easily than ever before. Cole found himself drawn out. Usually he let Burke do the charming and he just joined in for the sex. But he really talked to Jessa. He and Burke joked about their childhood and the twin pranks they'd pulled on friends and teachers alike. God, he'd forgotten the fun they used to have. He'd been so mired in the job, the danger. How long had it been since he just relaxed?

He took another long sip of the Scotch as a slow

Christmas song began. Burke got up and held out his hand to the woman in front of him. Damn, his brother was smooth.

"Dance with me?" Burke asked, a hint of a smile on his face.

Jessa looked around as though assuring herself that they were truly alone. "Sure, but on one condition. I get to dance with Cole, too. Don't say no. It's Christmas Eve, and I want a present."

He never danced. He wasn't sure he could. And yet after Burke finished twirling her around, Cole found himself standing and taking her in his arms, his hand curling around her little waist. He practically sighed when she put her head on his chest.

What the hell was he doing? This was a bad idea. But the moment she snuggled closer, he knew there was nothing he could do except sway to the music. The snow fell on the streets of New York just outside the window and, despite the danger and the world's seedy underbelly awaiting him, Cole Lennox felt happy for the first time in what felt like forever.

# Chapter Two

*Present Day – Virginia*

The chill in the air hit Burke's lungs like a knife to his chest. He forced the air in deeper as he moved them outside the house, toward the car.

Them. Not just Jessa, but Caleb, too. Their son. That truth hammered at him. If the tiny mop of black hair didn't give the kid away, there was the fact that Jessa hadn't been around any man for the last year except Angus. Who, it turned out, was a cat. So it was a pretty damn good bet that Caleb was theirs.

After all, she'd only had two lovers in her whole life.

How had the PI they'd hired gotten it so wrong? Another question for another time.

Cole stood by the car. "I couldn't find anyone else in the house, just that fucking cat. He's in the car. Obnoxious furball. I called the cops. Let's get Jessa away from the house in case that idiot of Delgado's is telling the truth." Cole frowned as Jessa hurried to the car, the baby swaddled in a blanket against her chest. "Is that another damn cat? No more. The first one has a seriously bad attitude. I won't mention his breath."

The blanket came loose, and Caleb gave a little gurgle, his tiny head turning to take in the newcomers. Unlike his mother's grim face, Caleb's was happy. He grinned, showing off a completely toothless mouth.

"That's a baby, Burke. What the hell?" Cole's mouth hung open.

If the situation hadn't been so goddamn dire, he would have reveled in his brother's surprise. Nothing ever fazed Cole. Even when they had been jumped by ten armed Taliban fighters in an Afghan backstreet, he'd merely killed his half, shrugged and said "I told you so" before popping open another black-market beer. Burke took the opportunity to snatch the keys from his brother's hands. "Your powers of observation are staggering. Get in the car. We need to reach the cops. Jessa, get in."

She shook her head. "I'll take my car. I have Caleb's car seat."

Burke felt his patience slipping. Did the gravity of this situation not register with her? "You will get in the car now. Goddamn it, Jessa, someone just tried to kill you. That asshole said he planted charges around your house. Charges mean shit blows up," he snarled. "We don't know how many eyes are on us right now. Get in the car."

Jessa's head swiveled as though she was looking for whoever stood in the darkness watching. Her hand went protectively over Caleb's head, cupping his whole body against hers. She eased into the front seat of the rented SUV and closed the door.

Cole simply stared at the spot where she'd stood.

Burke glared at his brother and opened the driver's side door. "Snap out of it."

He pointed back to the house. "We're just going to leave her husband to die? She won't forgive us."

"There is no husband. Angus is the fucking cat. She wasn't trying to save her husband, Cole. She was trying to save Caleb, her baby."

Cole frowned and shook his head. "That baby can't be more than a few months old. If there's no husband, that means…"

"Caleb is our son, yes. Well, one of our sons, biologically speaking." Biology didn't matter in their case. A simple paternity test would tell them nothing of importance. This was *their* son. It didn't matter who had actually provided the DNA. Like everything in their lives, it was shared and identical. Caleb was theirs.

"How the fuck did the investigator miss this?" Cole snarled. "We've been getting reports for a year, and he didn't think to mention that she was pregnant? And why would he think Angus was her husband? Can't the idiot tell the difference between a man and a cat? She had our *baby*. She's been dealing with this all alone."

Burke totally understood his brother's fury. He felt it himself. The idea of Jessa in a hospital giving birth without either of them to hold her hand made his heart clench and his stomach turn. "Not here and not now. We have to go."

Cole nodded. Burke could feel the anxiety coming off his brother in waves, but there was no time to calm him down. Burke breathed a sigh of relief when Cole acquiesced, getting into the back of the SUV and shutting the door with a hard thud.

Burke hopped in, his heart twisting at Cole's words. God, his brother was right. Jessa had been alone. They hadn't even known she needed them, despite all of the money and effort they'd put forth to have a PI keep tabs on her. How the hell had this happened?

He started the car. The night around them was quiet. The baby cooed. The cat meowed. But the tension between the human adults was thick and pervasive. Burke gunned the car, and it flew down the road.

"Which way to the police station? I'd rather not be sitting ducks here waiting for them." The station would be a good, safe place to stash Jessa and Caleb while he and Cole figured out which of Delgado's henchman had taken over the business and was looking for a little revenge.

"When you get to the road, take a left." Jessa's hands trembled. Caleb patted his mother's face as though he could sense her fear and was trying to soothe her. "Why are you two here? Who was that man? He came out of nowhere. I was cleaning the brushes after working on a painting, and he just walked in."

That explained the turpentine. "What did you hit him with?"

"I was using some ashes from the fireplace to mix with the paint. It was kind of a metaphor. I'd put them in a bucket and used a poker to stir them. Luckily, I'd brought those to the basement to clean, too. So that's what I hit him with."

Their Jessa fought tough when she had to. "You did the right thing, sweetheart."

"Who was he? What does he want with me?"

Burke opened his mouth to answer her, but the sound of an explosion cracking through the air cut off his reply. A loud boom split the night, and the rearview mirror showed the brilliant flash of orange and red as Jessa's pretty house went up in a ball of hot orange flames. He could feel the heat of it down the road. Burke fought to maintain control of the car as the earth shook. All around him pieces of the house rained down. They hit the top of the SUV like pellets striking tin.

"Oh, my god." Clutching Caleb, Jessa cut her gaze out the back window to gawk at the devastation that used to be her home. She gasped, and tears coursed down her cheeks.

Burke was about to reach for her hand when his cell rang. Goddamn it. He didn't need to deal with his secretary or a client now. Jessa was far more important. He ignored it.

"Answer it, Burke," Cole said gravely. His own cell was in his hand as he held it up so Burke could see it in the rearview mirror. "I just got a text. Marco Delgado wants to talk to you."

*Marco Delgado.* The bastard Ricardo's son. At least he knew who they were dealing with now. But it wasn't good—at all.

"Who are you talking about?" Jessa asked, panic rising in her tone. "Who is Marco? Is he the bastard who just blew up my house?"

Burke was glad to see Cole's hand on her shoulder. His brother whispered to Jessa, attempting to soothe her. Burke dealt with the problem at hand as he drove, gravel crunching under the tires, and answered. "This is Burke."

"Welcome back to the States, Mr. Lennox. You've been gone for so long. I trust your flight went well." There was a silky satisfaction to Marco's voice.

"You're the one who sent us the text." There was no

doubt. Jessa hadn't called them when she was pregnant. She hadn't texted yesterday. In fact, she'd never meant to talk to them again. He compartmentalized that realization to deal with at a better time.

"I thought it was time we talked. You killed my father."

"No," Burke corrected, his jaw tight with tension. "I put your father in jail for selling young women to bordellos in South America. Some guy doing life shanked his ass."

A fitting end, in Burke's opinion. It had saved them all the effort of a trial. He and Cole had seen what happened to the women the elder Delgado had sold to his friends in South America. He could still see their haunted eyes. Some had died. Others had lost their souls. He didn't feel a moment's remorse about that fucking bastard's fate.

"You might not have thrust the blade in, but you made it possible. Family means something to me. Did you think I would let this pass?" There was a slight pause on Marco's end. "Since your parents are gone, I went after the next best thing."

It took everything he had to keep his hands on the wheel. He knew what Marco meant. Jessa.

"How the fuck did you know about her?" Burke held the phone in one hand, his other tightening on the steering wheel. He didn't want Jessa to hear this conversation, but he didn't see a way around it. He had to figure some things out and quickly.

"You have several people on your payroll, Mr. Lennox. Employees are not family. I learned that the hard way. It's quite easy to bribe someone. You should know.

That's how you got to my father. By the way, I already killed Michael. He died squealing like a pig."

*Michael.* The young man had been an up and comer in the Delgado organization when he'd had an attack of conscience. Michael had been willing to push the man's drugs, but not to sell young women into prostitution. He'd become their informant. And his conscience had gotten him killed. "What do you want? I'll meet you. It was my doing. I took the case. I'll take the blame."

A disbelieving snort ripped across the line. "It's never just you, Lennox. It's you and that brother of yours. I thought long and hard about killing one of you, but that lets one of you off too easy. I wanted both of you to suffer as I have, grieving. Then I remembered the delectable Miss Wade. Unfortunately, by the time I tracked her down, she was pregnant. I believe in karma. Nor am I completely cruel. I don't intend to harm the boy."

"You don't think killing his mother would harm him?"

Beside him, Jessa gasped, a trembling sound full of fear. Burke tried to block her out and focus. Almost as soon as he wished for Cole to comfort her, his brother's hand caressed her shoulder again. Burke listened to Marco again.

"I'm making a deal here, Burke. I'm a reasonable man, but I like to gamble. I've been setting this game up for months now. The pieces are all in place. We begin soon."

God, this fucker was insane. But smart. Burke brought the car to a stop at the edge of the road. Once he had Jessa secured by the police, he would call in the feds.

He began to turn left.

"Do you really want to go that direction, Mr. Lennox?"

Burke stopped, pressing his foot on the brake. The asshole was still watching them? Of course. He must have eyes on the entire road that led up to Jessa's property.

Her gaze darted around them nervously. "What's wrong? The station is about a mile to the west. Let's go."

He shook his head. "We have eyes on us."

Cole's gun was back in his hand. Through the mirror, Burke could see his brother watching. His free hand came up, gently pushing at Jessa. "Get on the floorboard, baby. You and Caleb stay down."

Jessa went without a protest.

"I'm not coming to you as long as she's in the car," Burke insisted. "Let me take her and the child to the police, then I'll come in. So will Cole."

There wasn't a word of protest from Cole, but then Burke hadn't expected one. As usual, he and his brother were in synch. They loved Jessa. They would do anything to save her, even die.

Marco chuckled. "You can take her to the police, but as I said, I've been setting up this game for a while now. Ask Miss Wade if she knows a friendly deputy named Fred?"

He looked down at Jessa. "You know someone named Fred, sweetheart?"

She nodded. "Yes, he's the man we need to talk to. He's my friend. He's on the police force here. He'll know what to do."

No. He was a fucking small-town spy. A puppet, and

Marco was pulling the strings. He'd given them this one hint to prove it. Burke turned away from her, speaking into the phone again. "I get your point."

"Then you should also know I have friends in the FBI, DEA, and just about every other agency where there are underpaid employees. Oh, you might be able to find the good ones, but do you really want to take that chance?"

*Fuck*. His eyes met with Cole's in the mirror. He could see plainly that Cole was following the logic of the conversation without hearing it.

"No police? No feds?" Cole asked, his voice tight.

Burke shook his head slightly.

Cole cursed. He knew how fucked they were. They could take the chance and risk Jessa, or they could run on their own.

"What do you want, Delgado?"

Marco's voice went ragged. "I want my father back, but since that's not going to happen, I'll settle for you feeling just as fucking bad as I do. I am going to kill your girl. If you follow my instructions, I'll leave your son out of it. If you don't, then he'll be collateral damage. I've already given you proof of my good will."

"Really?"

"Yes. I waited to blow up the house until you'd taken the child out. I'd rather not kill the boy, but I will if you force me to. You have twenty-four hours to lose the kid. After that, I come in with guns blazing, and I don't care who gets a bullet."

"You do understand that if you hurt her, Cole and I will never stop hunting you."

"Ah, then our game can go on. I was rather counting

on that. Twenty-four hours."

The line went dead, and Burke felt his stomach roll. The road stretched in front of him. Three choices. Left to the police, right to the highway, or straight into god knew what. *Fuck.* What if he chose wrong?

"He wants to kill me." Jessa blinked up at him from her crouched position. It wasn't a question.

"Yes." There was no way to protect her from that. "You can sit back in the seat, sweetheart. We have twenty-four hours to stash our son someplace safe, or he'll kill Caleb, too. I believe him."

"Marco. The son. The gambler. Fuck. I hadn't even thought about him. He didn't seem even vaguely interested in his father's business." Cole scrubbed a hand across his face, his eyes bleak.

"He's interested now," Burke confirmed. "In revenge especially."

Jessa sniffled as she got back to her seat. "We need supplies. Everything I had for Caleb just blew up. We need a car seat and more diapers and clothes. Formula. He needs formula. He'll get hungry soon." She tightened her arms around her son. "God, please let me wake up. Please let this be a bad dream."

Burke's heart ached. "Sweetheart, I'm going to fix this."

Her eyes met his, anger making them flare. "Don't call me that. Don't *ever* call me that again. I want to go to the police, but I can't, can I? Some guy hates you and wants to take it out on me, and I can't go to the police because this jerk has them on his payroll. My nice friend, Deputy Fred, is working for this guy."

"According to Marco, yes." He would give anything

to take away the betrayal on her face. To remove the danger to her life. "All law enforcement is off the table if we want to be one hundred percent sure of your safety."

"Seriously? Even the FBI?"

He swallowed, bile in his throat. This wasn't how he'd pictured their reunion. "We can't go to them or anyone else. We're on our own, Jessa."

"And he'll spare my son if we take him someplace out of the way?" Jessa's voice caught, but she had so much strength. She was a mother protecting her child, but she was still listening, assessing, processing. She wasn't trained for this, but she was handling everything amazingly well. "If I give myself to him, he'll spare my son?"

"You're not giving yourself up." Cole barked.

"We won't let anyone hurt you," Burke assured her. "I believe him about not wanting Caleb involved. He would have blown up the house before we fled if he didn't. We need to get the baby someplace safe. I know you aren't going to like this, but we have friends, powerful friends. They'll absolutely protect Caleb. And we'll protect you."

He reached for her, but she pulled back. "I don't like any of this, Burke. But I don't seem to have a choice. It's just me and Caleb. My parents won't lift a finger to help us. My only friend here turns out to be working for the enemy. You two are my only option. I want to talk to these friends of yours. Call them. I can't just turn over my son to anyone."

Cole made the call, murmuring, "Gavin James will reassure you, baby. You'll want to talk to Hannah, his wife, too."

Burke watched Jessa as she glared at Cole, hand outstretched for the phone. They'd brought her to this place. God, she was never going to forgive them.

He made a right turn toward the highway that would lead them back to D.C. Gavin would come. Dex and Slade, his brothers, would do anything to protect Caleb, too. Hannah would cuddle and love their boy as soon as she heard the story. And if the worst happened, and none of them made it, the James family would take care of Caleb.

Burke resisted the urge to drive his fist through the windshield. God, he wanted to know his son. He'd already missed out on months of Caleb's life, and now he had to give the boy up? For how long—days? Weeks? He refused to think it could be longer. Or forever. And the thought of Jessa in danger made him even more insane. He began to understand Cole's violent streak.

His mind wandered as the miles flew by, images of Jessa laughing played through his brain. Happier times.

Would she ever smile for them again?

\* \* \* \*

*One year earlier – New York City*

Jessa hurried inside the little Mexican place, her portfolio in one hand. She was running late, but she couldn't help the smile on her face. The last few days had been amazing. Burke and Cole had spent Christmas Day with her, taking her for breakfast and lunch, then sitting in the bar while she worked the night shift. They'd had to work the next day. According to her friends on the maid staff, they had been at the hotel for a week, coming and going at odd hours of the night. She wasn't sure exactly what they did for a living. They had told her something about the import export business, but she just couldn't see them behind desks. They had too much energy. They were too…dangerous.

She hadn't figured them out yet.

And she might never. She really didn't care why they were here. She was just damn happy they were. The restaurant was loud, vibrant, and proudly proclaimed that they sold the largest margaritas in Manhattan.

"Jessa!" Burke stood up, waving her over to the small table he and Cole had claimed.

With a smile, she made her way toward them, brimming with excitement.

Burke's friendly smile lit up the place. Cole was darker. She saw them for what they were, halves of a whole. Just looking at them sparked her creativity. And her libido. Was she really considering doing something about that? Would she really have the courage to be honest with them?

"I ordered you a margarita. I hope you don't mind. I remembered you said you liked mango." Cole didn't smile as he offered the insanely huge glass to her. He was slightly grave, almost as though he expected her to refuse him.

She slid a hand over his, delighted at the relief that crossed his face, the way he relaxed. "I love mango. Thank you. And I have something to celebrate."

Burke sat back down. The two men surrounded her. She felt oddly safe when she was between them, which happened often. Whenever they took a cab, she found herself in the middle. Walking through Times Square the night before, she'd had a brother on either side of her, their big bodies a bulwark against the encroaching crowd. She fit between them. She wanted to see just how she fit between them in bed.

"You're blushing," Burke said with a grin. "Is this celebration turning naughty?"

She was sure she flushed even more. "I sold a painting."

Cole's eyes flared. "Jessa, that's wonderful. To a gallery?"

She nodded. She was going to have a work in a gallery in Soho. It seemed too good to be true. "I didn't really sell it, but the gallery owner agreed to put it up. I have a painting for sale! She wants to see more. I can't believe it. I know it's small, but it's a start."

She was practically humming with glee.

"It isn't small," Cole said, his voice a deep rumble. "It's huge. That's great."

"It's amazing, Jessa. I can't wait for your first show," Burke said with an enormous smile on his face.

God, if she wasn't glowing, it was only because it was impossible for human skin to do it. She was pretty damn sure she now understood what it meant to beam with happiness. They were so kind to her. She had spent the last several days basking in it, desperate for this giddiness to never end. She thought about them all day…and all night. Now she knew what she wanted.

Both of them.

She'd waited. Well, not exactly waited. Sex just hadn't come up. She'd spent so many years trying to please her parents by becoming the perfect student. She'd graduated from high school early. She'd gone to college too young to really fit in with her classmates. Since coming to New York, all she'd been able to think about was keeping a roof over her head and food in her belly.

It was time to have a relationship. This might not last more than a week, but she would know what it meant to belong to someone.

"We should celebrate," Burke offered. "I think dancing is in order."

Cole groaned. Though he hadn't been much of a dancer, she'd loved being held in his strong arms when they'd danced on Christmas Eve. He'd sighed and called himself an elephant with two left feet, but being close to him made all the grousing worthwhile.

"How about a movie?" Cole practically pleaded. "Or a show. I'll go see a show. See, I can compromise."

She took a long sip of margarita, wishing she had a tequila shot instead. Liquid courage, she needed it. Instead, she drew in a breath and plowed ahead. "I think we should all go to bed."

They both stopped, and in perfect synchronicity, swung their dark heads her way.

"What did you say, sweetheart?" Burke asked.

She licked her suddenly dry lips. "You heard me."

"I heard that you want us in bed." Cole stared at her like a lion about to pounce on something soft and furry. "All of us. Together."

Yep. They just stared in silence, those blue eyes hot, dissecting. Embarrassment swamped her. Had she been wrong about them? Had she let the fantasies in her head color her judgment?

Burke's eyes narrowed. "You want a ménage, sweetheart? Have you ever had one?"

She shook her head. Oh, she didn't want to admit more than that. Surely she could fake some experience. She'd seen movies. Mostly R rated, but Jimmy from concierge services had once had a party where some of the guys had gone to the back and watched porn films. She'd sneaked a peek. A long peek.

"Do you understand what you're asking for?" Cole asked. He'd completely closed his expression off. Burke had relaxed, his sensual expression almost decadent. But Cole sat stiffly, his whole body seeming to shut down.

Jessa fought the tears that threatened. She'd thought they both wanted her. Cole, it appeared, was just being nice. If she couldn't have them both, she wondered if she shouldn't just walk away. It would be like accepting half of something. Ever since that first night, she'd viewed them as a single unit. She forced a bright smile on her face, hating the sniffle that came out. She'd gotten herself in this mess. She could get herself out.

"Just kidding." She forced a laugh. "Sorry, guys. I'll stop telling bad jokes, I promise. Let's just have a nice dinner, then I'll head back to the hotel since I have to work tonight."

"No, you don't. Eric is working. I saw the schedule." Burke raised a dark brow.

She was a horrible liar. She couldn't hold the sunny pretense anymore, not with humiliation stinging every corner of her body. "Why don't I just go?"

Grabbing her coat, she stood.

"No," Burke barked with a ferocious frown. "Jessa, sit back in your seat. We need to talk about this."

Slowly, she set her coat aside and eased back into her chair. "There's nothing to say. If you don't want—"

Cole snorted, his gaze looking as if it had heated up ten thousand degrees in the last minute, though the rest of his body remained frozen.

But Burke spoke. "Sweetheart, we're not shocked by the idea. Trust me. We've done this a time or two. We prefer to share lovers, but you're very young."

"And very inexperienced." A fact that obviously made Cole grit his teeth.

"How would you know that?" Jessa challenged. It was true, but his assumption annoyed her. She fought the urge to get up and walk away—end this whole embarrassing evening. "You don't know my history. I could have had a bunch of lovers."

Both men snorted. Somehow they made it seem elegant.

"Sweetheart, if you've had more than a couple, I'll eat my socks." Burke watched her closely, then paled. "You have had a couple, right?"

She took another long swallow, wringing her hands. They could see right through her. No sense in lying now. "Fine. All right. No."

Cole clenched his jaw and sent Burke an accusing stare. "I told you the minute we met her that she was a virgin. Goddamn it."

Jessa suddenly felt alone. The twins were looking at each other, their eyes speaking while their mouths stayed closed. Sometimes they retreated into a private world where she couldn't follow.

Moments later, Cole stood, buttoning the jacket of his suit coat. "It's time for me to leave. She's too innocent for what I need. I can't put that on a virgin. Besides, she's more interested in you. I'll go back to the hotel. We do have work to do, remember?"

Burke's face fell. "Can't we talk about this?"

"What the fuck is there to say?"

She sat there watching them, wishing she hadn't ever spoken up. They could still be sitting here having a nice dinner and planning to go to a movie or a show together. But no, she'd needed to forge her own path. She always did. She could hear her mother complaining in her head about what an ungrateful daughter she was for turning aside all their plans for her and making her own. Painting, not international business. Two men, not one.

Jessa listened to them argue. She was on the outside now, but then she'd felt that way all of her life. Even at the lavish parties her parents had thrown, she'd been on the outside. When she'd tried to fit in, going to a school she didn't want to go to, studying what she didn't love, it had been terrible. Always on the outside.

The best thing she'd ever done had been defying her parents. She'd stood up and gotten kicked out, but it had been for the best. She would have suffocated if she'd stayed. She'd been happier since leaving all that behind and didn't regret her choice for a minute. So why was she retreating now instead of fighting for what she wanted? Wasn't she simply proving Cole's point that she was too inexperienced to handle him?

She wasn't a child. She might not have slept around, but that didn't mean she couldn't deal. She looked at him, really looked at him. She tried to look past her insecurity and see him as he truly was. Jessa gnawed at her lip. How would she draw Cole in this moment? His face was all broad lines and bleak angles, but under the pain she saw gentleness lurking. Yearning even. She would love to draw him, then transfer that image to canvas, the colors of her palate bringing everything to life. Time slowed for Jessa. She studied him as she would a subject she painted, looking deep. Bold colors. He required them. He wasn't as black and white as he tried to portray. He was a million shades, just like his brother.

He turned to her, and she realized his carefully blank stare wasn't about her. He was scared of something.

Maybe she was fooling herself or seeing what she wanted to see, but his sudden refusal didn't make a lick of sense. For four days, Cole had been right beside her, eating her up with his stare again and again, silently seducing her with the desire in his remote eyes. Burke was more blatant, but she hadn't imagined Cole's attraction to her. What was he afraid of?

"Goodbye, Jessa." His voice sounded ragged. "You have a good time with Burke. He'll take care of you, baby."

"No." The word slipped out. Now that she'd truly seen him, she knew deep down that if he let his fear win, it would haunt them all.

Burke smiled, but Cole scowled, suddenly on the offense.

"No?" Cole challenged, leaning in. "What is that supposed to mean?"

Stopping him in his tracks emboldened her. Jessa stood, certainty running through her veins, settling her face inches from his. She was still nervous, but no one got what they wanted by giving up. And she just knew she was doing the right thing.

"It means that you two are a packaged deal. I won't settle for half, and that's what I would get if I only gave myself to Burke. I would get the good and the gentle, but there'd be no balance."

"Fuck balance. Stick to Prince Charming. I'm a ruthless bastard." Cole's eyes narrowed. His fists clenched.

She was getting to him.

"I don't need gentle all the time," Jessa assured him softly. "I need what you can give me."

Cole sunk his hand into her hair and pulled slightly. "I don't have gentle in me. I'm brutal. I'll demand everything from you, then want more. I'll want to give you a little bite of pain, then I'll get hard at all your little cries. I'll want to tie you up, spank your ass, and share you with Burke. You're right; we aren't exactly whole. And we won't do this for fun. We'll consume you."

They needed to share her. They balanced each other in every facet of their lives, even sexually. As an artist, she understood symmetry completely.

She smiled at Burke who sat patiently, awaiting the outcome of their little skirmish with a faint smile. She drank in strength from his encouragement before rising up on her tiptoes and brushing her mouth against Cole's. The kiss was a soft, sweet caress of lips that had her longing for more.

"I'm game to try every dirty, dark thing you can think of," she whispered. "But can you ease me into it? Let me have a lover…" She grinned. "Or two. Then I'll be ready."

"Fuck." Cole fisted her hair in his hand and pulled, pinning her with a wracked blue stare for a long moment. She could sense the war inside him, the need clashing with the caution. Then he took her mouth.

Jessa held on for dear life. She'd been kissed before, but not like this. She'd been pecked and bussed, and a couple of boys had thrust their tongues at her, but Cole dominated. His kiss made her really understand the word. He was in total control. Using his tongue, he surged in, not asking but demanding entry. She gave it because she wanted him inside. She ceded control to him, riding the wave. Her body flooded with a hot swell of desire as his tongue rubbed against hers in a silky slide. She could feel her pussy tightening, her folds warming and softening. Moistening. It was unlike anything she'd ever imagined before. With those hard, sinewy arms, Cole dragged her in, his chest impossibly solid and wide against her breasts. His hips slammed against hers, and she could feel the long, thick line of his erection.

He wanted her. She trembled. God, she wanted him.

He lifted his head, his lips almost a snarl, his voice a harsh rasp. "Kiss Burke. Let me watch you."

Burke stood, smiling and open, as though something had blissfully fallen into place. "You should do what he says, sweetheart. He's incredibly bossy."

For all the dark passion she'd felt with Cole, a light-hearted joy stole over her as Burke took her in his arms. He kissed her every bit as passionately, but playfully. He nipped, flirted, toyed with her lips, his fingers sliding down her back to rest playfully on her ass.

Everything. She could have everything. It was right here in her grasp.

Burke's tongue found hers and they danced, a teasing waltz of desire. When he released her, his deep blue eyes found hers, and he kissed her forehead with such tenderness it brought tears to her eyes.

"Thank you," he whispered.

"Take me to your room. I want you both so much." She reached out to Cole. He hesitated only a moment before he took her hand. She smiled brightly at him. Their circle was complete.

# Chapter Three

*Present Day – Virginia*

Cole stared at the baby in his arms. The baby peered back with blue, blue eyes. God, he'd seen those eyes in the mirror thousands of times, but he couldn't remember a time when they'd looked so wide and trusting.

Caleb. Their son. God, they had a son. Would that fact ever just sink in, or would it constantly spark at him like a live wire?

The baby reached out, arms and legs kicking in his puppy-print footie pajamas. A tuft of dark hair covered the kid's head. He cooed, making all sorts of strange sounds that went straight to Cole's heart, which had been doing weird flip-flops ever since Jessa had asked him if he'd like to hold the baby when they had stopped for gas.

A big box store loomed in the near distance. While gassing up, Jessa had used the restroom. Now Burke was inside the store, grabbing everything Caleb would need for the next few days. Cole didn't like hanging out in the parking lot like a sitting duck, but he wouldn't leave Jessa or their son unprotected.

Thankfully, Gavin James was already on his way to a small, private airfield just outside of D.C. They had lucked out when they'd called him. The oil executive was in New York. He'd dropped everything to meet with them and take them to Dallas, where they would leave Caleb behind and start this nasty game of Marco's.

He only had a few hours with his son. The knowledge that he might never see the boy again carved a gaping hole in his chest.

"Da!" Caleb said with a grin on his face.

"Yeah, I bet you say that to all the guys," Cole joked grimly. Caleb also seemed big on Ma, Ba, and Na.

At his feet, the cat meowed. At least he'd stopped making that strangled choking sound. Angus didn't travel well, but with the car stopped, he'd decided to curl up on top of Cole's feet and purr like an engine.

How in the hell had he been left babysitting a cantankerous cat?

"Da," Caleb said with a forceful kick of his legs.

If anyone he knew could see him now, they'd laugh their ass off. Cole had to grin. And cuddle his son closer to his chest.

"He likes you," Jessa said as she slid back into the car. She was wearing Cole's coat, her small body swallowed by it, but he couldn't have her cold. Despite the chill outside, the car was still warm and toasty, so she shrugged out of the coat as she got in.

Cole had to swallow before looking up into Jessa's eyes. "I don't know why."

Jessa frowned. "I don't want to wait out here while Burke shops. I know what Caleb needs."

"We've already had this argument. You'll draw

attention since you're wearing pajama bottoms and a tank top. Without a bra. And yes, I can tell." In fact, he could see the outline of her pert little nipples even through the near darkness, and it was driving him crazy. Cole squirmed, but he couldn't let his dick do his thinking now.

She crossed her arms over her chest. As if that was going to stop him from looking. He snorted.

"I told Burke that if I'd gotten the 'we're going to try to kill you tonight' memo, I would have dressed for the occasion."

That sharpened his focus. "I'm sorry you got tangled up in this."

Those words weren't enough, but he couldn't say or do anything more at the moment. Caleb settled his little head on Cole's shoulder. The baby sighed, and Cole's hand covered the baby's back as he enjoyed the motion of Caleb breathing in and out, calming him, soothing him.

"What exactly am I tangled up in? Look, I figured out you weren't really businessmen. I wasn't ever sure if you were criminals or cops."

Something in between, perhaps. "Neither. If you thought we were criminals, why the hell did you get involved?"

Her eyes rolled, weariness plain in the green depth. The gas station neons illuminated her skin. "Stupid, I guess. I was a kid. I thought I was in love."

Well, he'd tried to tell her. She'd finally wised up, it seemed. She hadn't called or texted when she'd had their baby. She'd just cut them out of her life. "We're private investigators. We were on a case in New York when we met you."

"With all the lies you fed me, I figured there was something going on. Do you want me to take him?" Jessa asked, eyeing the baby.

No. This might be his only moment with Caleb. "He's asleep. I don't want to wake him."

"All right," she replied with a deep sigh. "I think you owe me some explanations. What kind of case were you on? When did it end? And why did you show up at my house tonight?"

"We were hired by three gentlemen from a country called Bezakistan. It's a small country just outside the Middle East."

"I've heard of it." She frowned. "Don't they practice polyandry, multiple men with one woman? Do you guys have a network or something? A *Craig's List* for sharing?"

He felt his eyes narrow. "I'm trying to explain. If you can't give me a little courtesy, then maybe you should wait for Burke."

She bit into her bottom lip, a sure sign that she was nervous. God, he loved that lip. "I'm sorry. I'm on edge. Please continue."

"We met Rafe and Kade after a mission. I'd helped their brother, Talib, out of a tough spot. When their cousin went missing, they called. She was only eighteen."

"A missing girl? Did you find her?"

"Eventually. Her name was Alea. She went to New York for college. Six months of daily phone calls to her mother, and then nothing. When we started looking into it, we realized that there was a pattern. Alea wasn't the only girl missing. She'd been working in a club. She kept her wealth and privilege a secret. Everyone thought she

54

was just another student living in an NYU dorm. That was what did her in. Ricardo Delgado ran coke for one of the big Colombian syndicates, but that wasn't enough for him. He decided to start trafficking women."

"Oh, my god." She put a hand over her mouth and sat back. "That's terrible."

"He would find pretty homeless girls or foreign students and clean them up. He would display them in his club, and if they worked out, he would sell them to private owners or South American bordellos. We posed as wealthy men looking for a private pet."

"That sounds dangerous. God, Cole, you could have been killed."

"Almost was a couple of times. We videotaped our meetings with Delgado when we purchased a young Asian girl. She's home with her family now. Delgado had friends in the FBI, but it didn't matter at that point. They couldn't risk their positions when we had everything on tape, ready for primetime news, so the fucker finally went down."

Jessa wiped at her eyes. "Why didn't you tell me about your mission when we met?"

"And get you involved in all that danger? Hell, no! We never intended to drag you into any of this. We thought we were careful, but Delgado's son found out about you. Do you remember the morning we had breakfast at the Waldorf? The morning after we first made love? Remember the man who walked up as we sat at the table?"

Her eyes widened. "Yes! Oh, my god, *that* was Marco? I heard Burke say his name when he was talking on the phone. He blew up my house?"

Cole nodded. Jessa was a sharp woman. "His father was the man we put in jail. He died shortly after, before he could go to trial. Burke and I were down in South America looking for Alea. According to the authorities, Delgado's murder in prison was payback from another cartel."

"And you found her?"

Cole took a deep breath, his hand going to the baby's back. So innocent. Fuck, he would do just about anything to protect this child from the shit the world could throw. "Finally. Shortly before his arrest, Delgado had shipped Alea off to South America. We went down there and spent three months just trying to find her. It took another month of greasing the right palms so we could eventually rescue her. We pulled her out of a Colombian brothel in one of the worst parts of Medellin. She was strung out on drugs and had almost wasted away."

He didn't tell her how she'd begged them to kill her. She hadn't wanted to go home, just get her next fix—or die. She hadn't looked a thing like the vibrant college girl in the picture her cousins had given them. She'd been a shell.

"If you found her within a couple of months, why were you gone for a year?"

He hesitated. Fuck, he didn't want to tell her how hurt he'd been after being told that she'd married. The kicker was, all that time apart—he and Burke had been almost entirely at fault. Eventually, they'd have to confess how stupid they'd been, just not minutes after seeing her house explode. "After we found Alea, we discovered there were another ten families who'd lost their daughters. We brought Alea back home, and her cousins opened their wallets to help us reunite these other women with their loved ones. The families didn't have the money to pay us, but Tal, Rafe, and Kade did. In the end, we found seven broken women and three bodies. We gave a year of our lives to this fucking case, and we barely scratched the surface of the misery Delgado spread. I feel like we failed. It wasn't enough."

Jessa sat back, solemn. "I had no idea. I thought you had just left."

"We've been buried in drug dealers, slavers, and pimps. I've felt so goddamn dirty for the last year, dealing with drug dealers, slavers, and pimps. And we didn't want to drag you in deeper."

"I can understand that you had a job to do, but tell me something, Cole. Do they not have phones in South America? You couldn't find one?"

*If you had been married, a phone call from your lovers might have pissed off your husband.*

But that hadn't been the only reason. Instead, he said, "And risk those bastards tracing the call back to you? No way, baby. You don't understand how corrupt these men are or how far their reach extends."

She nodded reluctantly. "Since they just blew up my house, I have to suppose you're right. You could have given me your real names before you left. All I had was a phone number written on a tiny piece of paper. Do you know how easy it was to lose that number?"

She'd lost it? "Did you try to call us?"

"When I found out I was pregnant, yes. But I shoved the paper into my jeans that morning when you left. Housekeeping took my jeans and washed them. No more number. So I waited. I was sure you would come back.

You said you loved me." She sniffled but kept her tough-girl armor around her. "I believed you."

Cole closed his eyes, feeling low and sad and twenty kinds of pissed off at fate. "Fuck."

"I used every dime I had saved up to try to track you down so I could tell you I was pregnant, but no one knew Burke and Cole Carlisle."

"It's Lennox. Our last name is Lennox," Cole conceded.

Jessa simply shook her head as though it no longer mattered. "When I was about seven months along, I gave up. I figured the whole song and dance about coming back was just a line to ease your way out of my life."

"Jessa…"

"Don't." She held up a hand, looking moments away from tears. "I understand why you did it. I'll concede that I would have tried to keep you. I would have cried and begged and been a general nuisance, so you were probably right to lie."

"We didn't want to lie, Jessa." His voice started to rise, but Caleb shifted. He had to stay calm for their son's sake. A son they had to protect above all else.

"All this dangerous stuff… This is your life, isn't it?"

"Yes." This was why he'd stayed away from women like Jessa. "Burke and I joined the Navy when we were just kids. Our parents died when we were fifteen. We had one relative, a cruel bastard of an uncle. He went through any money our parents had, not that it was a lot. When we turned eighteen and the state support stopped, he gave us twenty bucks each and told us to get out. We joined up and made the SEAL program. We served overseas and started our own security company when we were discharged. Burke took heavy fire in Afghanistan. He lost some use of his left arm. The Navy cut him loose. I followed. We take rough cases. It's the only life I know."

It was brutal and ruthless and never stopped.

"I can't live this way. You know that if we survive this, I can't be around you. I can't let Caleb be around you. He's my baby. He's my only family. I can't risk him. I want you gone as soon as possible."

Cole felt the cold like never before. He'd told her from the start. He'd warned her. He'd fucking tried to walk away from her, but she'd drawn him in. Damn it, he'd loved her. And now she was telling him he had no place in his son's life? Bitterness crept through his veins. Caleb was so sweet, so trusting. The kid's fathers had been in his life for less than two hours, and what did he have to show for it? His house in rubble, and he was on the run. He was about to be separated from his mother. Yeah, Cole saw that he'd been real fucking good for the kid so far.

Jessa's lip trembled. "I'm sorry. I didn't mean that. I'm twelve kinds of freaked out right now. I really did try to call you and Burke because I thought Caleb needed his dads. Can we not make any decisions right now?"

But she'd already made the smart one. Cole pulled Caleb off his shoulder gently and handed him to Jessa. "Take him."

As soon as the baby's soft, sleeping weight left his arms, he clenched his jaw and exited the car. Fuck. He might never hold his son again, but she was right. Caleb deserved better.

Jessa followed, the coat back around her body. She'd

tucked Caleb inside, only a tuft of hair visible. "Cole?"

"I'm no good for him. I never wanted a kid in the first place."

He hadn't—at least in the past. But now he wanted Caleb desperately. He wanted Jessa. Even that stupid cat who had thrown up everywhere. He wanted the goddamn white picket fence, but his life didn't work that way.

Caleb turned his little head, pushing at the coat around him. His sleepy eyes sought Cole. That innocent gaze felt like a stab in the fucking heart.

"Just do what we tell you and you'll be with him again. You won't see me after this." He would disappear. He would walk into Colombia and save as many abducted girls as he could until he found that bullet with his name on it. Burke would stay. He'd said as much that day in the Mexican restaurant. Burke had been willing to take Jessa without Cole. Burke loved her. He was way fucking smarter.

"I got everything on the list." Burke approached, pushing a full cart. At the tension in the air, his eyes shifted, narrowed, quickly figuring out the situation and assigning blame. "What did you do?"

Cole shook his head. He wasn't having this fight. She was Burke's now. Burke would charm her, say all the right things. He would take care of her and Caleb.

And Cole would protect them all from afar.

When Jessa started to cry, Burke wrapped his arms around her. Cole turned away.

This was for the best. He wasn't good for anyone. His uncle had drummed that into his head for years, and given the ugly things Cole had done to survive and put money in the bank, he couldn't disagree. Jessa and Caleb would be better off if he disappeared from their lives forever.

* * * *

*One year earlier, December 28 – New York City*

Jessa wanted to have sex—with both of them. Burke was pretty sure his cock was going to explode. And he was pretty sure his heart wasn't far behind.

She was different. He'd known it the minute he'd set eyes on her. Cole was just a stubborn bastard. But Jessa had quickly figured out exactly how to take him down.

She turned as Burke closed the door to their suite. "Is it okay if I use the bathroom first?"

He practically laughed. She looked so soft and sweet. She was perfect, and right now she was perfectly scared.

He pulled her into his arms. The minute he drew her close, she softened against him. "Yes, sweetheart. Take all the time you want. If you want to wait, we'll wait. We can still go out, you know. Nothing has to happen right now."

"Burke is right, Jessa. Nothing has to happen at all. We're not going to be mad," Cole assured, his voice low.

"I'll be mad." Jessa frowned, turning her face up to his. "I'll be very mad. I was promised sex."

He kissed the tip of her nose. "I think we can handle that."

She nodded and pulled away. "I just want to freshen up is all. Give me a couple of minutes. I promise you that I want this. I want you both."

She disappeared into the bathroom.

"This is a bad idea." Cole was always the voice of

doom.

"Shut up, Eeyore. She's made her decision." Burke looked at his brother with a sigh. "I really like this girl."

"You think I don't?" Cole challenged. "I'm crazy about her. I don't think I've ever…"

Cole didn't finish his sentence, but he didn't have to. Burke understood precisely how he felt. He felt it, too. Jessa was special. In fact, she just might be the one. The ease with which she'd handled Cole's withdrawal into himself proved it. She understood and accepted that they were a strange package deal. Burke couldn't remember a time when he hadn't had his brother to rely on—and in many ways to take care of. Cole was more thoughtful, but he brooded. He'd let their fucker of an uncle crawl in his head, and he carried scars on his heart. Burke often had to pull him out of the darkness. Maybe Jessa could finally convince his brother that he was not only worthwhile, but perfect.

Of course, Cole was the one who had Burke's back and had risked everything to save him in Afghanistan. Cole was the one who had taken care of his ass, leaving his own military career behind when Burke had taken an IED. Burke might be more functional, more charming, but he couldn't do much without his brother.

"I know the timing sucks," Burke offered.

"We have a meeting soon where we're basically buying a human being. These people are dangerous."

"We're saving a girl. We're not the bad guys here." And he wasn't about to let the best thing that had happened to them slip through their fingers. Jessa didn't have anything to do with their undercover work. They would catch the bad guys, save the girls, then come back and claim their own woman. End of story.

"And what happens if we find out Alea has already been transported to South America? You know it's unlikely that she's still in New York. We have to find her. We owe it to her cousins. Fuck. We owe it to her."

That was Cole in a nutshell. He wanted to save the whole fucking world. He might be dark, but he truly believed in the light. "We'll find Alea and bring down Delgado, but I want Jessa. Don't we get some reward for all the shit we do? Doesn't the universe owe us one little slice of happiness? A goddamn future?"

He knew it sounded selfish, but he had to believe that the battles he'd fought for his country and his fellow man would net him a little happiness. He needed to believe that one day he could lay down his gun and sink into a happy marriage and family, even if his picket fence didn't look all Normal Rockwell.

"Hey." Cole put a hand on his shoulder. "I understand. I want her as much as you do. I want her so fucking bad. But I'm scared. I don't think I can change. I need some dark stuff. Maybe not tonight, but sooner or later." He paused. "I don't want to hurt her. I'll leave her to you. I'll handle the business, and you can be happy."

Always the damn martyr. "I don't—"

"What about what I want?" Jessa asked.

Burke turned and saw her standing in the bathroom door wearing nothing but the luxurious robe the hotel provided. Her auburn hair lay against the soft white velour. She'd tied the robe at the waist, but it still gaped, showing porcelain skin and the hint of round breasts.

"He's being a self-sacrificing idiot," Burke said. There was no other way to describe it. His brother huffed and sent him a dirty look.

Jessa merely smiled, looking on with a lazy, sexy indulgence. "He's good at that. But I won't have it."

"Jessa…" Cole began, his brow furrowing.

"We covered this," Jessa said. "I want you, Cole, no matter how brooding or dark. I don't just want Burke's vibrance. I can be difficult, too. I'm not always sweet. Seriously, I'm on my best behavior. But I can be stubborn. When I feel like I'm in a corner, I come out scratching and clawing. I can get lost in my work and forget people exist. I'm not perfect. Can you handle that?"

"I can." Burke was so fucking proud of her. He'd known her for such a short time, but she'd filled up his whole heart so quickly. Sweet and funny and brave. She was smart and talented, and she knew how to handle them. That was so fucking sexy to him.

"You're sure?" Cole asked.

Burke watched her gather her patience. "Yes."

Cole hesitated, drew in a deep breath, then... "Strip."

His brother's inner caveman had emerged, and for the first time, Jessa's confidence faltered. Her hands came up to the flaps of the robe, nervously pulling them together.

"Don't, sweetheart," Burke coached. "You've handled him beautifully so far. Don't stop now. Drop the robe. He wants to inspect you. I want to look at you, too. I want to see the body that's going to belong to us soon."

"You made your choice, Jessa," Cole said, standing shoulder to shoulder with Burke. "This is how it's going to be. We're in control. We'll treat you like a princess. We'll indulge you, but here in our bed, you're going to submit to us."

"I promise you'll enjoy it, sweetheart. We'll take care of you. Just trust us."

With trembling fingers, she pulled at the ties of the robe and let it fall to the floor.

Burke caught his breath. She was beautiful, all luscious curves and breasts and perfect skin. She stood there, biting her lip, waiting for them to say something.

"You're gorgeous, sweetheart." Burke couldn't take his eyes off her.

"Turn around," Cole choked out, twirling his finger to mimic what he wanted.

Jessa took a deep breath and turned, giving them a spectacular view of her backside.

"God, that is a gorgeous ass," Cole said.

"Perfectly heart shaped." Burke was calmer now. This was going to happen. His brother was in. Now that Cole had seen her naked, heard from her own lips that she wanted him, and she'd shown him trust in baring herself, there was zero chance of him walking away. "We need to prepare it."

Jessa looked over her shoulder. "Prepare what?"

"Your ass, baby," Cole explained. "We won't take you together tonight, but eventually, we want to fill you up."

"I'll take your pussy, sweetheart," Burke explained, voice low. "I'll work my way into your tight little cunt. You'll think you're full then, but then Cole will start in on that sweet backside. Then he's going to fuck your ass while I take you pussy. Over and over. Or the other way around."

Her mouth opened. Then she closed it in apparent

shock, but desire lurked there, too. "I'm glad you're not triplets."

"Turn around again," Cole commanded.

Jessa turned and stared at them. "It would really be easier for me if you two were undressed as well. I'm feeling a little lonely here."

Cole ignored her, eyes narrowed and focused right between her legs. "Her pussy is shaved. How many virgins are bare?"

Jessa's skin flushed a pretty pink.

True, but Burke sure liked the view. "Her skin is exquisite. Imagine what her ass is going to look like after we paddle her."

Burke could see her, bent over and accepting Cole's discipline. His cock twitched. Maybe he would wield the paddle, too. He'd never really wanted to before, simply enjoyed watching his brother do it, but he wanted to be responsible for Jessa, as well.

Cole walked over to her, still staring down at her perfectly naked pussy on display. "Did you shave for us?"

She nodded. "I read that men like it."

"Do you know why men like it?" Burke asked, enjoying her slightly nervous demeanor.

He'd never thought about virginity before, he and Cole having lost theirs at sixteen to an adventurous woman who lived in the same trailer park as his uncle, but now he could see the appeal. Later, when Jessa came into her sexuality, she would be a force to be reckoned with, a goddess. But he loved this brave little nymph, too. All of Jessa's sexual self would belong to them—the temptress and the girl just opening her wings. The thought did strange things to his heart.

"Uhm, I think they like to look at it."

A knowing grin stretched across Cole's lips. He'd finally relaxed. "I do like to look at it. I'm a little perverse."

"A little?" Burke prodded.

Cole shrugged. "Okay, a lot. But that's not the only reason. I think she knows, and she just doesn't want to say it. Tell me the truth, baby, why did you shave your pussy?"

They were crowding her, one on each side, but she didn't back down. Burke leaned in and kissed her lips, a soft little touch of flesh on flesh. He played, his lips skimming hers, then retreating. When Burke released her, Jessa turned and accepted Cole's kiss. His brother's tongue surged in, never one to simply play. Jessa was breathless when Cole let her go.

"Answer me."

Burke touched her, his hand skimming down from her shoulder to her hip, leaving goose bumps along the way. Her nipples tightened, and Burke swore he could smell the musky scent of her arousal permeate the air.

He let his hand slide from the delicious curve of her hip to the mound of her pussy. Sweetly wet. He closed his eyes. His mouth watered as he leaned in, letting his nose find her neck. "Tell Cole why you shaved your pussy."

"I heard that men are more willing to do things down there if there's no hair."

He felt a grin split his face as he slipped his fingers through her folds. More arousal coated his fingers. She was getting hot. He was already blazing. "What things?"

She sighed. "You know."

"I don't," Burke teased. He found the jewel of her clit and ran his thumb over it. Jessa jolted, a little cry falling from those plump lips.

"I do. She wants you to eat her pussy, Burke." Cole's hand slid beside his own.

"Cole," Jessa gasped. "That sounds so dirty."

"It is dirty. But I want to hear you say it. Do you want Burke to eat your pussy? He'll get his tongue in deep. He won't miss an inch of your cunt. He's going to lap up all that cream you're making and demand more. I'm going to love watching. How's that, baby?"

Her voice was shaky as she replied. "I—I… That sounds incredible."

"Then ask him nicely," Cole commanded, face stern.

Jessa turned to Burke. "Will you…kiss me?"

Cole raised his brow, then landed a sharp smack across Jessa's ass. She jumped, a little huff leaving her mouth.

"He spanked me." Wide-eyed, Jessa smoothed her hand across her bottom.

"You disobeyed," Cole pointed out. "And there's more where that came from if you're a bad little girl. Now ask correctly."

She turned to Burke a bit nervously, her green eyes so beautiful and clear. "I'd very much like for you to eat my pussy."

Joy threatened to overtake him. He lifted her up, his arm going under her knees, pulling her against his chest. She was a pleasant weight in his arms, and suddenly Burke was goddamn excited about the future. He set aside all his worries about Delgado and the case. No one would think a thing about Jessa. As far as Delgado knew, he and Cole were only interested in very young, well-trained slaves.

Jessa was perfect for them. She was the one. He knew it deep down. They'd claim her tonight, and as soon as this case was over, they'd return and claim her forever.

Burke settled Jessa on the enormous bed, satisfaction pouring through his veins. Wearing a smile as primal lust pounded inside him, he took her ankles in his hands and spread her wide.

* * * *

Jessa felt the soft comforter at her back, contrasting with the hard man on top of her. Burke had spread her legs and settled himself between them. She stared up at him, wondering how she'd gotten so lucky. These men called to her in a way no single man had or could. They were pieces of a puzzle she'd been looking to solve her whole life. She fit. She finally fit.

Burke lowered his mouth to hers, his lips brushing them. She could feel his erection gently nudging against her. He was big, but she wanted him. She wanted to do away with the whole "virgin" thing and be their woman in every sense of the word.

As she wrapped her arms around his neck, she silently admitted that she wasn't being smart. She'd only known them for a few days. But they were already in her heart.

She returned Burke's kiss, need sweeping over her, and bucked her hips to his in silent entreaty. She was fooling herself if she thought a few nights with them would do. Already, she wanted a lifetime.

Burke broke away and started to kiss his way down her body. She shivered as his lips swept over her neck, his tongue grazed her collarbone. He caressed her, seemingly fascinated by her skin. Then he touched her nipples, a tender glide of his thumb. She gasped as he pinched one while his tongue circled the other. She'd never guessed how much sensation the little buds could feel. When Burke pulled her nipple deep in his mouth, she felt it in her aching pussy. She was getting wet. So wet. She closed her eyes and let Burke's touch bathe her in heat.

And then Burke's fingers were replaced with another mouth. She looked down. Cole nuzzled her other breast, and she arched helplessly at the hot, jagged need they created. Two dark heads worked over her, sucking at her nipples, their hands playing at her mound. Someone's fingers slipped inside her while another toyed with her clit.

With a last long suck, Burke released her nipple. His tongue delved into her navel, licking a line all the way down to her pussy. Cole growled at her breast, the sensation rumbling along her skin. He bit at her sensitive little tip, taking it between his teeth.

A little pain was all right by Cole. The way he did it, she liked it, too. When he'd slapped her ass earlier, all she'd been able to think about was what it would be like to lie across his lap, immobile, and take the sting of his palm on her bare backside. Even the thought excited her.

Cole sat up and began unbuttoning his shirt. Jessa stared. With every inch he revealed, she couldn't help but notice that he was ripped with pure, hard muscle, every inch of flesh a testament to his strength and

determination. Broad shoulders. A sculpted chest. Big
biceps. Flat, tight abs. He was a work of art. A tattoo of a
dagger, the hilt ornate and detailed, decorated his left
arm, and she touched it. Someone with a very steady
hand had spent hours crafting this image onto his skin.

"You don't get out of the Navy without a little ink."
Cole shrugged out of his shirt, letting it fall to the floor.
"Burke has an identical one."

*Naturally.*

The thought died when Burke pulled her folds apart
and licked at her clit. Then she couldn't think at all
anymore. Tingles erupted across her skin. Fire spread
through her system.

"Does that feel good, baby?" Cole's hand was on the
buckle of his belt. Jessa watched as he slowly pulled it
open and eased his slacks down.

*Good?* Burke tormented her. His tongue lashed at
her, then he suckled the sensitive bud. He traded little
teasing licks with long sucks at her clit. A burning wave
of feeling built inside her. It was huge and foreign and a
bit overwhelming.

Cole stopped his slow striptease and growled at her.
"You stay still. Let Burke have his way."

She'd been moving, she realized, unconsciously
trying to escape the need starting to overwhelm her. "It's
too much."

"You're just getting started. You move again, and
I'll spank you red. Do you understand? Burke, let's finish
her off."

As though they had planned it, Burke moved lower,
spreading her legs even wider with his shoulders, and
fucked her with his tongue, filling her and making her

writhe and cry out. She stayed still, Cole's warning still ringing in her ears.

And then she couldn't move at all. Cole covered her torso with his big body and the warm press of his skin. He leaned toward her pussy. *No, he couldn't…* But he did. In a move of practiced seduction, his mouth claimed her clit as Burke speared his tongue high into her pussy. Sensation ramped up, and she began disintegrating under the onslaught. It was too much. It was everything.

"Come, sweetheart. Right on my tongue. I want to lick you up." Burke's hands tightened on her thighs as he thrust his tongue back in.

Cole sucked her clit in between his teeth, pulling hard.

That was all it took. Sensation tightened, seizing her breath and heartbeat, blood pounding. Then she exploded, thrashing and screaming as the orgasm took her. It was more than she'd ever imagined. Pleasure thrummed through every inch of her body as they suckled and fucked her with their mouths until she lay in a boneless puddle.

As she came down, the twins licked more leisurely, as though they simply enjoyed her taste. She panted, melted, feeling drugged by their very presence. This was where she wanted to be. This was what she'd waited for.

Her body jerked in little aftershocks. Cole got to his knees. Burke looked up, his stare locking on hers.

"That was delicious, sweetheart." He pushed up and started to undress.

Jessa watched him. Burke stripped out of his pants. His cock jutted from the *V* of his thighs. It was big and intimidating, just like the man himself, reaching almost to his navel. She couldn't take her eyes off the graceful lines and plum-shaped head. What would he taste like? Pearly pre-come seeped from the head.

"I need you, baby." Cole's voice was deep and honest.

Desire was stamped on his face, and she could tell this was more than just needing her body. He needed *her*. Whatever insane feelings had overtaken her heart, that expression said she wasn't alone. She was the only one he wanted. Jessa held her arms out, welcoming him.

"Lift up, sweetheart. I want to be a part of this." Burke helped her sit up, then slid in behind her, his body half under hers. He wrapped her in his arms.

Cole tore open a condom and began working it over his cock, his hands shaking.

"He wants you. He wants you so bad, sweetheart," Burke whispered in her ear. "He's never wanted anyone like he wants you. You know how I know? Because I feel the same way. We're crazy about you."

She let her head roll back, finding a place in the crook of his neck. His words both soothed and aroused her. His breath played over her skin. His palm cradled her breast.

Cole's eyes glittered a dark, fathomless blue as he gripped her thighs, cock just barely touching her pussy. "There's no going back from here."

She nodded, her gaze tangled in his. "I don't want to go back."

"Then you're ours now." He thrust up, joining them in a single, smooth move. Her recent orgasm had made her folds soft and swollen. Jessa cried out at the tearing pain as he broke through her barrier and kept sinking deeper. Then the pain faded, replaced by a foreign, delicious fullness that grew with each second.

"You feel so good." Cole groaned and thrust into her with slow, short strokes. An inch in and then out. Another inch, burning, unstoppable. He fucked her carefully, moving in and out, giving her time to take him comfortably. She welcomed the burn. He was so big, stretching her relentlessly and making her writhe.

Burke's hands cupped her breasts as he whispered, "Take all of him. Yes, that's beautiful, sweetheart. So fucking beautiful. You'll take me next, and I'll sink so deep…"

Jessa let her hands find Cole's back. His skin was hot, smooth, bunched with muscles as he invaded her, his strokes burning and filling her, becoming more and more urgent. Burke pressed kisses along her neck. She was surrounded by them, every inch of space taken up with their feel and scent.

She belonged to them.

Cole picked up the pace, his face contorting as he worked over her. "You feel so damn good, baby. So tight. So…ours."

Burke's hand slipped between them and pinched at her clit. Cole thrust faster, hitting some place deep inside. The kind of pleasure they'd given her with their mouths built all over again, but deeper, more demanding. Jessa whimpered and wrapped her legs around Cole, rushing up to meet his thrusts. She gave herself to him completely.

"That's right," Cole said on a groan. "Give it to us. Come, baby. Let us have it."

"I can hear you panting," Burke whispered. "Feel your rapid heartbeat. Your whole body is tensing. Come, sweetheart. Cole won't resist joining you. You're too sweet."

Burke rubbed her clit with every low word he spoke, and she exploded, pleasure wracking her. Cole held her hips, driving in with hard thrusts, teeth bared, as he came. He called out her name and shoved in as deeply as he could, as though he wanted to fuse them together. His body shook then fell against hers.

She was pressed between them, Burke's arms wrapped around her, Cole's head buried in her neck. She moaned, feeling absolutely exhausted—and at utter peace.

"Don't think we're through yet," Burke whispered. "It's my turn, sweetheart."

With his soft, subtle warning, her body went on alert.

"We're not even close to through," Cole added, his lips brushing the space between her breasts before taking a nipple in his mouth tenderly. Between them, she felt special, beloved.

No. They weren't through. She would never be through with them.

Gingerly, Cole withdrew from her pussy. Almost immediately, Burke loomed over her, his sheathed cock in hand. Cole disposed of his own condom, then he eased into the spot Burke had occupied just moments ago, wrapping his arms around her. Her breath caught. Burke smiled seductively as he covered her, slid inside of her, then let out a long moan. "That's it, sweetheart. This is fucking heaven." Another deep stroke, another groan. "And I'm never going to want to leave."

# Chapter Four

*Present Day – Dallas, Texas*

The jerk of the plane hitting the runway brought Jessa out of her dream. She blinked, forcing her eyes to focus. Moments ago, she'd been back in a world where everything had seemed warm and perfect. She'd dreamed of the night she'd first made love with Cole and Burke. She'd been surrounded by them, feeling safe and cherished.

It had been a dream—all of it. Oh, she'd lived it, but it had been her fantasy. In reality, she had been nothing more to them than a way to kill time while they worked a job. She'd been fooling herself, and the proof of her gullible nature was currently sleeping in his new car seat. The bouncing of the plane hadn't woken Caleb. Nor had it awakened Burke, who slept beside him, hand resting on the baby's little belly.

"My brother can sleep through anything. I think that's what happens when you spend too much of your life on cargo planes." Cole rubbed his eyes and stretched.

"Burke could sleep through Armageddon," Gavin

James drawled, then eyed Angus in his new carrier. The feline gave a guttural *meow* of supreme displeasure. No surprise since he'd spent most of the flight throwing up.

With a grimace, Gavin unbuckled his belt, stood and buttoned his jacket, then picked up the cat carrier. "The car is waiting for us. Hannah has everything ready. You don't need to worry about Caleb. Or this charming cat you've got."

*Not worry?* The thought of leaving her child behind with strangers tore at Jessa's gut, threatening to rip her open.

"I'm sorry," Gavin James said, his eyes hooded. "That was a thoughtless thing to say. I can't imagine what you're going through. Of course you're going to worry. I have two children of my own, a boy and a girl. I would die a little if I were in your shoes. But I want you to know that I will protect Caleb as though he were my own."

Tears pricked at her eyes. She believed him. The man in the thousand dollar suit seemed genuine, despite the fact that everyone around him jumped to do his bidding. He'd been waiting at the private airport outside of D.C. with a Learjet cleared for takeoff. He'd huddled near the back of the plane while Cole filled him in on the situation. She'd heard Gavin try to talk Cole and Burke into staying at his home in Dallas, but she agreed with them. Staying far away from Caleb was safer. She couldn't risk his little life.

Burke came awake as the airplane screeched to a halt. "Are we here?"

"Yes, princess," Cole replied. "And you managed to get your beauty sleep in, as usual. Jessa rested a little, too. We're going to say goodbye to Caleb and take off before Marco can catch up with us. Did Dex find a car for us?"

Gavin frowned. "Yes. He's waiting outside with it. He also tried to get hold of Mick Landry. He's the PI you had watching Jessa for the past year, right?"

Cole unhooked his seatbelt. "Yes. He's the good-for-nothing son of a bitch who didn't do his goddamn job. I have a few words to say to him."

"That's going to be difficult. He was murdered two days ago." Gavin's words fell like a ticking bomb waiting to go off.

"Fuck," Burke said.

"Well, we knew Marco was serious," Cole muttered.

"Why did you hire a PI?" Jessa asked.

She didn't understand them. They had walked away without even giving her their real last name, making it impossible for her to find them. But they'd hired someone to keep tabs on her? It didn't make any sense.

"When we realized how long we were going to be in South America, we hired a PI to make sure you were okay. We just wanted to keep tabs on you," Cole explained. "He wasn't supposed to do anything but check on you. Make sure you were safe and had everything you needed. He sent monthly reports to our office. Our secretary forwarded them to us." He greeted his teeth and cursed. "The bastard was obviously working for Marco. He told us you married Angus in Scotland this past spring."

"*Married?* Seriously?" Jessa shook her head. "No. I went to Scotland because I sold some work at the Soho gallery, and the owner liked me so much she let me spend some time in her house there in exchange for painting it. It's an old monastery on a gorgeous piece of land. When I came home, I was still only a few months along, so I adopted Angus from the animal shelter."

"We had no idea you were pregnant," Burke said, bitterness dripping.

She shrugged. "Would it have mattered? You still had a job to do."

It wasn't fair, but she was jealous of their mission. They had spent a full year saving other people's children while their own child had been born in a county hospital. She could still remember standing outside the hospital with Caleb in a car seat, waiting on a taxi to take her home. She'd been the only new mom with no one to take care of her.

She could feel Cole's stare burning through her. "One of us would have come back while the other stayed and did the job. We wouldn't have left you alone."

The door to the Lear opened, and a big man wearing a cowboy hat charged in. He wore a long-sleeved western shirt, jeans, and boots. The casual outfit didn't hide the man's air of authority. A lovely blonde followed behind him, her pretty face grimacing with worry.

"Dex? Seriously?" Gavin James stared at the cowboy. "You brought Hannah?"

"She's earned a couple hundred licks." Dex scowled. "But she wouldn't be left behind. Slade's back at the house making some calls. He's working his way up the FBI ranks, screaming all the way. Unfortunately, no one can prove that this Marco asshole has taken over his father's business. He's been perfectly clean for years. We're in a bind."

"It wouldn't matter," Cole said, standing to shake hands with Dex. "Marco has FBI contacts. We could go into protective custody, and it would be a crap shoot. In fact, I think that's exactly what the fucker wants us to do."

The men started talking strategy, moving to exit the plane. The pretty blonde stepped forward and sat down across from Jessa, looking both concerned and kind. She was dressed in white slacks and a colorful sweater that had come straight off a designer's rack. She was soft and natural, and there was no doubt this woman was well loved.

"He's beautiful. Caleb, right?"

"Yes." This was the woman who would take care of her baby. The blonde reached over and gently touched Caleb's cheek, a tender look on her face. Jessa liked her right away. She had "experienced mother" written all over her.

She turned back to Jessa, holding out a hand. "I'm Hannah James. I'm married to those two and one who's still at home. We have two babies. I promise, I will take care of yours. I love your men."

Jessa shook her head. "They aren't mine."

They had never been.

Hannah's perfectly manicured eyebrow rose on her face. "Say that all you like, but I promise you, those men have barely taken their eyes off you. They're not going to give you up. But that's an Alpha male for you. They can be obnoxious, but I wouldn't have mine any other way."

Hannah was married to three men? Jessa leaned in, her curiosity getting the better of her. She stole a glance at the two men talking to Cole and Burke. They looked...difficult. "How do you handle them?"

Hannah's smile was brighter than the lights on the plane, her laughter tinkling through the cabin. "Oh, they don't make it easy. They gang up on me. I rarely win a fight... But making up is worth it." She turned serious, tears pricking her eyes. "Trust me. As difficult as this kind of relationship can be, it's worth every moment. I wouldn't know a damn thing about love or happiness without them."

Jessa turned away, the look of adoration on Hannah's face too much for her to bear. "Well, you got lucky."

Hannah touched her knee. "I've known Cole and Burke for a couple of years now. They would talk about you on their brief trips home. I have never seen them as crazy about a woman as they are about you. Of course, they also haven't had a case as bad as the one they've been working for the last year. If they say they didn't know about Caleb, then they didn't."

Did that really matter? They had left her, walked away, and not returned for a year. They had only come now because they thought she was in danger. Great. They didn't want her to die. She bet she could find a whole bunch of people who didn't particularly want her to die. That didn't mean they cared. And now that they knew about Caleb, whatever they said or did would be colored by the fact that she'd given birth to their son. Jessa didn't want to be tied to them simply because her reproductive organs worked.

She glanced at Cole. He stood, looking so masculine it hurt. And Burke's eyes strayed to hers. She looked away, too confused and angry to meet his stare.

Burke walked over, his face a grim mask. "We have

to go now."

Jessa put a hand to her mouth, stifling her cry. She was leaving her baby, her very soul. A moment later, Cole stood beside his brother.

"I'm so fucking sorry, baby." Cole started to reach a hand toward her. She flinched. Cole's face went blank. "The faster we get out of here, the less chance Marco has of following us. We have cash. We have an untraceable vehicle. We have new IDs. I promise, I will keep you alive or I will die trying."

With tears falling, she leaned over and kissed her sleeping child. All this time, Caleb had been her strength. How had she ever thought differently? Shame filled her as she thought of those first, dark days when he had seemed like a burden. Now, he was the light of her life. His sweet smile, his sunny disposition, had kept her going through some very lonely times. Would she ever seen him again?

"I love you, baby boy," she whispered against his cheek. "I love you."

She stood and followed Cole and Burke out of the plane, her heart aching, threatening to seize up. God, she'd give anything to return to a happier time.

\* \* \* \*

*One year earlier – New York City*

Cole looked around the richly furnished dining room of the Waldorf Astoria, an ornate echo of its grander past. "So, this is your idea of breakfast?"

Jessa's bright smile lit up the fucking room. What the hell had she done to him? One night with the curvy redhead, and he was practically her lapdog.

"Well, after you insatiable men ravished me all night, I'm starved," she said with a wink. "I'm ready for the whole 'treat me like a princess' thing."

Oh, he could do that. He slipped his hand into hers and leaned over, kissing her. His whole body still hummed from the hours of their lovemaking. He couldn't fool himself. It hadn't been simple fucking. Or even mere sex. He'd made love to her. He hadn't even understood what the phrase meant until last night.

"Then that's what you'll get." He nodded toward the hostess.

"What is our sweet thing going to get?" Burke asked, looking happier than Cole had seen him in a long time. Burke's arms wrapped around Jessa's waist, and he buried his face in her hair. "Probably everything. Poor baby, we gave her all she could take."

Sweet Jessa had finally begged them to stop. They'd been relentless, easing into the snug heaven of her sweet pussy and loving her over and over. Cole had also introduced her to some ass play. He could still feel the way her virgin hole had clamped down on his finger as he'd worked to open her backside up. Soon, he'd take her there, and it would be a supreme pleasure.

But all their vigorous attention had worked up her appetite for food. And made their poor sweetheart more than a little sore.

The hostess's eyes widened as she took in the three of them, but she showed them to a table without staring too much.

"Isn't it beautiful? I love New York at holiday time." Jessa looked around the dining room, all decorated for the season, pleasure evident in her eyes. The haunted look he'd seen in her eyes when they'd first met was gone. A smile of contentment lingered. He and his brother had given that to her. Cole stared across the table at his brother and shared a single thought.

*She's the one.*

He felt it, knew that Burke felt it, too.

"You're having one of those silent conversations." Jessa shook her head as she gave them both pointed stares. "That is so not fair to me. I don't have a telepathic link with anyone."

Burke snorted. It was something they did almost unconsciously. "It's not telepathic, exactly. When you spend your whole damn life chained to someone as ugly as that, you just get to know what he's thinking. Right now, he's thinking about bacon."

Cole rolled his eyes. "No, but I am thinking about ham. You, brother."

Burke shrugged. "I've been called worse. By you mostly."

Jessa slapped lightly at Cole's chest. "You boys behave. I'm going to run to the more than likely outrageously decadent bathroom, then grab some of that smoked salmon. It all looks so good."

She stood. Both he and his brother rose to their feet. She kissed them both lightly, then walked off, her sweet curves swaying.

"We're in trouble," Burke said, sitting back down.

Cole lost his smile. He'd had twenty-four hours to forget why he was in New York. Reality came crashing down, and she was a bitch. "I know."

"We have to meet with Delgado tomorrow."

"Yeah." Months of negotiating, and tomorrow they would finally meet the man. Up until now, they had dealt with lackeys. The day before they had met Marco, the big guy's son, who apparently ran the legitimate side of the business. It had been a terribly civilized meeting with absolutely no mention of the business at hand. The super small recording device that Burke wore in the button of his suit coat hadn't had anything to pick up. The recording would show nothing but three men talking about business interests and recent sporting events. Every time he or Burke would try to get the man to say something incriminating, he would simply smile and turn the conversation toward something less illegal.

But tomorrow there would be no avoiding it. Tomorrow they met with the man himself, and there would be no way around the fact that they were negotiating to buy another human being. The thought had bile rising in his throat. He wanted to keep Jessa far, far away from this shit.

"It won't be over tomorrow. Finishing this up will take days, maybe even a week. We have to take custody of the girl to prove our case, let her tell her story, turn over the recordings and any other evidence we collect. We may have to help set up a sting…" Burke sighed and toyed with the perfectly placed silverware. "Fuck, the timing couldn't be worse, but we can't veer now."

Neither of them wanted to do this. Cole knew what his brother was thinking. He wanted to be with Jessa, in their bed, passing her between them. He wanted to be happy with the one woman who handled and completed them both.

"Look on the bright side," Cole said. "Yes, we're

going to spend an enormous amount of Rafe and Kade's money on a slave, but at least one woman will be safe and free very soon." But Burke was right; they couldn't back away now. If they did, Cole knew he'd never be able to sleep at night. He would always wonder where Alea was, regret not trying harder to save her. She was only eighteen, for fuck's sake.

From the moment he'd seen the snapshot of her young, vibrant face, he'd known that they had to save her. They were bigger and stronger than most men. And he was a predator. His life could have gone one of two ways. He was built to hunt, to kill. He could have taken advantage of those who were weaker. Instead, he chose to protect them.

It would take everything he had to walk into the fucker's office tomorrow and not blow a hole through his skull. Delgado deserved it. He'd ruined so many lives. He lived in luxury while the families of the women he'd abducted lived victimized, without hope. He wanted nothing more than to take vengeance on the man. But they'd been hired to find a girl and collect evidence. He'd been hired to save a life.

"We could try the feds." Burke toyed with the fork in front of him.

Cole shook his head. "No. Everything we have right now is circumstantial. And you know this bastard has some men on the inside. They would squash the case, and Delgado would probably kill all the girls he still has in the States. Even if we got lucky and found the good guys, the feds won't move overnight. If we fail to make that meeting tomorrow, Delgado will fold up his tent and disappear for who knows how long. We can't risk either one happening."

Burke nodded miserably. "And we can't risk Jessa, either."

The thought of Jessa in danger turned his stomach. All that amazing food had looked so tempting a moment before, and now he couldn't stand the thought of it. "I pray he doesn't know about Jessa, but this guy hasn't risen to the top of a crime family without being ruthless and smart. I know he's vetted us already."

"Our cover will hold. I put it in place myself. There's zero chance he can figure out it's all made up. I'm a damn good hacker."

"I know." Burke was the best in the business. If he hadn't gone into the Navy, Burke might have been a fine criminal. Cole stared at the hall where Jessa had disappeared. "He can believe our cover and still have someone watching us. You know he had someone at the airport. He knows where we're staying. He hasn't stayed in business for so many years without playing it smart and getting to know his clients. I'm worried that if he has someone watching us who I haven't made yet, he's going to find out about Jessa."

"I don't want that any more than you do, man," Burke replied. "But it's done now. We can't go back and undo last night. I wouldn't want to. All we can do is lay low. If anyone asks, she's just a nice piece of ass."

Cole clenched his fists. Fuck that. She was so much more. Smart and funny, she'd worked hard for her independence and scraped by, upholding a life and a passion she believed in. Despite her youth and inexperience, she'd done her best to tackle the big, bad world her way. She deserved more than a lie, but he couldn't give her the truth right now. It would put her in too much danger.

Jessa bounced back to the table, her smile vibrant, a plate of food in her hand. "I caught our waitress. I ordered coffee for us all. There's a juice bar, too. There's just about everything. I love this place."

Her obvious joy brought out his own. He'd always felt like he was simply existing, moving from one job to the next, but Jessa made him want to stop and enjoy life for a change. The world had seemed like a shithole before, but that was because he went to all of its dark, terrible places. Jessa reminded him there was goodness, too. She shined her bright light on all of the reasons he had to fight. For her. For all the girls Delgado had manipulated and abused.

"Then we'll definitely come back soon." Cole put a hand on hers.

God, he loved the way her fingers felt threaded through his. Burke reached for her other hand, and their circle was complete. Jessa accepted them. Her warmth was a balm for all the rejection of the past. His uncle had beaten into his head for years that no woman could ever want someone so guarded and angry. Females had used him before to get closer to Burke, then ditched him like trash once they thought they had his brother's attention. Jessa simply held on to them both in the golden glow of her adoration.

She squeezed his hand. "If I eat here too often, I might end up weighing four hundred pounds."

And he would still love her. Fuck. He was in love with her. He loved her smile and her rich auburn hair and the curve of her hips. He loved her quirky view of the world. Seeing everything through her eyes was a startling revelation. Jessa had been through hell with her parents. They'd rejected her true soul and cut her off when she'd refused to conform. Still, she'd managed to move on without being bitter or vindictive—or letting their crappy games play with her head. When his uncle had died, Cole had spit on his grave and gleefully continued hating the bastard. Now, he winced. Definitely, he could take a lesson or two from Jessa.

He and Burke had been drifting emotionally. And they'd guarded their hearts. Jessa hadn't. She'd been through hell, yet she had opened her heart and asked for love. Jessa was perfect.

He brought her hand to his mouth, Burke did the same thing, having the same instinct. "Go on, then. Weigh whatever you like. We'll still want you."

She would always look like this to him. His eyes would be broken, lost in this moment. When she was eighty and frail and wrinkled, he would look at her and see her the way she was today. Vibrant. Beautiful. His heart thudded in his chest. He was in love for the first time. The last time. They would never love anyone the way they loved Jessa Wade. She was the end of their journey. His eyes met his brother's. Not grim this time. Burke was happy and full of love.

A lifetime of joy spread out before Cole when he'd expected so much less. He'd never once thought that he'd have or deserve this sort of devotion. But it was his. Jessa was his.

"Well, I never expected to see the two of you here."

Cole looked up, a dark voice yanking him out of his thoughts. He felt his eyes flare as he caught sight of

Marco Delgado standing at the end of their table in a perfectly tailored suit. Marco was the picture of a well-groomed businessman, right down to the bodyguard who hovered behind him.

Cole felt his stomach turn. He dropped Jessa's hand, hating the fact that he had to do it. "Marco. It's nice to see you. What are you doing in this part of the world?"

He should be in lower Manhattan. There were about a thousand restaurants in the city, but he chose this one?

Burke's whole frame had stiffened, his hand dropping Jessa's, too. "Marco."

Marco smiled, a reptilian expression. "I have brunch here all the time." His eyes went to Jessa. "I find it a good way to restore my energy after a busy night."

"We're doing the same." He prayed Jessa would smile and go along with them.

"Hi," Jessa said brightly, holding out her hand. "I'm Jessa Wade. They have no manners. Oh, well, they have to have some faults."

Marco smiled, satisfaction oozing from his pores, as if he'd found a chink he'd thought he'd never find. "I'm glad to hear that, dear Jessa Wade. Such a pretty name. Do you live around here? How did you meet the twins?"

Cole leaned forward, pulling Jessa back. "She's just in town for the weekend."

Jessa's frowned. "I live here. In Manhattan. I'm an artist."

"I live here as well. On the Upper East Side. It is so nice to meet you. I am a business associate of Cole and Burke. How very nice to make your acquaintance. Enjoy your breakfast." Marco moved off, his bodyguard moving behind him.

"What's with you two?" Jessa frowned. "He was nice, and you two were terribly rude. Eat something and feed your inner beasts." She picked up her plate. "I'm getting some smoked salmon."

The second Jessa strode toward the buffet, her sweet curves swaying, Burke turned to Cole, brows furrowed. "What the fuck just happened?"

"Marco knows Jessa is important." There was no denying it. Marco Delgado had just seen into his soul, and there was nothing he could do about it. "Which means Ricardo will know soon, too."

Burke's whole face tightened. "Fuck."

Fuck was right. Cole had to hope that Marco wouldn't remember Jessa. He had to pray that he would write her off as another bimbo who'd fucked a couple of hot guys with too much money to blow. Marco hadn't been listening in. For all he knew, he'd caught them indulging in a one-night stand. It was okay. It had to be.

Cole watched Jessa, resisting the urge to pull her into his lap and never let go, and prayed he was right.

# Chapter Five

*Present Day – Dallas, Texas*

Burke put the nondescript sedan in park, well aware of just how tired he was. The neon lights of what had to be the skankiest motel he'd seen in a long time—and he'd seen a few—blinked off and on as though they couldn't decide to just give up the ghost and die.

"We're here," he said, aware that his voice was gravelly, his tone bleak.

Jessa stirred in the backseat. She'd climbed in when they had left the airport, dragging the small suitcase Hannah had brought for her filled with clothes, a toothbrush, and shampoo. Then she'd curled up and cried a few silent tears after leaving Caleb. He'd seen the quiet shake of her shoulders in the rearview mirror—and it had nearly ripped his heart out. But she'd refused all comfort. She'd shut them out.

"I don't know that we should stop," Cole said, rubbing a hand across his eyes.

Burke shook his head. "We all need sleep. We have to figure out what we're doing and where we're going to stash Jessa while we do it."

Cole took a long breath, then got out of the car, his acquiescence plain.

Burke turned to look at Jessa. Her face was puffy from crying. God, she was making his heart twist and hurt. He wanted to hold her. It wasn't going to happen. "We're going to make sure you're okay. Cole and I won't allow anything to happen to you. And Caleb is safe. The James brothers will kill anyone who looks at him sideways."

She nodded without showing a hint of emotion on her face. It was as though she'd simply turned her feelings off after a river of tears. "I know. I liked them. I believed them."

He reached for her, catching her hand in his before she could pull away. "Then believe in us, Jessa. We would die before we let anything happen to you."

She tugged her hand free. "Unless, of course, you need to work. Can't let a little thing like a girlfriend get between you and a paycheck, can you, Burke?"

"Jessa, we thought you were married," Cole growled. "It's not—"

"Important," she cut in. "Just get this guy so I can have my son back and start rebuilding my home and my career."

She opened the door and slid out before he could say another word. Burke smacked the steering wheel, wishing it was Marco Delgado's fucking head. They should have killed the fucker that morning at the Waldorf. He'd been a loose end that they should have taken out.

Fucking hindsight was twenty-twenty. He got out of the car and palmed the key he'd been given just moments before when he'd registered under the name Brian Palmer. Like the sedan, it was suitably bland and nondescript. He'd paid cash. It was one of the reasons he'd chosen this particular lodging. The Hilton would want a credit card on file. Given the fact that Delgado seemed to have been planning this for nearly a year, he would almost certainly be on the lookout for their credit card to ping.

Cole opened the trunk and pulled out their bags. Burke couldn't help but notice an addition to the duffel bags he and Cole had carried with them from South America. When Dex James had seen them off, he'd handed over a couple of bags he'd packed from the condo Burke and Cole shared. No doubt, the small briefcase-like bag contained Burke's computer and an untraceable Internet hotspot device that linked to a satellite. He was pretty sure Dex had also packed some heavy-duty guns and plenty of cartridges, along with the hard drives from Burke and Cole's office.

But the beaten brown bag currently in Cole's hand had another purpose entirely. Burke just knew that it contained ropes, handcuffs, lube, condoms, and other wonderful things needed to restrain and fuck pretty little submissives.

"You're kidding?" Burke jibed as he made his way up the stairs.

Cole turned and glared at him over the top of Jessa's head.

"That's some awfully positive thinking, brother." Burke shook his head as he hit the landing and opened the door to room fourteen. He turned on the light—and wished that he hadn't. It was clean but old and worn.

There was a sadness to the room. Neglect.

It wasn't at all what he'd envisioned when he'd fantasized about reuniting with Jessa.

Cole followed him in, toting his bag of tricks. "Dex is the positive thinker. He brought it. After a whole fucking year, it may be full of cobwebs."

Dex, true perv that he was, had picked up Cole's BDSM bag when he'd gone to their place to get the essentials. Clearly, Dex considered the numerous devices with which to sensually torture and pleasure a woman really fucking vital.

As Burke went back outside to watch over Jessa, Cole set the bags aside and immediately searched the room.

"Can I go in?" Jessa asked. "It's not as cold as it was in Virginia, but it's still nippy."

He shrugged out of his coat and had it around her shoulders before she could protest. "Not until Cole says we're secure. It's not a big room. It won't take more than a minute."

She nodded, her head turning toward the Dallas skyline. It twinkled in the distance like a jewel just out of reach. "It's pretty. At least you didn't lie about living here."

God, they were in such deep shit with Jessa, they'd probably never dig out, much less get to that bag of tricks. "We only lied to protect you from this."

She laughed, an utterly humorless sound. It seemed that all of her life and happiness had been left behind with her son. "Yeah, you didn't do a very good job."

He closed his eyes briefly, the pain that flared almost overwhelming him. They had failed her on every level.

"We didn't mean for any of this to happen."

She shrugged, continuing to watch the horizon. "It wasn't so bad once I got my trust fund. My folks wouldn't give me a loan. They told me I'd made my bed so I should lie in it. Dad offered to pay for an abortion, but only if I came back to the company and behaved the way his daughter should."

How close had Caleb come to never being born? He'd only met the little guy a few hours before, but he already loved their son, missed him sorely. It would have been smarter for Jessa to end the pregnancy. She would have been able to get on with her life. But Burke was glad she hadn't.

"I'd like to meet your father someday," he ground out.

She shook her head. "It wouldn't matter. He's never going to change. He truly believes he's doing the right thing. In his mind, being an artist is one step away from being a mental patient. Don't ask about that logic. Despite the long, convoluted lecture, I don't understand, either. I had assumed they would want to know their grandchild regardless, but no. I don't care anymore. I have the trust my grandmother left me, and my art is starting to pay. Caleb and I are going to be fine. Well, if I'm not dead in the next couple of days."

Burke couldn't stop himself. Jessa wasn't going to like it—but she needed what he could give her.

"Come here." He put his arms around her and brought her close. She didn't fight, but she didn't return the embrace, either. That was all right. She needed comfort; he would provide it. And just being close to her, feeling the heat of her body, calmed him, too. "I'm never going to let that happen. I swear I'll die first."

She softened slightly, giving him some small measure of hope.

"The room's clear." Cole stood in the doorway, watching them with burning eyes. Burke could see plainly that his brother wasn't jealous, but envious that he was hugging Jessa. Cole wanted to do the same thing. Burke felt his twin's frustration and worry. Cole didn't trust himself to stop at a hug. If Cole touched her, he would try to mount her, seal their bond again. He wanted to dominate her, sink into her, make her remember who her Masters were, and he didn't feel he had the right.

"Let's go inside, sweetheart," Burke murmured.

She jerked away from him and stomped past Cole. "I told you not to call me that."

"I've never been good at taking orders." Burke followed her in. He watched Jessa's face as she took in the sad room. Though painfully clean, there was only one very large bed. No wonder they charged by the hour rate.

"Where are you two going to sleep?" Jessa raised a brow as she sat on the bed.

"I'm planning to wait until you're asleep, then climb in with you," Burke admitted.

"Uh, no." Jessa crossed her arms over her chest. "I'm not sleeping with you ever again."

Several charged retorts ran through Burke's mind. He swallowed them down. Challenging her when she felt like her back was against the wall wasn't productive. But god, how he wanted to make her eat those words.

"I won't try to touch you. But we all need rest."

"Then you can sleep on the floor. I don't exactly trust you to be a man of your word since everything you told me a year ago was a lie."

"Goddamn it, we've explained that!" Burke felt his temper slipping. Anxiety, adrenaline, and a burning need to fuck Jessa weren't good for his mood.

She jumped up and got in his face. "Only because Marco forced you to. Otherwise, you'd still be working, and Caleb and I would still be at the bottom of your priority list. I'd still know that you'd seduced and abandoned me, but at least I'd have my beautiful Victorian home, my son, and some really beautiful memories of the night he was conceived. Now, all I have is some asshole trying to kill me and the two…" she fumbled for a word, "mercenaries who abandoned me saying they're going to save me. Forgive me if I'm not thrilled with your sudden honesty."

"Both of you, enough," Cole growled, his voice deep, low, and dominant. "This argument is pointless and over. I concur with Burke's plan. You will fall asleep in the bed, then we will crawl in with you and rest. All in favor say aye."

Burke smiled. "Aye."

Jessa glared at them in turn, her mouth hanging open. "You can't vote on this."

"We just did," Burke said. "And guess what? We win. Ah, the joys of democracy."

She rolled her eyes. And there it was. A hint of a smile, albeit reluctant. The faintest trace of the Jessa that Burke had been worried was lost forever. "Fine. Gang up on me. But don't be surprised if I toss and turn in my sleep and kick. There definitely might be some kicking."

"There might be some spanking, too," Cole vowed. "Think on that."

Burke's cell rang, cutting off a very interesting turn in the conversation. He pulled it from his pocket and checked the number and frowned at Cole. "It's Hilary."

"Who is she and why does she have this number? I thought no one had it." The chilliness of the question made Burke repress a smile.

"Our assistant. She's been running the office in our absence. She procures all the phones we keep around the place, and she has the numbers in case of emergency. Dex picked them up when he got the hard drives. It's fine." He swiped his hand across the phone, answering it. "This is Burke."

Cole stood over Jessa. "Are you hungry? I'll get you something."

Burke stepped away as Jessa replied, confident his brother would take care of her while he dealt with Hilary. For some reason, Cole and Hilary didn't communicate well. Then again, Cole didn't communicate well with a lot of people. Hilary was competent and punctual. She always did exactly as asked. Burke simply made sure he was the one who dealt with her, just as he dealt with most of their clients. They were reassured by Burke's affable manner. Cole's snarling...not so much.

"Burke. I'm so glad you're here. You are back in the country, right?" Hilary's voice was tremulous.

"Yes, we're both here."

She sighed with relief. "I'm glad you're back. Something strange happened. A man came into the office asking all sorts of questions about you and Cole."

Marco or one of his henchmen. Burke's blood ran cold. While Burke wasn't terribly surprised the bastard would question Hilary, he hadn't expected Marco to do it so openly. So brazenly. Marco would only do it if he felt entirely confident he could win this game.

"Don't talk to anyone. I can't say more, but you need to close the office and work out of the Black Oak building for now. Tell Dex James I said to put you up in a hotel."

Marco hadn't said a word about going after anyone besides Jessa, but Burke didn't need any more guilt if the fucker changed his mind.

"I don't understand. Please, Burke. Can you just come back and tell me what's going on? I need to see you. You've been gone so long, and I need your signature on about a hundred documents. I don't want to work from Black Oak. Dex James was here earlier today, and he was very rude."

Dex? Rude? Yeah, not a shock. If Hilary had given Dex the slightest bit of grief, he would have steamrolled right over the petite blonde. Dex got things done. He didn't let little things like procedure or protocol stop him. Procedure and protocol were two of Hilary's favorite words. "I'm sorry about that, Hilary, but Dex had to move fast."

"Why didn't you just call me? I would have gotten you whatever you needed. I run this office. I didn't need some brute to come in and take over."

He sighed. This was the trouble with Hilary. She sometimes sounded like a fainting Southern belle. And sometimes she protected her territory like a rabid pit bull. He didn't need this shit, but he'd left her a lot to deal with.

Much like Jessa.

"I'm sorry, Hilary. We had to move quickly."

"I don't even know what he took. He simply detached a couple of the computer things. He even demanded that I give up my laptop. I barely managed to convince him to let me get my CD out. It was rather like a burglary. He should be happy I didn't call the police."

He could practically see her frown. Hilary Stevens was only thirty-two, but sometimes her disapproval made her seem much older. She really should have been a school teacher since she often made those around her feel like naughty children. "It's a good thing you didn't. I don't think Dex would have taken well to that."

"At least his brothers are polite. I don't see how brothers can be so very different, but you and Cole are proof, I suppose. Anyway, why don't you come into the office? Or I can meet you. I don't know what's going on, but it sounds dangerous. It's best if we stick together."

Yeah, that would be great. Adding a woman with a perpetual stick up her ass and a little crush on him to the mix would be awesome. No. Marco's target was Jessa, and Burke had to concentrate on her. "No. We're involved in something bad, and I'm worried that anyone close to us will be hurt. Do you remember Mick Landry?"

"Isn't he the investigator you hired to keep track of that woman in New York?"

"Jessa, yes."

He could practically see her shrug. "What does Mr. Landry have to do with any of this? He was supposed to submit a report two days ago. He's late and won't answer my calls. Do you see what I've had to deal with?"

"He was murdered."

That shut her up. "I-I had no idea."

"So call Gavin James. Get to a hotel. Don't tell anyone where you're going. And don't call again unless it's an emergency." He flicked the phone off.

"I only had to hear half that conversation to know that Hilary sounds an awful lot like a jealous girlfriend." Jessa watched him, her feet curved under her as she reclined on the bed.

"Hilary has a thing for Burke. She can't stand me." Cole looked up from his work. He had wires going everywhere. "I'm a caveman. I shouldn't be allowed in polite society."

Again, that tiny hint of a smile. "So she's met you, then."

"Many times."

Burke stepped up. His brother might be the better tracker and better with weapons, but he was going to screw up the computer. "Give me that."

Cole seemed damn happy to defer. He stared at Burke for a moment, sharing the link that bonded them together. His brother was happy that Jessa was no longer spitting and fuming. Burke nodded, but wasn't so sure that their little kitten had quite put her claws away yet.

"Get some sleep, you two. Well, Jessa, you get some sleep. The faster you drop off, the faster Cole can slink into bed."

"I hate you both." But she was shaking her head as she crawled under the covers. "Just get in, Cole. But stay on your side."

Burke had never seen his brother move so fast. Cole shrugged out of his jacket, pulled off his shoes, and had his hand on the fly of his jeans.

"Don't you dare. The pants stay on." Jessa settled in

and turned out the light on her side of the bed.

Cole sighed, but didn't remove his jeans before he climbed into bed.

Burke turned back to his work, his mind on the last time he'd been in a hotel room with Jessa. New Year's Eve. The night he was pretty sure Caleb had been conceived.

\* \* \* \*

*One year earlier, New Year's Eve – New York City*

Burke watched as Jessa walked through the door, her breasts practically falling out of the little black dress she'd poured herself into. She walked into their suite and sank down on the couch, a seductive little smile on her face.

She was so fucking gorgeous. He felt his brother step in next to him. Desire practically poured off Cole.

How did she do this to them? They'd been with her for a week. They had been sleeping with her for four days. Despite their misgivings over this terrible case, they hadn't been able to stay away from her. They were addicted. They'd tried to lay low, spending most of their time in the suite, in their bed, inside her.

"I know we've talked about going to Times Square," Jessa said, crossing her legs slowly.

That wasn't a good idea. And it certainly wasn't what Burke wanted to do. "We talked about it. We didn't agree to it. It's going to be very crowded."

"I know. I think I had enough crowds at dinner tonight."

Thank god. Burke could feel Cole relax a little. He

hated big crowds, hated not being able to watch his back. "We can watch it on TV or go down to the bar, if you like."

She shook her head. "I don't like. I thought we could...experiment."

Burke's cock jerked in his slacks. They had taken Jessa over and over, but they hadn't taken her together yet. They had spent nights preparing her, working fingers and plugs high into her perfect ass, forcing her to take more and more. "Be very explicit, sweetheart."

She grinned saucily. "You two perverts love it when I talk dirty."

"Yes. And I want you to talk dirty now," Cole said, expressing exactly what Burke wanted. "Say it. Tell me every little detail, or you might not get what you want."

Her nose wrinkled up, a sweet little expression. "You make things so hard, Cole. It would be so much easier if you'd just pounce and do nasty things to me."

Cole shook his head. "But I need to know exactly what you want so I can give it to you."

Burke patted his brother's back. That wasn't exactly true. Cole feared his own tendencies. Jessa could give Cole what he needed most: Permission. His brother never simply took what he wanted. He snarled with and fought his nature to conquer, to bring a woman to her knees. Cole didn't want to hurt, but he craved the consent to let loose his inner restraints and utterly possess. And Burke himself simply needed to be wanted for something other than his cock, body, and smile.

Jessa cocked her head. "No, you need me to tell you that I want to be dominated. Isn't that right?"

With a faint smile, Burke wondered how Jessa could,

despite her relative inexperience, be so intuitive, so wise. But he was so damn glad she was. She was everything they needed.

She leaned forward, taking Cole's hands—and giving them both a great view down her dress. "I want you to dominate me, Cole. And Burke, baby, I want you to be the loving, indulgent man you are. I want you both. I want the possessive caveman and the tender seducer. I want the whole package, especially since you come in two gorgeous bodies. I want you together and apart, and every way you'll have me."

Tears swam in her green eyes, glistened on her cheeks.

A melee of emotion surged and swarmed. It overflowed inside Burke. Fuck, he loved her. Absolutely loved her. The sentiment had never made sense before. Love had been elusive, something written about, but it had never meant anything. He understood now. Love was this ridiculous feeling of acceptance and hope and security. This was his family. These were the people he would grow old with, count on, build a life with.

"I'll have you every way you'll let me, sweetheart." Burke was caught between his raging hard-on and his soft fucking heart. The rest of the world was a piece of shit, but Jessa...oh, Jessa made it all worthwhile.

Cole still held back. "Think carefully. I've been as gentle these past few days as I know how. But if you give me permission, the gloves come off, baby. And I can be damn dark."

He could. Burke didn't need a woman's submission the way Cole did, but he understood his brother and often assisted so Cole got what he needed. "Sweetheart, I'll keep him in check. He never pushes too far. Don't be scared."

Jessa stood and inched closer. "I've read up, looked at some videos. I'm ready to try more. I trust you." She stared right at Cole. "Both of you."

Burke watched his brother's eyes close briefly. When they opened, the Dom had taken up residence in his brother's body, and Burke knew they were in for an amazing night.

"You need a safe word, one you can say to stop everything. Pick one now."

She blinked, hesitated. "Resolution?"

Cole nodded. "Resolution is fine. Now undress. Slowly. Take off your clothes and get to your knees. If you've done your research, then you know the slave pose. I want to see it."

Burke took a long breath at the thought of their Jessa truly submitting.

She rose, a fine tremble in her hands, but her eyes were steady, resolute. Her hands went to the back of her dress.

"Will you help her, Burke?" Cole said, his gaze never leaving Jessa.

He stood behind her an instant later. "Allow me, sweetheart."

Grabbing hold of the zipper, he dragged it down slowly, revealing her creamy skin. As he pulled, he kissed his way along her spine. Then he eased the dress down to her waist, trapping her arms at her sides. With a practiced hand, he flicked the clasp of her bra open, allowing her breasts to fall free.

"Is this what you wanted to see?" Burke asked, his

hands coming around to cup her breasts. He watched
Cole over Jessa's shoulder. She wiggled a little, her ass
grazing his cock. "Stop, sweetheart. Patience. Let me
present you to Cole. He wants to see your breasts, pussy,
and sweet ass." He whispered in her ear, "We're going to
take your ass tonight, Jessa. We're going to share you in
every way possible."

"I want that," she managed to choke out a whisper.

"You'll have it," Cole said, backing away and
sinking down into the plush chair across from them.
"Eventually. But we do this my way tonight, Jessa."

She nodded, gasping a little as Burke flicked her
nipples, sending tingles and a bite of pain through them
until they hardened. "Yes, Sir."

Cole shook his head. "No. No 'Sirs.' My name,
Jessa. Say my name. Tell me that you want both of us to
take you. Together."

That naughty backside of hers was moving again,
twitching against him. "Yes, Cole. I want you and Burke
to take me at the same time. I want you in my ass, Cole,
and Burke in my pussy. I want to serve you tonight, to
worship your cocks."

"I like the sound of that." Burke continued rolling
her nipples between his thumbs and forefingers. Her skin
was flushing, her breasts swelling. He'd bet anything that
pussy was nice and wet.

"It's only fair," she murmured. "You've worshipped
me. I wouldn't have believed it could be so good, that I
would feel so…cherished."

He kissed her neck. "You are cherished, Jessa."

"Precious pet." Cole consumed her with a stare. "So
fucking precious. Show me that pussy. It belongs to us,

and I want it on display."

"Let's do what he says, sweetheart. He'll make it worthwhile."

Burke let his hands skim the curves of her hips, dragging the dress down. He knelt behind her, helping her step out of the dress. Her lacy black bra, previously tangled with her hands, came free, leaving her in nothing but a tiny black thong and some spectacular fuck-me heels. Burke tossed the dress and bra away and really looked at her gorgeous ass. He traced the line of her thong from the little triangle at the top of her ass down the valley where the little string of black lace disappeared. So fucking sexy. And in his way.

He hooked his fingers under the straps. "This has to go, too. But keep the shoes. I like them."

"Gee, thanks, Burke. They'll keep me warm," Jessa snarked, looking over her shoulder at him.

Cole growled, his eyes narrowing. That look let Burke know just what his brother wanted him to do.

"Damn," Burke said as he pulled the thong down her legs and helped her balance while she stepped out of it. "You obey or you'll get in trouble. And you have to listen carefully. He gets to a point where he communicates entirely through grunts and shoving his cock somewhere."

"Your sarcasm is duly noted," Cole said.

Burke ignored him, preferring to kiss the dimples right above her ass. He loved that little valley and how it dipped and curved. "Luckily for you, I speak Cole. He's not happy with the snarky attitude, sweetheart. He'll love you for your sass outside the bedroom, but he won't put up with it here. Get on your hands and knees. We'll start with a count of ten. When I'm done, you'll find your slave pose and ask Cole very nicely to forgive you."

"I will?" The question squeaked out of her mouth.

"Absolutely." Cole sounded supremely confident.

Burke nodded, confident, as well. He knew something Cole couldn't yet. "The minute I told her we'd start with ten, she got aroused as hell. I can smell her."

Jessa tried to take a step away, but he caught her. "Burke, stop embarrassing me."

Her skin was flushing, and he smiled. It wasn't polite. "I would think after having one of us deep in your pussy almost constantly for the past four days that you'd be over the embarrassment. I love the way you smell. I want to stick my face in your pussy and drown." He caressed her hip. "Sex is dirty and nasty, sweetheart. Do you really want some nice boy who will politely fuck you once a week in a standard missionary position and never, ever spank you? Or refuse to shove his cock up your ass while he shares you with his brother?"

She glanced at him over her shoulder, cheeks stained pink. "No."

"Good. If you want two men who will obsess over you, treat you like a princess and a hot sex toy all at once, then get on your knees and take our discipline."

Jessa dropped immediately to her knees and presented herself. Cole's eyes glittered, and Burke smiled. Yes, she was exactly what they needed.

* * * *

Jessa felt the plush carpet beneath her and tried to breathe through her excitement. God, what were they doing to her? Five days ago, she'd been a virgin. Sex had seemed so unimportant when compared to everything else. Now she was on her hands and knees waiting for two hot men to spank her and fuck her and take everything she had to give.

Why?

Because she loved them. She let the thought flow through her as Burke settled himself behind her. She looked up, and Cole sat like a king on his throne, watching her with those deep blue eyes that reminded her of the night sky right before a storm. He wore a satisfied smile that made her womb clench, one that told her he meant to fuck her ruthlessly and often tonight.

"This is the right choice, sweetheart. We'll take care of you." Burke's hands soothed over her backside.

She knew that and couldn't resist baiting them. "There's a lot of talking and not a lot of action."

She heard the smack before she felt it. It cracked through the air, stinging her. She bit her bottom lip to keep from crying out. It hurt a little, but nothing she couldn't handle. Instead, she opened herself to the sensation, the visceral heat of it, letting her senses really take it in.

Another smack, this time on the other cheek. She groaned. Fire licked at her skin. Yep. She'd definitely felt that one. Eight more.

She breathed in as Burke struck again, this time a bit faster, a bit harder. She memorized the sound of his hand hitting her ass, the sharp breath he took with each slap, Cole's tightening posture. She let the smells wash over her. Burke and Cole's cologne came first, masculine and clean. But her arousal, musky and pervasive, settled underneath that. No way to hide it. Getting her butt spanked was doing something for her. Burke struck again and again, moving around, laying his hand on every part of her ass, the tops of her thighs, forcing her to spread her legs, then landing a blow directly on her pussy.

The physical sensations astounded her. Her ass was burning, but it was an oddly sweet heat, reminding her how alive skin could feel, reminding her that every part of her body was connected. Burke's every blow washed like a wave from her ass to her pussy, drenching her. Her nipples tightened. She fisted her hand into the carpet, and she whimpered.

But she was dazzlingly alive. This was what she'd found in the last week. Lights seemed brighter. Sounds louder. Smells more decadently tempting. And her painting…oh, she'd found her passion again. When she wasn't with them or working at the hotel, she was painting with a purpose she hadn't had in a long time. Passion. Love. Acceptance. They'd opened doors Jessa hadn't known she'd closed.

Another blow, and she moaned, unable to stop the sound. She didn't even want to. She wanted them to know that she felt it. Burke smacked again, striking in the center of her ass, lighting it up. Jessa waited for the pain to bloom into something else.

"That was ten, sweetheart." She could hear the approval in Burke's thick voice.

"She took it well. I was right." Cole smiled down at her. His body was poised back in the chair, but he'd opened his slacks and released his cock. He stroked the thick column in one hand while he watched her, the very picture of decadence. "She's very submissive sexually."

"You only know the half of it. She's so wet."

Burke's hand stroked her ass now, tracing the flesh he'd struck until he skimmed down to her pussy.

Jessa gasped with pleasure as he forced a finger past her swollen folds and up her hungry cunt. She felt so empty. She hadn't even realized it until just now. She wanted one of them inside her. "Please..."

Burke chuckled behind her, his finger teasing lightly. "Please? What would please you, sweetheart?"

"You. Or Cole. Or both. I need you." She wiggled, trying to tempt that finger deeper inside and maybe to bring a friend.

Burke pulled away. "Not yet. You have something to say to Cole."

She looked up. Cole was still leisurely stroking his cock, the enormous organ standing straight up like a temptation she was dying to taste. Yes, she had a few things to say to Cole. Things like, "take me now" or "I'm going to scream if you don't fuck me." But that wasn't what he wanted to hear. Jessa sat back on her heels, wincing a little at the ache in her ass. After she'd figured out that Cole was into BDSM, she'd looked it up on the web. She'd found thousands of images, articles, and videos on the subject. She understood the single thread that bound every piece of BDSM information together: trust.

She spread her legs wide and lowered her head, trying to keep her spine as straight as possible. The slave pose was a way of greeting a Dom. It showed a submissive's trust and respect. She'd been aroused by the pictures, but a little afraid until she'd understood that this was an exchange of power. It wasn't a stronger person taking from someone weaker. It was a mutual decision meant to bring peace and pleasure to both parties. Jessa hoped she had the pose right. She wanted to please him so much.

"Beautiful, baby. You have no idea how exquisite you are to me." Cole's deep rumble rolled over her. She felt his hand on her head, sliding into her hair. Burke still hovered at her back. She heard the rustling of clothes, but she kept true to her role, leaving her head submissively down when all she wanted to do was watch Cole undress. "Do you have any idea what it means that you figured out how to do this yourself? That you cared enough to study?"

She smiled, though she knew he couldn't see it. Cole was so insular, always waiting for someone to reject him, thanks at least in part to their bastard of an uncle. Burke wasn't far from him, but knew how to hide the insecurity better. But she suspected these two gorgeous men had been rejected before. How many women had used them for the pleasure they could give but refused their love because they couldn't function apart? How many of them had spurned a ménage relationship most of the world would reject? The world could go to hell as far as Jessa was concerned. The world could shrink to just the three of them, and she would be happy.

"Jessa, I have never felt about a woman the way I feel about you."

It took everything she had not to look up. Cole sounded tentative, and despite his deep voice, vulnerable. It took a lot for him to admit that. She kept quiet and listened carefully out of respect.

"I want to be responsible for you. God, I want to be your Master."

It was the equivalent of "I love you" in the BDSM world. Jessa felt tears prick her eyes. Burke made no qualms about his feelings, but Cole had been far more reserved. He'd clearly taken every rejection to heart, while Burke's sunny disposition allowed him to shrug it off more easily and move on.

Cole's confession now warmed her and gave her strength.

"I want your mouth on me while Burke prepares your ass." Cole settled a hand under her chin and lifted it gently. She let him lead her slowly up, enjoying every inch of his body from his muscled legs to that cock that made her mouth water, all the way up to his beautiful blue eyes. "We don't have to play this way. I'll still be here, Jessa. It means a lot that you would try."

She shook her head. She didn't want a Cole who simply tried to please her. She wanted every dark bit of him getting what he needed. "I took my spanking. I want the rest of it, too."

A smile of pure joy lit his face in the form of a bad-boy grin. He leaned down and kissed her, touching her lips sweetly to his. "Then I'll give it to you, baby."

He took his cock in hand, and Jessa sighed, leaning in. She really wanted this, to please him. They had spent days worshipping her. It felt right to revere one of them now.

"All right, baby. Lick the head for me."

The head as he called it, looked enormous, and there was a pearly drop on the tip. Dying to know how he'd taste, she leaned forward and did as he bade, running her tongue over the bulbous tip. Cole tasted clean and woodsy; his masculine scent filled her senses. His hissedin breath made her smile.

"Open up for me, sweetheart," Burke said, pressing down on her back. "I need to plug this pretty ass. We bought this one two days ago for just this occasion."

Cole got to his knees as Jessa went back to all fours. Burke forced her legs farther apart, making a place for himself there. Cole offered his cock as Burke caressed her backside.

She licked at Cole, running her tongue around the head again. She loved the soft skin covering all that hardness. Cole's hand tangled in her hair, forcing her to take him deeper. She opened her mouth, allowing him to invade. He was so big. She could barely get her tongue to swirl around the thick stalk, but she managed it, slowly whirling. He groaned, and the hand in her hair guided her with lazy insistence.

The hand on her hip gripped her, too. The brothers held her firmly in place. Something cold and wet dribbled down the crack of her ass. Lubricant. They had been playing with her ass every time they made love, preparing her for what they wanted. One of them would distract her with pleasure while the other stretched her for the sharing. She'd thought they would simply do it, but they had taken care of her patiently and with great care.

She didn't even move when Burke started to rim her with his fingers. She was used to the pressure. He massaged her ass with the lube, forcing the tight ring of muscles to accept his invasion. She shivered at the pressure and the jangly feelings of heat and tingles he gave her.

"Take me deeper, baby," Cole's voice had gone guttural, his strokes into her mouth quicker. "God, I love how good your mouth feels. So hot and tight on my cock."

"And your ass is so lovely." Burke's words joined with Cole's, a stereo of praise that made her feel wanted and sexy and beloved. "You keep that cock in your mouth. Don't lose Cole. I'm going to work this plug into you. God, I can't wait to get my cock in here. She's going to be so fucking tight."

Cole's hand softened on her hair, petting her. "Ease up, baby. I don't want to come until I'm deep inside you."

Something harder than Burke's finger started to push against her. She groaned around the cock in her mouth. She found a soft place on the underside of his thick stalk, where the hard column met the head. She worked it, worrying it with her tongue to take her mind off the way Burke shoved the plug in and out of her ass.

"You're a bad girl, Jessa," Cole said, pulling away. "I told you to ease up. You're trying to make me lose control. You tried to make me come in your mouth."

He leaned in until his hands found her breasts.

Jessa moaned. "I was trying to forget about the fact that Burke is shoving a piece of plastic up my ass."

Cole pinched at her nipples, twisting. "You obey me in the bedroom, Jessa."

"Or he'll spank you all over again." Burke's silky smooth tone gave away his deep pleasure at his task. "And this bottom is already a perfect pink."

"Keep disobeying, baby, and I'll clamp your nipples. I'll pull out the clover clamps and the chain that goes between them. They'll bite into these sweet little buds, and you'll feel the burn when I tug on the chain as I force you to ride my cock."

Jessa let her head fall forward as he tugged on her nipples. Each little wrench of his fingers flashed fire down to her pussy. So hot. She'd never been so aroused, and his words were just adding kindling to the fire. She suddenly wanted to try those clamps. Apparently, she was a little bit of a freak, but with Burke and Cole, it made sense. They accepted this side of her, wanted it. She was with men she trusted. Men she loved.

"I'd like that, Cole."

"Oh, baby, you're so fucking perfect." His hand slid down, and suddenly she felt him pinching at her clit.

"Oh, oh." She couldn't stop it. It felt too good. Cole still plucked at her right nipple, squeezing harshly, then rolling it. His other hand played in her pussy, sliding all around while Burke seated the plug deep in her ass.

"Give it to her, Cole. I want to watch her come."

Jessa nearly screamed when Cole took his hand away. "Don't stop!"

There was a smack to her ass that made her moan. The plug shifted, causing waves of jagged sensation to streak through her.

"Hush, Jessa," Cole said, his voice a sharp bark. "You'll get what you need when I decide you need it, not before."

As though she weighed nothing at all, he lifted her up and she found herself falling on top of him, sprawled across the big bed that dominated the suite. The shades were open, and the twinkling lights of Manhattan lit up the room.

"I told you I would force you to ride my cock. I mean what I say, baby. Burke, I need a condom."

Jessa shook her head. "No. You don't. I'm on the pill. I want to feel you. I'm clean."

"Obviously," Burke said, standing next to the bed, a concerned look on his face. "Cole and I never have sex without a condom. And you might not believe it, but we're not out there every night with a different woman. We're clean, but maybe we should still..."

"No," she said, practically pleading. "It's safe. I don't want to stop. I want to feel you, skin to skin."

Cole gave her his answer by thrusting up and joining them in a single smooth move. "Oh, god, that feels so fucking good."

It did. Nothing between them but shared breaths and bare flesh. She was so glad she'd decided to go to the clinic and get on the pill. No stopping for protection. No latex. Just her and them, the way it should always be.

"That sounds heavenly, sweetheart." Burke shoved his pants down and off. "I want a turn, too."

"You'll get it," Cole replied. "Soon. I had her pussy first. You take her ass."

Cole surged up, pumping inside her. With his hands, he forced her to grind down on him. He was so damn deep, she gasped, mouth open, sensations washing over her as her pussy clasped and grabbed at him, pulling him even farther inside.

"Fuck. I want that. I want that so goddamn bad." Burke reached for the lube.

"Come for us, baby. Let go for us before we take you together. I want you soft and happy when we share you the first time."

She gave over to him and rode that big cock. The plug took up a lot of space, making her feel fuller than ever before. She slid up and down, Cole's hands on her ass, a finger on the plug, holding it deep. She slid down on him, her clit hitting his pelvis as he surged up, hitting just the right spot inside her once, twice, again. Then she came with a mewling cry, the pleasure crashing through her system. She fell on Cole's chest, and his arms closed around her, making her feel safe and warm.

"Get that plug out and get inside her, Burke. I don't know how much longer I can last. Fuck, she feels so good." Cole groaned against her ear, spreading kisses across her cheek, brushing his lips over her mouth.

Jessa felt the bed dip as Burke climbed on. His hands moved tenderly over her ass, and the plug slid out. She sighed, tightened. Cole was still thick inside her body, holding her impaled against him, but now she felt the loss of the plug. Her ass felt empty.

But not for long. Cole soothed his hand down her back as Burke spread her cheeks. She whimpered as she felt him spread more lube on her anus, preparing her to take something far larger than the plug.

"It's going to be so good, baby. We're going to fill you completely," Cole murmured, his hips moving in lazy, teasing thrusts.

Every time he rubbed her clit, a little aftershock sent more pleasure through her that just added to the sweet aftermath of her stunning climax. As they touched, soothed, and worked, she felt boneless and momentarily sated. She let them have their way—just like they'd planned.

Cole's hands tightened around her, hugging her as she felt Burke's cock at the rim of her untried hole.

"Sweetheart, you're so beautiful," Burke said as he

gently stroked himself in, taking her in increments, forcing his cock inside in neat little thrusts. "You feel *so* good."

"It burns." Far more than the plug, in fact. She gritted her teeth. It wasn't pain exactly but it wasn't comfortable.

"It's all right," Cole whispered. "It's going to be okay. Let him in, baby. Arch your back."

She lifted her ass a bit higher, pressing her breasts against Cole's chest. His heart beat loudly with hers as the burn of Burke's dick sinking a bit deeper seared her. He worked his way inside her, bumping against the tight muscles of her ass.

"Push out against me," Burke gritted out, taking her hips in hand and lifting her ass higher.

Jessa pushed out, wondering if he would really fit inside her. A moment later, he popped past the barrier and slowly filled her with his cock.

God. She had to force herself to breathe. They were everywhere, so deep and all around her. Her world was filled with Burke and Cole.

"Are you all right, sweetheart?" Burke's voice was tentative. His hands gripped her hips, betraying his tension as he thrust gently.

"Please be all right, Jessa." Cole's face was tight, his brow knitted together, jaw clenched.

Something about the big bad Dom begging her to accept them made her smile. She pushed back, wiggling against Burke. Nerves she'd never known she had lit up. She shook with the sensation, and as they filled her in tandem with deep breaths and guttural moans, she trembled with need, quickly rushing to the edge of pleasure. She cried out.

"Oh, that's it, sweetheart. Let it go. Let it happen." Burke clutched her hips as he thrust in.

Cole groaned when she seesawed back his way. "This is perfect, the three of us together. The way it should be."

Every way she moved brought her pleasure. Cole filled her pussy, his thick dick striking at her G-spot when he pushed up. Burke dragged his cock out almost to the rim of her asshole, marking the path with burning pleasure, before he shoved deep again, forcing her to grind her clit against Cole.

They set a brutal pace. Jessa gave up trying to control it. She became what they had warned, their pleasure toy, a soft, sweet thing they passed between them. She would have fought it if they'd treated her that way outside the bedroom, but instead, they treated her like a princess, with courtesy, always thinking of her wants and needs. They made it easy to give over to them here, to be pulled and pushed as they fought for pleasure. She felt like they'd been fused together, formed into one unit as they worked inside her. As they made love, they were whole.

All the languor from her previous orgasm was gone. A new driving pressure built again, surging, searing, until little pleas and whimpers fell from her mouth.

"Help her, Burke. I'm dying here," Cole growled.

Burke's arm wrapped around as he drove into her, one relentless thrust after another. He reached between her and Cole and found her clit, rubbing it with sweet friction. Cole thrust up. Every sensation in her body turned molten and converged. They sent her flying again, this time higher and longer than ever before as she screamed their names.

Jessa bucked against them, trying to prolong the pleasure. Cole thrust up, his face contorting as he came inside her. She could feel the hot wash of his seed flooding her.

Burke groaned behind her, his grip on her hips punishing as he held her tight and forced his cock in until she could feel his balls against her ass. He thrust in and out, filling her ass with his come until finally he fell forward, his front plastering her back.

They relaxed into a heap, Jessa safe and warm between them. She fell asleep, happy to have a piece of each inside her.

* * * *

Jessa woke slowly, reaching for them. Every muscle in her body felt deliciously used. She stretched and yawned. She kept her eyes closed, letting her mind wander a bit. It was New Year's Day. She was looking at a whole new year, a whole new life—one with Burke and Cole.

"Sweetheart?"

She opened her eyes. There was a reason she hadn't felt them next to her. They both stood by the bed, fully dressed in suits and ties and expensive shoes. She could smell coffee and the deliciously savory scent of bacon. She sat up, pulling the sheet with her, anxiety starting to penetrate her brain.

"What's happening?"

No answer.

Not only were they dressed, their faces were grave.

They didn't look like two men who were happy that they'd spent the night making love to their woman. They looked like men who were leaving. They looked to each other, having one of those silent conversations. She just knew they were trying to figure out how to deal with her.

Her stomach turned. "At least you didn't sneak out. I guess that's something."

Burke got to one knee. "Sweetheart, we are not sneaking out."

"But you are leaving." She could see it plainly on his face.

"Yes," Cole said.

She could always count on Cole to state the facts without sugarcoating. Burke would try to put the best sheen on it. Cole didn't bother. She turned to him. "Do I get an explanation, or do you just say 'thanks' and walk away?"

"I don't want to leave you, Jessa," Cole stated, a stark look on his face. "I do *not* want to go. If there was any other way, I wouldn't ever leave that fucking bed again. But I made promises."

Tears pricked at her eyes. "What kind of promises?"

Burke took her hand. "We have some friends, sweetheart. They're having some problems. Family problems. Their cousin is in trouble."

"What does that have to do with you?"

"We have contacts. We can help her," Cole stated. His jaw was a stark line, his eyes sunken, as if he hadn't slept.

Jessa swallowed. What was going on? Were they telling her the truth? Had this all been a scam to get her in bed? If it was, she reasoned, they would have just left.

"You have to go now?"

Burke nodded. "Yes. Part of why we were here in New York was to make some inquiries for our friends. We got a call an hour ago. We've got a really good lead on her location."

"I can help. I'll go with you."

Cole's eyes widened with horror. "No. You are *not* coming with us, Jessa. You will stay here, and you will be safe. That is an order."

The Dom was back. At least he seemed to care. "How long will you be gone?"

Cole sighed and sank down next to Burke, reaching for her other hand. "I hope it's only a couple of weeks. No more than a month or two. I can't tell you more than that."

"What you're doing…it's dangerous." She didn't make it a question. She knew.

Burke brought her hand to his lips. "That's why we're keeping you out of it. The less you know the better."

She tried to pull away. How was this happening? Last night had been perfect. She'd been safe and loved and looking forward to building something beautiful and lasting with them. Now they were leaving.

"Jessa." Cole sounded tortured. "Jessa, I love you."

"Don't you say that when you're leaving me."

He took her face in his hands and fused his stare with hers. "I love you."

"We love you, Jessa. You're the one for us," Burke said, caressing her arm. "We're going to finish our mission and come back for you. You better be ready to move since our business is in Dallas."

"We want to marry you, Jessa. We want a life with you. Please don't think we're leaving you lightly." Cole pulled her between them and kissed her.

But they did leave. Two hours later, Jessa showered. She dressed and walked out of the hotel room where she'd lost her virginity and her heart. She went back to work and prayed they would come back to her.

# Chapter Six

*Present Day – Dallas, Texas*

Burke woke to the sound of the door slamming. A blast of chilly air smacked him. He sat straight up in bed, shaking off the dream. He'd been back in New York, making love to Jessa, her silken body moving against his. She'd told him she loved him. She'd looked at Cole and whispered those sweet words to his brother, too. Then she took every kiss, touch, and thrust they had to give. He'd replayed that night over and over again in his mind. That last night with her had been the best of his life. The next morning had been one of the worst. Every night since, he'd dreamed about her face as he and Cole had walked away.

"Sorry," Cole said gruffly, his hands full as he walked into the tiny room. His face was red. He'd obviously been standing in the cold for a while. "I didn't mean to wake you. The wind is pretty bad out there. It looks like a storm is coming in tonight. I made a couple of calls."

Jessa was still beside Burke, stretching and rubbing

her eyes. Her hair was slightly rumpled from sleep, and she looked perfect to Burke. Despite the danger, all he wanted to do was haul her into his arms, kiss those sensual lips, and sink into her until they were both warm and satisfied. His cock didn't give a shit that she no longer wanted him.

"Did you call to check on Caleb?" Jessa asked, her voice a little hoarse.

"He's fine, Jessa," Cole assured her. "Dex said he slept late, and now he's having a ball playing with their kids. He's eating fine, had some cereal and a bottle. He pooped, too. I thought that was weird. Dex just tossed that out there. Was he supposed to tell me that?"

A smile pulled at Jessa's lips. "He's obviously a well-trained dad. We moms like to keep up with stuff like that. Babies have touchy digestive systems. He's in a new place, and his schedule is all messed up. It's a good sign that he's eating and playing and pooping."

"Oh. All right, then. Good information." Cole put some bags on the table. "I got some breakfast. Just biscuit sandwiches. There's a fast food place next door. Sorry it's not—" *The Waldorf*—"anything better, but I didn't want to be gone long."

Burke winced at his brother's mental stutter and got up to grab some coffee. He would need it. There was no doubt in Burke's mind what his brother had been thinking.

After he'd set up the computers the night before, he'd started downloading everything he had on Delgado. He'd read late into the night, looking for clues, any weakness, before Cole had awakened and made room for him beside Jessa's soft body, demanding he get some sleep.

She mumbled her thanks. "How long do we have before Marco's timeline kicks in?"

Burke was brutally aware that the bastard had given them twenty-four hours before this little game began. If they could trust him to wait.

"Seven hours at best. We have some decisions to make." Cole opened the bag and pulled out a sandwich.

"Can we make decisions with our pants on, please?" Jessa asked, frowning Burke's way.

Burke shrugged. She hadn't minded when they were sleeping. Despite her warnings, after she'd dropped off, she'd rolled into Cole's arms. They'd slept entwined until it was Cole's watch. Then she'd merely cuddled back against Burke. She might not trust them when she was awake, but when she was vulnerable, she sought out comfort and the security of their embrace.

"It would have been too hot with my pants on." He declined to mention that it would have been too hot because her body had been pressed to his. He could be a gentleman.

"Burke, those tight little boxer briefs don't do much to hide the fact that you have an enormous erection. Am I the only one this bothers?"

Cole grunted out a laugh, but Burke simply turned to her, giving her a full view of what sleeping next to her had wrought. She wasn't going to let him be a gentleman. "Well, sweetheart, that's what happens when I sleep with my cock nestled against your beautiful ass."

She gasped, sounding a little like the virgin she'd been before she met them.

Cole smiled her way. It was the smile that always let

Burke know his brother was about to throw him under a bus. "Don't let him fool you, baby. He wakes up like that every morning."

"Fucker. Like you don't. We both have the same dreams." He pinned Jessa to the bed with his intent stare. "We dream about you, sweetheart, and we wake up hard."

Her gaze slipped back and forth between the two of them, then dropped. "Could I have some coffee please? From someone wearing pants."

Damn it, he should have kept his fucking mouth shut.

Cole brought her a cup and a sandwich. "Cream and sugar. Two spoons. And please eat, Jessa. You didn't eat on the plane last night."

Burke knew that Cole wanted to demand, order her to eat, but they didn't have the right to command anything of her that didn't pertain to her immediate safety. Curbing himself, holding back from Jessa, hurt Cole like hell. Burke didn't like it any better.

She accepted the coffee but put the sandwich down. "I don't feel much like eating."

Burke didn't either. He wanted to work through their problems with Jessa somehow. But now wasn't the time. And he wanted to see Caleb. God, a single day as a dad, and he was already freaking out about his kid. He shook it off. Their son was safe with the James family. They were insanely wealthy and very powerfully connected. They would take care of Caleb. But the James brothers weren't the only powerful people they knew. "Did you get Rafe or Kade on the phone? I tried last night, but no one answered."

Cole nodded, finally looking away from Jessa.

Thankfully, the question directed his brother's attention elsewhere. "They were…busy last night."

Burke took a long sip of the fast food coffee. Swill, but still better than some he'd had in the past. He could bet how Rafe and Kade had been occupied. They had business interests in the States, but they loved American women. Lots of them. And they loved to share. It was just one reason they had all bonded as friends. "What did they say?"

"They're in town. They have some meeting with Black Oak about the new refineries in Bezakistan. They're going to come out here and bring some equipment with them. Sat phone, better computer equipment, new car, and a whole lot of cash. And cell phones. I don't want Hilary to know our number after we get out of town. It's better for all of us. They're bringing some credit cards, too, and passports in case we want to leave the country. I know we can't stay in one place too long, but I think it's worth the wait to meet with them before we move."

Jessa turned, her eyes wide. "I can't leave the country without my baby."

"Jessa, we'll do what we have to do to keep you alive." Burke didn't want to leave her again. He was sick at the thought, but she stood the best chance of staying alive somewhere far away.

She shook her head frantically. "No, I *can't* leave the country."

Cole frowned. "You'll be surprised what you can do when I tie you up and shove you on a private jet."

Burke looked at Jessa for a moment. She was still tired, despite her sleep. It was written in the circles under her eyes. She was still the most beautiful thing in the world to him, but she looked fragile, haunted. And very afraid. She clasped her hands tightly in her lap. "What haven't you told us, sweetheart?"

"How did you know?" Jessa asked.

Because he'd made a careful study of her. He had a brilliant mind and a very good memory. Every exchange they'd ever had, he'd kept vibrant and alive in his brain. "You wring your hands when you're upset or unsure."

She also did it when she didn't want to admit things. Like she had that night she'd admitted she was a virgin.

Jessa unclasped her hands. "Damn observant men. Someone texted my phone last night. I had my purse in Caleb's diaper bag, and when we had to leave him, I grabbed it. The phone has pictures of Caleb, and I thought keeping it was harmless. I wasn't planning to call anyone. I thought if you knew he'd contacted me, you'd take the phone away, so I didn't say anything. But then you started talking about what sounded like leaving the country…" She sighed, then reached into the small bag Hannah had given her and pulled out her phone. Jessa held it out, her eyes full of tears. "I knew I needed to say something. I just want my pictures."

Cole grabbed the phone.

Burke sat beside Jessa. He would let Cole do the investigative work while he handled their woman. Even if she refused to be, he still thought of her that way. This was one of the joys of sharing. There was always one of them to handle the necessary business, which freed the other to comfort or protect the female.

"Sweetheart, no one's going to take your pictures, but we're going to turn off anything that sends or receives a signal. You'll still be able to look at the pictures and use a few apps."

"Motherfucker!" Cole's curse reverberated through the room. "Goddamn it. I'm going to kill that dog-fucking son of a bitch. I'm going rip him into little fucking pieces with my bare hands and shove them down his shit-sucking throat."

"Wow, he knows a lot of bad words," Jessa said, eyes wide.

"And he's not afraid to use them," Burke drawled. "What does the message say?"

Cole put the phone down and picked up his own—the disposable, untraceable phone Dex had given him. He dialed a number and continued cursing.

Jessa watched Cole, but spoke to Burke. "It said that he knew you two would try to get me out of the country, but that if you called in favors to have me taken abroad, he would have no choice but to go after Caleb."

Burke closed his eyes, cursing mentally, using all the same words his brother had. "Marco knew we'd eventually come up with this plan."

"You were really going to send me away?"

He hated the way her lips trembled, the hurt in her voice. He hated the fact that she was so scared. "Yes. We talked about it while you were sleeping. We were going to send you with some friends who could have kept you safe. Once you were in their country, Gavin James was going to fly Caleb to Bezakistan himself. We didn't have enough time to pull it off at the onset, and the fucker knew it. That's why he only gave us twenty-four hours. But it still might be the best plan."

She shook her head. "No. I believe him. He'll come

after us."

Burke raised an arrogant brow. "He couldn't get to you in Bezakistan."

"I can't stay there the rest of my life," Jessa said, frustration evident in her tone. "He wants to kill me. I don't get why, but I have to fight this. I can't risk letting him come after my son, not even for a second. Unless you manage to kill this asshole, we'll be looking over our shoulders for the rest of our lives, worried that he's gunning for us."

"I will kill him, Jessa. I won't let anything happen to you or our son," Cole vowed, hanging up the phone.

She was quiet for a moment. "Exactly who is this man?"

"Fucking dead," Cole said, his face still red.

Jessa turned to Burke. "Could you please tell me? Without the gorilla chest thumping."

He didn't want to. It would have been so much easier if he'd just been able to pack her off with Rafe and Kade, then pick her up when it was over. Then he wouldn't have to admit just how much they'd screwed up.

"Tell me! I have the right to know why this man wants me dead."

"We usually handle security problems for corporations," Cole explained. "But in this case, we were helping our friends from Bezakistan find their cousin, like we explained."

"Alea, yes." She waved him off, hugging the blanket to her chest. "Now give me the rest of the story."

Burke took a long breath and plunged in. "Marco believes we're responsible for his father's death."

"That's bullshit. I wish I had been. I would have

fucking enjoyed pulling the trigger," Cole growled. "But no, I was a good boy and sent the asshole off to prison. If I had known he'd be dead so soon, I would have put a bullet in him myself—and Marco right after him—and ended everyone's goddamn misery."

Burke stared pointedly at his brother. "What Cole is trying to say in his Neanderthal way is that the elder Delgado was a very bad man and that a rival stabbed and killed him behind bars."

"He deserved everything he got. The fucker trafficked young women. He filled client orders and sold them to brothels all over South America. He bought and sold girls to fulfill male fantasies, made them prostitutes and sex slaves." Cole never flinched.

But Jessa did. She paled visibly. "Oh, my god. It's so horrible."

"A single word can't describe that kind of hell." Cole continued. "We got involved because we did some security work for Bezakistan when we were Navy SEALs. Some extremists kidnapped Sheikh al Mussad, and we rescued him."

"Why? Is he a dictator? How does Delgado come into this picture? Were they in business together?"

Burke laughed at the thought. "Talib? No. He's not a dictator, and he would never harm a woman. And he'd certainly never go into business with Marco. Though I will admit his family has a long history of kidnapping females. The women all ended up being very happy brides, however. Tal and his brothers were educated in London, so he runs Bezakistan like a business. A ridiculously profitable business. They're a small country, but they're sitting on a wealth of resources. Talib's father decided to spread the wealth many years ago. Every citizen in the country gets a portion of the money from the oil they put out. It's the single wealthiest country per capita in the world."

She bit into her bottom lip as she considered what he'd said. "Then why would someone kidnap him?"

"The region doesn't look kindly on the way the royal family runs the country. They cling to some very old practices."

"Oh. The polyandry. Yeah, I know their neighboring countries think it's a mortal sin."

"Yes." Cole smirked down at her. "But the mortal sin of all the brothers in a family sharing a single wife means there's no need to divide the kingdom or the wealth. Anyway, my team was sent in to rescue the sheikh. Our government didn't like the idea of a less friendly leader in control of all that oil."

Cole's eyes went dark as they always did when he thought of that day. Burke was pretty sure he was the only one to whom Cole had told the whole story. "Tal was in bad shape by the time we rescued him. We were trapped for a couple of days under fire until we got away."

"Until you managed to kill everyone." His brother still had nightmares.

Cole shrugged it off. "Same difference. We got cut off from my team, and I got him out of there. Anyway, we got to be friends. He does a lot of work with Black Oak Oil, the company Gavin and Dex run with their brother, Slade. When they were looking for a firm to handle outside security, Talib recommended us."

"So when his cousin disappeared in New York City,

he asked us to look for her," Burke explained. "The morning we left you, we'd just gotten word that Delgado had a girl for us."

"So you used a fake last name while you were investigating Marco's father," Jessa said. "You didn't tell me the truth because…?"

"We were posing as men looking to buy a slave," Cole said bluntly. "We had to build a whole cover story that would check out to Ricardo Delgado's people. Any loose end could have unraveled the whole case."

Burke winced at the indelicate way his brother put everything. "We had to work very carefully to even get the elder Delgado to talk to us. It was months before the cautious bastard agreed to a meeting. We took possession of our 'slave' about three hours after we left you that morning. When the buy went down, we recorded everything and turned it over to the feds. It started a whole shit storm. The FBI stormed the Delgado compound and arrested Ricardo. He was dead in prison six weeks later."

"And now his son wants you to feel his pain." Her fists clutched the folds of the blanket.

"Yes. He figured out that you were our weakness. I'm sure he started investigating us. It wouldn't have taken much to find out that we'd hired a private investigator named Landry to keep tabs on you while we were gone. And apparently he bribed the PI to keep us apart."

"What do you mean?" Jessa looked between the two of them as if searching for answers.

Cole scrubbed a hand through his hair. "We got regular reports, Jessa. We knew you went to Scotland,

and Landry said that you'd gotten married there."

Bitterness welled inside Burke. So much time lost. Marco Delgado had cost him in ways Burke couldn't have imagined. Marco Delgado had made sure he hadn't been there at the birth of his child. That he hadn't held Jessa's hand and comforted her. That he hadn't been there when Caleb woke up in the middle of the night. Fucking Marco had played them like pawns on a chessboard.

Jessa rolled her eyes, a little huff coming out of her mouth. "He's the reason you kept insisting that Angus was my husband. So this PI was on Marco's payroll?"

"Right." Burke sighed. "And Landry didn't bother to mention your pregnancy. We would have come home. We were going to leave South America after we rescued Alea and come back to you. But he said that you'd married..." He shrugged. "We didn't have anything to come home to but a fucking empty condo, so we decided to stay on and rescue as many as we could."

She shook her head. "I went to Scotland early in March. That was long after you left me without a single phone call or e-mail. Or even a shred of real information about you. Don't try to cover your asses now. You could have contacted me, asked me about my 'marriage' yourselves. I get that you were doing something important. I really do, but I was important, too. Well, I thought I was. I realize now that I misunderstood. I was a stupid little virgin who thought sex meant love."

This was what he'd wanted to avoid. "Jessa, we told you we love you. I still love you. Cole still loves you."

She stood, leaving the coffee and food behind. "You also told me you would come back for me, so you'll forgive me if I find your undying devotion hard to believe. You lied about everything, Burke. You're two dangerous men who amused yourselves with a little virgin who was dumb enough to get pregnant. I'm sure I was an interesting conquest, but that's all I was. I'm going to take a shower. No, you are not invited. Just get this guy so I can get back to my son, and you two can get on with your lives."

Cole reached out and grabbed her arm. "If you think we're going to let you go at the end of this, you don't know us at all."

She pulled away. "Yeah, well, since I just found out your real last name and occupation in the last twenty-four hours, I think I can safely say that you're right. I never really knew you. Now let me go. Don't you need to clean your gun or shoot bad guys or something?"

As if he'd been burned, Cole released her. She turned and walked to the bathroom, her face set in stubborn lines. The door closed with a little slam.

"That went well. You know you could tone down the caveman act." Burke looked down at his sandwich, but his stomach turned. He understood why Jessa didn't want to eat.

"Yeah, well, your nice guy act isn't working, either. I'm not letting her walk away. She belongs to us. She's the mother of our child. I'm not going to sit back and wave as she leaves."

So stubborn. "Neither am I, but I don't think tying her up is going to work in this case."

"I don't see why not. She can't leave if she's bound to the bed with both of us deep inside her."

His brother's skull could be so fucking thick that not

even a chainsaw could penetrate it. "We fucked up. We got scared for her safety and fucked up. We didn't want her to know about our work or tell her how often we get our hands bloody. We should have told her everything, but we kept our mouths shut."

Cole's eyes turned down. "Yeah, well, would it have mattered? You saw how she reacted just now. Someone as sweet as Jessa doesn't need a man as hard as me. Our job is dangerous. I'm not good for her and Caleb."

"She's not pissed about our work. She's furious that we didn't call. And the minute we thought there was an obstacle, we let her go. We shouldn't have believed Landry or given up on Jessa without checking out this 'husband' ourselves. We caused this. We have to make it right."

Cole's whole body deflated. "You should work it out with her. I love her, but I'm too rough. I don't fit into the life she deserves. I sure as hell can't raise a kid, not when his mom thinks I'm nothing more than a gun-toting motherfucker."

"Do *not* let Uncle Martin win. Whatever shit he told you, you aren't unwanted and unlovable. Were you listening to her, damn it?"

But Cole was done. Burke could see it plainly. His brother turned away. "I need to make a few more calls. Did you get what you needed off the hard drive?"

Burke felt his hands tighten into fists. He knew how much Jessa meant to his brother. Cole had gone off on a two day drunk the day they got word she'd married someone else. Burke wasn't sure Cole hadn't been trying to kill himself since. He'd been reckless. Dangerous. Never around the women they had saved, but since he'd learned about Jessa's marriage, he'd taken chances he wouldn't have before.

Cole had accepted the loss not because he didn't love her, but because he didn't think he deserved her or that she could ever love him in return.

His mouth a flat line, Cole turned back to him. "I'll kill Marco. My wedding gift to you two. I'll kill him for her if it's the last thing I do."

Burke was suddenly afraid that Cole's words would prove all too true.

\* \* \* \*

*Eleven months earlier, February 14 – New York City*

"What did you say?" Jessa asked, her mind not able to really register the doctor's words.

The middle-aged woman looked entirely competent in her white coat. "You're pregnant."

*Pregnant. With child. Knocked up. Left behind.*

"But I was on birth control," she sputtered.

The doctor shrugged. She worked a low cost clinic for women. She'd obviously heard it all before. "No birth control is one hundred percent effective. I noticed on your chart that you came in and got the prescription about seven weeks ago. Did our pharmacist explain how it worked? You have to take them every day."

She wasn't stupid. "I know that."

"And you should use condoms for the first month. It takes some time for the hormones to take effect in your body." The doctor raised her eyebrows over very sensible looking glasses. "Did she go over all of that with you?"

Jessa shook her head, the reality starting to set in. "I

told her I didn't need a lecture. I was running late to a meeting. I thought I knew what I was doing."

"You've never had girlfriends who were on the pill?" the doctor asked, crossing her arms over her chest.

"No." She'd never had real girlfriends, period. Not since sixth grade when her father decided she was far too smart to stay behind with her friends. She'd been accelerated, moved through grades with no thought to her social life. She hadn't had one. She'd studied and when she could, worked on her art. She'd been far too young to be friends with her classmates. She'd gotten used to being alone.

Except for one week when she'd thought, just for a moment, that she wasn't any more. Tears spilled on her cheeks.

"Oh, sweetie," the doctor said, her demeanor changing in an instant. "It's going to be okay. Can you call the father?"

Which one? She shook her head. She wasn't going to go into her ménage relationship now. "I lost his number."

The doctor took Jessa's hand in hers. "You should look him up. He should know what's happened. Look, you have options."

"No. I want my baby."

"Good. You're not a child. You have a job. You can come here for your appointments. It's going to be okay. But he should know."

The doctor gave her hand a reassuring squeeze and left her to get dressed.

Twenty minutes later, she walked out, the frozen blast of Manhattan air hitting her straight in the chest. What she hadn't told the doctor was that she'd already tried to find them. After she'd realized she had lost the number, she'd tried looking them up. She knew they lived in Dallas. She knew the name of their business.

Except it didn't exist. Neither did they.

She walked back toward the hotel where she had to tell her sweet but flighty aunt that she was in trouble again. She was jostled and shoved by the crowd. She was surrounded by a throng of humanity, but she was alone.

They weren't coming back. They had used her, and in what seemed to be the cruelest way possible. If they had just told her what they wanted, she might have gone along anyway, but she wouldn't have fallen in love. She would have guarded her heart.

But they had told her they loved her.

A ruthless little lie.

She was alone. Except she wasn't any more. Her hand went to her belly. She would never be alone again. She would have someone who needed her, whom she couldn't let down. She'd spent weeks drowning in her own misery with tears, but she couldn't do that now. She had a baby to think of.

She had a life to build. She turned. She wouldn't talk to her aunt yet. The gallery owner had made her a very interesting offer. One she'd turned down because it would take her to Scotland, and she had been waiting for them.

No more waiting. They had left. They had lied. They were out there somewhere, and it was a good bet they had moved on with their lives, found another woman or two.

It was time to build her own life—and one for her baby.

# Chapter Seven

*Present Day – Dallas, Texas*

Jessa finished drying her hair and stared in the mirror. She wasn't sure she recognized the woman staring back at her. She looked tired and older than she really was. She sniffled. She'd cried in the shower, the pressure just too much to handle. Her whole world had upended in the course of a few short hours, and it was damn hard to handle.

She missed Caleb. His absence was a gaping wound in her chest. It was mid-morning, the time she usually brought her canvas into the living room to catch the soft, pure light that came through her windows. She would hum and talk to Caleb while he played and napped in his blue and white playpen. The hours would fly by as she mixed her colors and brought the pictures in her head to life. But she wouldn't work today. And her latest series was gone, destroyed by a man she'd met for less than a minute over a year ago. Five large canvases all burned. Two smaller ones, too, meant for a gallery.

She tried to shake it off. She didn't need the money

now. Her bank account was healthy. And she would never have sold the large works. She wouldn't have put them out there on the off chance that someone would recognize the men she'd painted with bold lines, broad strokes, and vibrant, vivid colors. Her agent had seen them and called them modern and erotic. She'd said she could sell them in a heartbeat for a pretty penny, but Jessa had refused.

Now the point was moot. They were gone, like her pictures and her videos, like all of Caleb's toys, and the crib she'd had to put together herself.

She wasn't just tired. She was angry, too. Furious.

Jessa pulled the robe she'd discovered in her small bag around her body. The bathroom, despite the hot water she'd used, was chilly. She'd forgotten to get her clothes, but the robe was large and warm. Not as warm as she'd been when she'd awakened in the middle of the night with Cole's big arms around her. She'd heard Burke working quietly nearby, his hands tapping at the keys of the computer. She'd felt his eyes settle on them.

And she'd cuddled closer. Despite all the trauma of the night, with Cole enveloping her, she'd felt safe enough to go back to sleep almost instantly. When she'd awakened this morning, Burke's arms had been wrapped around her.

There was a knock on the door outside, and Jessa nearly jumped out of her skin. She took a deep breath as she heard Cole greet a man he called Kade.

Their friends from Bezakistan. The ones with whom they had wanted her to go into hiding. Jessa opened the door and walked into the cramped room. If she let Burke and Cole, they would completely steamroll her, and she wouldn't have any say in her own protection. She wasn't about to let that happen.

Two insanely gorgeous men with dark hair, dark eyes, and golden skin sauntered in, one carrying a duffel bag stuffed full. She stared. They could have walked off the pages of a magazine. Tall and lean, both men were dressed impeccably. One was slightly broader than the other, with a hawk-like air about him. The other man seemed a bit younger than his brother, his solid face handsome. He wore a faint, mischievous smile.

"Hello. You must be Jessa," the younger man said smoothly, somehow instantly setting her at ease as he crossed the room in two long strides. "I am Kadir al Mussad. It is my greatest pleasure to meet you."

Oh, she believed him. He was one of those men who could just make a girl feel like the only woman in the world. He took her hand in both of his, surrounding her. "Hello."

He smiled, his lips curling, making his whole face come alive. "You are most beautiful."

"Cut that shit out now, Kade." Cole yanked her away from Kade.

Damn it. Even as beautiful as this man was, she found herself attracted to two goddamn men who looked exactly alike, one a smooth talker, the other this Neanderthal glaring daggers at his friend.

"She's not going to Bezakistan with you," Burke said.

The taller man frowned. "Pity. She would do well there. I could give her between three and five husbands very quickly. In fact, Talib would love her. He has a thing for redheads. She could save our kingdom. We only have another year left, you know."

"She's ours," Burke said with a little growl.

"Between three and five men?" Jessa gaped. "I can't handle two."

The older brother's lips curled up, but she wouldn't exactly call it a smile. Instead, the expression promised all manner of decadent delights. "I think you would be surprised what you could handle if you were properly prepared. Trust me. I know how to prepare a woman."

"And I know how to prepare a body for burial," Cole scowled.

"He really does," Burke added, his voice deep and dark. "I do, too."

The other man ignored them. "I am Prince Rafiq, second in line to the throne of Bezakistan. And because my brother owes Cole his life, I regret that we must forego carrying you off to my country to seduce you."

Kade raised a brow. "Seducing her is a tempting thought, but she is the mother of their child. We will honor our debt."

"Indeed." He turned to Cole and Burke. "Reconsider sending her with us. We will keep her safe and make certain no one touches her. She can disappear into the palace. Our jet is fueled."

"I appreciate the offer, but I can't leave the country," Jessa explained.

Rafe's handsome face turned down with what Jessa thought was disapproval. He waved a hand toward her, but spoke to Cole and Burke. "You will allow your precious gem to make such a decision unaided? Why is she not tied up? I have rope if you have need of it."

"And a gag," Kade offered. "It would be terrible to

close that pretty mouth, but she looks quite capable of screaming."

"I bite, too," Jessa promised. Yeah, she could see why all these guys got along with the Lennox brothers.

"I am sure Cole has his own rope, and I would be shocked if he hadn't gagged many a woman over the years," Rafe offered.

Jessa shook her head. "It doesn't matter, guys. I can't leave the country or this man will come after my son. I'll never have my life back until we deal with this bastard. I won't leave. Now, I would like to know exactly what's going on. Are we moving? Have we found out anything about where this Marco person is?"

Burke crossed his arms over his chest. "That's my girl. And Rafe is right about Cole. He's damn good with a knot. Now, what have you two found out?"

Kade straightened up, suddenly looking more professional. "First off, Cole called earlier about your phone, Jessa. We have confirmed that no one has turned on the tracking device. You should be safe. Now, about Delgado, we have uncovered a few things. We know that he has a private jet. The FAA shows the Delgado jet filed a flight request late last night for a small town outside Albuquerque. They landed. I don't know where they went from there, but on a short flight, they wouldn't have to file another request. But you should know that I also discovered Delgado owns several businesses in the Dallas-Fort Worth area."

Jessa's heart rate tripled. "He's here? In the same city as my son?"

Cole held a hand out. "Caleb is safe. Gavin is moving the whole family to his penthouse. They own a floor with a private elevator. They can shut the floor off from the rest of the building and lock down the stairwell, if need be. And if we get really worried about Caleb, Gavin promised to take him to Alaska. No one gets in and out of River Run without the whole town knowing it. It's going to be okay."

But Burke was frowning. "We have friends in Albuquerque. A couple of our old SEAL team members live out there. From Delgado's perspective, it would be a good bet that we'd run there and potentially stash Jessa with them."

Rafe's fingers tapped along one of the briefcases he'd brought in. "Or it's a ruse. When I hunt, it is good for the prey to believe you are in one place when you're really in another. All I'm saying is you should be careful. It would be easy for him to drive here from Albuquerque or to change planes."

"I covered our tracks," Burke argued. "I haven't used a credit card. The car can't be traced back to us. He could have followed us from D.C. and figured out we flew to Dallas with Gavin James, but after that, he'd have no way of knowing where we are. Dallas is a big city."

"Unless he has someone on the payroll at Black Oak," Cole mused.

"I'll talk to Gavin about that." Burke frowned, but opened one of the briefcases and pulled out a new phone. He held it up to her. "We have about ten of these now. We'll toss out the ones that came from our office, just in case one of the bastards gets to Hilary. We use one for a day or so, then we toss it. Stay here with Rafe and Kade for the moment. Cole is going to change the plates on the car. I'm going to scout the area. In a couple of hours, we're going to leave here and head to Louisiana. We have a Cajun friend there, a real security pro, and a damn fine Dom. He has a place in the swamp. We're going off the grid, sweetheart."

"He has a lot of rope, too," Cole drawled, selecting a new license plate from those Kade had carried in. In fact, the Middle-Eastern hotties had brought a veritable grab bag of items to help hide a person's identity. After selecting one, Cole stared, his gaze heavy, somber— completely closed. "I know you're afraid and angry, Jessa. Just let me get you through this. Then you don't have to see me again."

Well, he'd given up pretty easily. So maybe she'd never meant much to him. Hadn't she wanted them to go away? Yes. So why did those words make her heart hurt?

Jessa swallowed down the anger and forced herself to shrug, refusing to give him the satisfaction of seeing that he'd bruised her feelings. "Perfect."

Burke's whole face shut down, and his shoulders squared. "Let's go, brother. We need to leave tonight. Jessa, stay here. And for god's sake, eat something. I know you don't want to. Neither did I, but don't hold us back because you can't see past your own misery. We've already got one member of the team who seems intent on doing that. I don't need another."

Burke slammed out after his brother.

He was right. As terrible as food sounded to her turning stomach, she needed to stay strong so she could get back to her son. Caleb mattered to her. Cole and Burke didn't. She had to keep telling herself that.

"So you're Jessa." Kade sat down in the chair at the room's single table. It was a wobbly thing, but Kade made it seem almost elegant.

"I am." She wished one of the twins would have stayed. Suddenly, she was brutally aware that she was alone in a motel room with two very virile strangers who shared their women and all she wore was a robe.

"We've been listening to those two moan about you for a solid year," he explained. "Well, Burke moaned. Cole simply brooded more than usual."

She picked up the last sandwich. Her stomach turned. "I thought they were in South America for the last year. Not the Middle East."

Rafe stared at her. His easy charm seemed to be gone. "We're not really the Middle East, at least according to our neighbors. They don't like our…customs." He shrugged. "We hardly care. The Lennox brothers *have* been in South America. Because of the rescue operation they undertook, we talked to them on a regular basis. You seem to be under the impression that those men have been throwing a party."

Talk about accusations. At least the idea of a good argument made it seem easier to eat. She swallowed the first bite and reached for a bottled water. "I realize they were working."

Kade leaned forward. "They risked their lives every single day. We hired them, so we feel a bit responsible for the situation they find themselves in. After all, they were looking for our cousin."

"Alea." She remembered the name they had given her and wondered about the woman. "Is she all right?"

Rafe sighed, a deep sound of regret that filled the room. "She is alive."

"She was brutalized." Kade threaded his hands

together as though steeling himself. "She hid her ties to our family because she wanted a normal life. She is a beautiful girl both inside and out. Our little cousin was always a rebel."

"Sometimes I think she left Bezakistan because there weren't enough down-trodden people for her to help." Rafe paced as he talked. "She wanted to save the world. The world showed her that it doesn't want to be saved."

"That's not true," Kade argued.

Rafe shook his head, a tiny, somewhat brutal gesture. Jessa would have bet this was a well-worn argument.

Kade nodded his brother's way. "Forgive him. He's still angry. I am as well, but I know that Alea will eventually come out of this. She will live again. Her mind and her heart will heal. But only because Burke and Cole Lennox saved her." He massaged the place between his eyebrows as though trying to soothe away his frown. "She refused a security detail when she went away to school. She isn't in line for the throne, so we didn't think she'd truly be in any danger. She disappeared six months into her school year. They took her because they thought she had no family and the whoremongers needed a woman of Middle-Eastern descent. The brothel Ricardo Delgado sold her to liked to keep a variety of women for their clientele."

There went her appetite again. The idea of a young woman being sold made her shudder. Her heart went out to the woman. "I'm so sorry to hear that."

"She was drugged. All of the girls were fed a steady diet of chemical crap." Rafe bit the words out like bullets. "She begged for the drugs for weeks after she came home. She was down to skin and bones, but all she wanted was another hit. That's just one of the many things they did to her. She still has terrible nightmares…"

"When Burke and Cole found her," Kade continued, his voice going hard for the first time, "she was being held with fifteen other women. It pleases me to lie awake at night and think about everything your men did to the bastards who held those girls against their will. Their descriptions were pleasingly detailed. I have a vivid picture in my head."

"I can't imagine what Alea went through." She shivered despite the robe, feeling so terrible for the young woman. Even after she'd been saved, it was obvious Alea still had a hard road ahead of her. Delgado had ruined many lives, and now his son seemed determined to keep up the family business.

"No, you can't," Kade replied. "I wouldn't want you to. But I am asking you to take into consideration that their work was vital to us and the families of the other girls they rescued. Yes, they sacrificed. But Burke and Cole also saved lives."

Jessa stiffened her spine. "Of course their work was important. I don't disagree. And I would have understood the truth. But the fact is, they lied to me."

"Would you have understood? Really?" Rafe asked, his tone slightly arrogant, as if he'd already determined the answer to the question.

So they had judged her. "I would have done my very best. Maybe it sounds selfish to you, but I wanted to be important, too."

"They believed you had been claimed by another man," Rafe said.

"Something that could have been cleared up if they

had given me a real name or had called me even once."
She felt tears threatening. God, she didn't want to feel
this aching, gaping hole in her chest. She wanted to feel
nothing at all for them. "If I had known what they were
doing, I would have sat up at night praying for them. I
would have loved them, but they didn't give me the
chance. They didn't trust me enough."

Rafe's eyes softened slightly. "Men are sometimes
not the smartest of creatures. We make decisions that we
think are best to protect those we love. And sometimes,
we make mistakes. It doesn't mean we don't know our
hearts. If they have told you they love you, then they
mean this."

"They are good men. The best I know," Kade said
softly. "They are rough at times, but that doesn't mean
they don't have tenderness for you, for your son. It would
be a shame if that son never knew his fathers."

She glared at Kade. That just wasn't fair. She was
just supposed to forgive Burke and Cole the instant they
walked back into her life? They had cost her a terrible
year of heartache and pain, and never given her a choice.
"The funny thing is, if they had asked me to take the risk
and go to South America with them, I would have. Or I
would have stayed here and waited, as tough as it would
have been. I would have done whatever they asked. But
they didn't give me a choice."

Yes, she was probably being stubborn, but the more
she thought about it, the angrier she got. Of course they
were heroes; there was no question about it. But did that
mean she was just supposed to take them back without a
qualm? What happened the next time they had a
"mission" they believed in? Would they leave her behind

for months or more at a time with no communications? Would they decide that their son was safer without them and simply walk out again, this time for good? They wouldn't simply be leaving her behind. They'd be breaking Caleb's heart, too.

No. She didn't think she could risk that. She wasn't sure she was ready to trust them again.

And that made her brutally angry because she wanted to. She wanted to throw herself in their arms and beg them to love her, never leave her again. Though they had left her pregnant and alone, she still dreamed of them. She still woke up calling out their names.

She swiped angry tears away. She wasn't listening to her stupid heart this time. She couldn't afford to. She wasn't a child anymore. Now she was a mother.

Rafe straightened his coat. "I'm sorry if I overstepped my bounds. I merely hoped to give you something to think about. Know that if you need anything at all, we will help you."

Kade stood. "Indeed. All you need to do is call."

"You don't know me. Why would you do that?" These men confounded her. They were obviously powerful, yet they seemed to genuinely care about Cole and Burke, who were basically employees. They were royal, in line for a kingdom, yet they were risking their lives to help others out.

"The royal family of Bezakistan owes the Lennox brothers a debt for saving one of our family. Actually, two, since Cole also saved my brother, Talib," Kade explained. "When I asked how we should repay them, do you know what your men asked for?"

Rafe shook his head. "My brother would have given

them millions. Anything they wanted."

More tears. Would they ever stop? "I know they didn't ask for money."

They wouldn't. They would want to be paid for the job, but not for saving a life. She knew that deep in her soul.

Rafe regarded her seriously. "You know them better than you think. They asked us to bankroll the rest of their operation, though they did not take pay for themselves. They wanted to save as many women as they could. Seven women have been reunited with their families. And another three families at least no longer have to wonder what happened to their daughter or sisters."

"They drove a rough bargain," Kade explained. "We not only had to pay for their travel and expenses, but for these women to see a counselor and for their drug rehabilitation."

"I would pay millions more for it to have never happened." Rafe regarded her somberly. "I have never told Cole or Burke this, but we do not consider our debt paid. This is something we would have done regardless. One day, we shall repay them. You say you do not know these men, but when asked that question, you knew immediately that they wouldn't do what was easy. Search your heart. Perhaps it is yourself that you do not know."

The door opened, and Burke walked in, rubbing his hands together. His face paled when he looked at Jessa. "Sweetheart? Why are you crying?"

"We'll leave you alone now," Rafe said, gesturing for his brother to leave.

Kade followed him. "I wish you well, my friend. In all things. Bring your family to the palace when this is over—or sooner. You are always welcome in our country."

They left, slapping Cole on the shoulder as he walked in, his face blank.

"The car's ready, but I'd rather lay low until it's dark. If they've got a visual on us, it will be much harder to follow us once the sun is down. It's about six hours from Dallas to Lafayette and another hour to the swamp. I've made all the arrangements." Cole spoke, but there was no inflection in his tone. He could have been talking about the weather.

It was so easy for Cole to shut down. He seemed to be a pro at it. But what would happen if she broke the barrier down and got to the real man? Something angry took root in her gut. Something wicked and restless was making her heart twitch.

"Jessa, sweetheart, tell me why you're crying." Burke gripped her hand, his eyes seeking hers.

Cole crowded in on the other side, looking ready to make demands. Her body leapt. For whatever reason, she'd always be attuned to them. She felt their fear for her, their fury with Delgado. Their need to keep her safe. And to hold her.

God, she wanted the comfort they silently offered. That connection she felt to them reached out in a silent scream with almost painful yearning. She ached for just one hour of nothing but their reassurance, their touch. She wanted to break past Cole's defenses.

But she couldn't accept their tenderness. And couldn't admit that she wanted them, would probably never want another man. They'd construe either as surrender, and she'd have to work twice as hard to convince them to let her out of their lives. If she accepted tender kisses and soft words, cutting them out of her heart again might be impossible.

But she wanted them again, one last time. She pulled her hand away from Burke's and glanced at the clock. It was hours before dark. Hours before they would flee. She smiled to herself. She wanted Burke and Cole now. On her terms. And she knew exactly how to persuade them to give it to her.

\* \* \* \*

*Eight months earlier, April 5 – Dallas, Texas*

Cole stared at Hilary. No way he'd heard her right. He didn't like the woman, but she was smart and ran the office well. Still, she had her blonde moments. She had to be wrong about this.

"No." Burke shook off Hilary's touch. "I don't understand."

She put a hand on his brother's shoulder, her eyes going soft with sympathy. When she looked like she was about to repeat herself, he felt his own go cold and dead. Exactly like his heart.

"That woman you're having Mr. Landry follow, she got married," she murmured.

The words still didn't seem to compute to Burke, but Cole heard them. Loud and clear. They echoed in his ears. Married. To another man. Their Jessa. No, not their Jessa anymore. Less than four months after they had left her with kisses and vows to return, she not only started dating another man, she'd married him, tied her life to him. Given him her eternal love.

"I am so sorry, Burke," Hilary said, taking a step back. She looked to Cole, her eyes sliding away silently.

She always addressed Burke, the gentleman. Cole couldn't remember a time Hilary had looked him in the eyes, as though she was afraid of what she would find there. No surprise. She viewed him as a violent barbarian.

Hilary placed a manila folder on the desk in front of him. "I don't know what it is about this woman that has you all tied up in knots, but according to this report, she's happily married, so if she's one of your little projects, you don't have to worry anymore."

Burke grabbed the report before Cole could. He wasn't sure he wanted to see it anyway. If there were pictures of the happy couple, the image would probably sear itself into his brain. Already, he could picture too vividly Jessa with someone else, speaking words of devotion. Making love, giving her body to him night after night. Her gifting him with all of her luminous smiles and her warm laughter.

Cole turned away. He didn't want to see the fucking report. He wanted to see Jessa. He could be on a plane and in New York in just a couple of hours. He could stand in front of her and ask her if they'd ever meant a damn thing to her. He and Burke had loved her. Neither one had even thought of touching another woman since they'd left Jessa. She'd apparently done a hell of a lot more than think about it. Fuck.

Burke slammed the folder down.

"I really am sorry, Burke," Hilary said. "I didn't want to send that file to you. But I had to be honest. Who is she?"

Burke shook his head, his gaze hardening.

"Apparently, no one special."

No one special. Just a woman he would love for the rest of his life. His heart ached. Though it made him furious, the voice in his head asked: *Did you really expect her to wait for you? No one gives a shit about you, least of all a gorgeous, talented creature like her. Stupid bastard.*

Wincing, he looked at his brother. Burke's face had shut down.

"Burke? Is there anything I can do?" Hilary asked. "You must be so tired. I can make reservations for dinner. You need to eat."

Burke shook his head. "No, thank you. Not hungry. Get us back on a plane to Colombia."

Hilary's eyes widened, her lip forming a pout. "But you just got here. Burke, your wounds aren't completely healed."

A cold professional mask slid across Burke's face. Cole was fairly certain that his own mirrored that desolation. "Give us a moment."

Hilary nodded reluctantly and walked out of the room.

"I want to go to New York," Cole blurted.

"What would it prove? And according to that report, she's moved."

"I want to lay eyes on this fucker. What's his name?" Cole demanded.

Burke's laugh was humorless. "Angus. He's from Scotland."

She'd married someone named Angus? "She can't be serious. We've got to go."

They could talk to her, force her to tell them just why

she'd promised to wait when she'd obviously had no intention of being there when they came home.

Fuck, he still loved her. He didn't want to let her go, but he couldn't bear to see her with this man who had replaced them in her heart. He couldn't see a ring on her finger and know he hadn't put it there.

"We can't go, Cole." Burke scrubbed a hand over his hair. "She never called."

"We didn't call her, either." He regretted that fact on a daily basis, but it had been too dangerous.

"When were we supposed to call, man? We've been deep undercover for months. We have to face facts. She didn't love us. It's over. Fuck." Burke turned away. He stalked to his desk and picked up the phone. "Rafiq al Mussad, please. Yes, tell him this is Burke Lennox, and he needs to call me soon. We're heading back to Colombia soon. We need to meet with him."

Cole stared out his window. Miles separated him from Jessa, but even if she stood in front of him now, he wouldn't be able to reach her.

His future was over. He needed a drink.

Burke continued to make plans, but Cole could see the rest of his life mapped out in a neat plan. Fight. Fight. Die. Alone. Maybe he would save a few people, but the only woman who could have saved him was lost.

# Chapter Eight

*Present Day – Dallas, Texas*

Cole watched Jessa, his every instinct on overload. She was thinking something, up to something. She glared at him, then paced the small room, her feet padding across the floor in a quick step that told him all about her anxiety—and her anger.

Of course she was angry. In her head, they had lied, but it hadn't really seemed like a lie at the time. It had been a cover. They went undercover enough that it was just part of the job.

But this particular cover had blown up in their faces. Burke could be as optimistic as he wanted. She wasn't coming back. Not now that she'd decided what they really were.

*Mercenaries.*

He hated that fucking word. It sounded selfish, made them seem like men who sold their services to anyone with cash, who used their power and strength, no matter the cause and no matter who got hurt. That wasn't him, but he wouldn't be able to convince Jessa. Did he even deserve a chance to try at this point? He sighed. And how would their son regard them when he got older, grew up?

"So, how long do you expect me to live in a swamp?"

Cole watched her pace, her hands clenching and unclenching. She was ready to explode, and he was going to let her. Maybe if she bled off some of her tension naturally, he wouldn't be tempted to throw her onto the bed and force orgasms on her until she relaxed. He liked that plan much better, but she didn't want him. Uncle Martin had been right; he wasn't good for anything. No one would ever love him.

Burke crossed his arms over his chest and stared straight at Cole. "Well? Don't you have some caveman comeback to that one?"

Cole just shook his head.

"Not a single word?"

"No."

Fuck. Burke wanted to bait him into losing his temper, and Cole refused to let him. Burke wanted him to grab Jessa and push pleasure on her until she melted in his arms, then pass her to his brother so he could give her more of the same. But Cole wasn't going to give his brother the satisfaction of showing Jessa how much he loved and wanted her. Or of trying to break her down and soften her up for them. It was pointless. She wasn't coming back.

Burke's growl came from the back of his throat. His brother was getting really angry, a surprise since Burke rarely lost his temper. That was Cole's job, but Burke seemed willing to take over for him. "Fine. I'll do what I always do. I'll fucking speak for you. Jessa, you'll stay in the swamp for as long as it takes, until we tell you it's all right to go."

Her eyes narrowed. "Or maybe I'll call the cops myself. He can't possibly own every single one of them. Maybe I would be better off taking my chances with them than the two of you. At least they won't lie to me."

Cole felt his whole body flinch, like she'd hit him with a bullet. No, a bullet would hurt less.

"You're not calling anyone." Burke crossed his arms over his chest and intentionally crowded Jessa. He got right into her space, towering over her. "Do you honestly believe we haven't tried everything we could in the short amount of time we've had? We have people calling the feds, the US Attorney's office, the DA of New York. These things take time. That's what Marco is counting on."

"Or maybe he's counting on the fact that he's had months and months to prepare for this and he knows exactly what you'll do at every turn, like just sitting here and waiting for him to come get us." Her body was practically vibrating with anger.

"Do you think I like sitting around? Do you honestly believe I wouldn't rather be out looking for this bastard? If I knew you'd be safe, I would. But I don't know if this asshole is nearby, and driving around in the middle of the day is just asking for someone to spot us. So until dark, we're staying. What the fuck else do you want me to do, Jessa?"

"Go back a year ago and change everything. Hell, if I could go back, I'd be smarter, see through you two. I should have known exactly what you were. I can see it so clearly now." Her fists were little balls of barely contained emotion. Even her toes seemed curled, biting around the cheap carpet.

"And just what are we?" Burke challenged. "Lay it out, sweetheart. Put it all out there."

"You're liars."

Cole closed his eyes. That hurt almost as badly as the idea that they were mercenaries. Did she think they lied to everyone or just sweet virgins like her, looking for affection? Did she believe they really made money off saving or taking human lives? Probably. He'd been called worse, but never by someone he cared about.

"We were undercover. Did you want us to walk around giving the bad guys business cards?"

"In the end, it didn't matter. They seemed to have figured out who you are. They were way smarter than I was."

"Of course, they figured it out. We had to file a ton of paperwork to get the feds to accept the evidence we'd collected. We had to put the bad guy away. Don't act like we're the villains in this scenario. We were the ones *saving* the women, and you know it."

"Well, you didn't save me, did you?" she said acidly.

Cole felt his fucking heart almost stop at the question. Unlike her previous rantings, this question came out of her mouth with a hint of vulnerability that broke his heart. The hurt in her eyes was raw, like it had been scrubbed to bleeding with steel wool. Guilt churned in his gut.

Burke softened up a bit. He reached out for her. "Sweetheart, we didn't know you needed us or were in danger. The minute we thought you were, we came for you."

The vulnerable girl was gone in a heartbeat, righteously angry female taking her place. "I wasn't talking about that, you asshole. I was talking about the fact that you left me alone and pregnant, and if Marco Delgado hadn't decided I would make a spectacularly good Judas goat, you would never have come back for me."

"We would have checked." Burke's hands came back down, his fingers twitching as though they really wanted to be on her. Cole knew his brother. Burke thought if he could get his hands on her, he could smooth their way back. Cole didn't think Jessa wanted to be placated. She wanted to fight, and they were the only available targets.

"Would you? Or would you have just moved on to the next job and the next female who was stupid enough to buy into your routine?"

"It's not a routine, and we would have checked on you."

She turned those big green eyes on him. Cole felt his heart stutter. "Would you, Cole? Really? Would you have come looking for me, a woman you thought was married?"

"No." He'd died a little the day he'd heard about her marriage. A piece of himself had shriveled, and he'd buried it. He wouldn't have gone back. He wouldn't have wanted to see her with her husband. "We'd already discussed it and decided to leave you in peace."

"Goddamn it, Cole. Can you think for two seconds before you say something? Why are you sitting there? I know you love her. Why are you just letting her tear us apart?"

"We can love her all we want, but we're not together, Burke. I can't tear us apart because she's not going to let us close to her again."

And it hurt like hell. Cole had never felt more alive than when he'd been with Jessa. With her, he'd felt like he'd been good at something other than his fucking job. He'd been good at loving her.

Then he'd fucked up.

He watched as Burke spewed angry words her way, and she yelled right back. Yes, he'd fucked up. Brutally. He had told Jessa the truth. They wouldn't have gone back. Cole knew he would have taken job after job after job until it killed him. That fucker Landry had lied to him about Jessa's marriage, and he'd swallowed every damn word. He would have gone to his grave heartbroken, loving her…and believing that she belonged to another man.

"Have you thought about the fact that Caleb is our son?" Burke challenged.

"He's probably Cole's son."

"You think that matters to me? That I give a shit?" Burke shot back. "We've shared everything since the moment we were conceived. In my heart, that is my son, and I'll be damned if I let you shove me out of his life."

She was toe to toe with Burke, her face more alive than he'd seen in hours. She was flushed, her hair sliding out of its ponytail with every shake of her head. Little tendrils of red hair escaped to flutter around her face. She was so goddamn beautiful. Even when she was screaming at them, Cole was utterly fascinated with her.

Could he really let that go—her go—because he was worried he was everything she accused him of being?

Was he going to let his uncle keep taunting him from the grave? Jessa wasn't married. She'd given birth to their son. Cole still fucking loved her. She'd cared about him once. Maybe…Burke had a point.

Cole paused and really watched her. He'd been mired in his own misery and hadn't looked beyond her beauty, her anger. But now he did. His eyes narrowed. It was as if she wanted to…provoke them. For a fight? Or something else?

"You shouldn't be in his life at all," she insisted.

"How can you say that, Jessa? He's our son. We're his fathers."

"You didn't care enough about me to call and find out that you had a son, but I'm supposed to believe you're suddenly going to be dads of the year?"

Burke gritted his teeth, clearly nearing the end of his control. "I've explained that."

"You gave me an excuse. How hard would it have been to pick up the damn phone?" She turned to Cole. "There were three months between the time you left and I returned from Scotland with my supposed husband. Three months. Ninety days in which you could have called me. Ninety days of me waiting and believing that you'd abandoned me."

She said it with an angry growl, but there was something else underneath. Burke continued to argue his case. Cole frowned, working to shove aside his own guilt and misery, his uncle's destructive words. He watched her. She just kept picking at them, getting more frustrated with every one of Burke's comebacks.

"Just admit it, Burke. You found a dumb virgin who gave you two exactly the kink you two wanted, then you left with no intention of ever coming back. You'd gotten what you wanted and you were through. And you." She turned to look directly at Cole, her gaze laced with some sense of anticipation, like she sought something. "You're sick. Perverted."

Cole absorbed her words, but he was calmer now. Thinking. Watching. She was after something, and he didn't think it was simply the means to let out her anger. If that was all she sought, he'd take her rage. But there was something about the way she sidled closer and stared at him that made him question the reason behind her tirade.

"Yes. I'm very sick, baby." He gentled his tone. If he could calm her down by agreeing with her, then he would. But his guess was that his composure would only piss her off more. If so...he'd know exactly what she needed. "I'm damaged. I'm not good for you."

"Goddamn it, Cole." Burke's anger came off him in waves, blasting at his brother who had always been able to sense his strong emotions.

Jessa stiffened, her rage seeming to escalate, not dissipate. "Do you spank all your stupid little conquests? Poor Cole, can't get it up without a little kink. He has to tie up women or they might run away."

Jessa wasn't just spewing anger. She was painting him a picture with her words. If all she wanted was for him to admit his sins against her, he'd done that. But she kept poking.

"What? You don't have anything to say? You just don't care, Cole. I guess I shouldn't be surprised. Under all that aggressive attitude, you give up. You back down, don't you? You're just going to stand there and let a girl tell you off." She shrugged like it didn't matter.

But it did, and he was beginning to get the picture.

Burke opened his mouth to start defending Cole's honor, but he stopped his brother with a shake of his head. Burke didn't need to waste his breath. All this bullshit of Jessa's wasn't really about him.

"Big, bad Dom, huh?" She scoffed, baiting Cole even more.

The pieces slid together, unmistakable. She'd clung to him in the night, and for part of it, she hadn't been asleep. He'd been able to feel her breath take on an uneven rhythm as she'd awakened, restlessly moving until he'd wrapped his arms around her to force her to be still. He'd felt her stiffen for a moment and worried she would reject him, but she'd simply melted back into him and fallen back to sleep, their arms and legs entangled. She'd woken this morning wrapped around Burke. She'd wanted comfort, but she wouldn't ask for it.

This argument was no different. She was fighting, battling against him when he'd laid down his arms and given her the victory. Yet she still poked him, as though picking a scab she couldn't let heal over. Because she didn't want it to. Fuck. If he was right, then she was in a corner, wanting something from them, but having no idea how to fight past her pride to simply ask for it.

So she'd maneuvered him into taking it. She might need him far more than he'd expected.

"Not so tough without handcuffs and a ball gag, are you?" She glared with disdain.

Cole tested the waters, crossing the room to tower over her. He laced his arms over his chest and got in her personal space, leveled a dark, heavy stare at her. A thousand dirty thoughts of Jessa naked and under him, between him and Burke, crossed his mind. He let every one of them show in his eyes. Relief and arousal flared across her face. She should be backing away, but she wasn't, because Cole could clearly see that she didn't merely want to stir his ire. She'd been looking to rouse his dick, maybe even his heart. She wanted them. Needed them? The next few hours would tell.

This might not solve anything, but he wasn't giving up his forever without a fight. He hoped that his uncle rotting in hell was gnashing his teeth. He was done stewing on all the swill the old man had shoved down his throat. Jessa might not love him, but she cared. That would be enough for now. It was a start.

"Jessa, turn off your mouth, or we're going to have some serious punishment."

Though he'd spoken quietly, both Jessa and Burke shut up immediately. The air froze.

"You don't have the right to punish me." Her breathing picked up pace. Her cheeks flushed.

Stubborn little sub. "I'll take it if I have to. You don't top me, baby."

"You don't touch me."

"Oh, but you want me to." He edged closer, satisfied with her sharp intake of breath.

Then her shoulders relaxed, and her eyes softened, as though she knew she was going to get what she wanted. "You're wrong."

Oh, she was so digging her own grave with those breathless words. He smiled.

"You won't admit the truth. I suspect you're going to fight me, even though we both know you want this. You want me to take you, Jessa. I showed you a whole world, then I left you alone to suffer. You haven't been with anyone since that night, have you? Don't you dare lie to me."

"I'll lie to you all I like, Cole. Our whole relationship has been a lie."

"That's bullshit, but I understand why you feel that way. Now, we have a few hours before we can leave. Do you want to sit down and rationally figure out how to deal with this or do you want to play this game out to its inevitable conclusion?" He felt so much calmer now. The guilt was still there, but now he could see plainly that she needed what only he could give her.

Burke stood silently beside his brother, allowing Cole to take the lead. He stared at Jessa, his eyes hooding. Yeah, his twin was finally in the know and on board.

"What game is it that you think I'm playing?"

"You're topping from the bottom, baby." And normally, he wouldn't rise to the bait, but if this was his only way back to her, he'd bend his rules this once. "You're doing your damnedest to manipulate me to a place where I simply take you and you don't have to consent. You want us both, but you're too hurt to ask for what you need. There's only one problem with that scenario. This has to be consensual. I won't rape you, not even to pretend."

"I don't want to make love with you."

"No, you want me to fuck you. If I took that robe off you right now, would I find your nipples hard? Would they be standing up straight, all peaked for me? If I slid my hands down your body and buried my fingers in your pussy, would I find you wet and ready for me?"

She swallowed, then tried to pass off a shrug. "If I was, it doesn't mean I love you. It just means I haven't had some in a long time."

"Baby, I haven't touched anyone since I walked out of that hotel room. I won't touch anyone else for the rest of my life. I love you. I love you with every ounce of my being, and I'll die before I ever take another woman."

Her eyes flared with hope. He watched her squash it quickly with pain and fear. "I don't believe you."

"He hasn't, Jessa," Burke murmured. "I haven't touched anyone in a year, either, sweetheart. In my head, in my heart, it would have been cheating. Even after we thought you had gotten married, we couldn't look at another woman. You're it for us. We fucked up. We let our work and our own misery and guilt defeat us. If I could do it again, I would have told you everything."

"You can't fix this, Burke." She crossed her arms over her chest and fought tears. "Not now."

"No, he can't. I can't fix the past either, Jessa. I can only promise that the future is going to be different. Now, you need to decide how this is going to go. We can talk. I can be gentle. Or I can give you what all three of us need."

"If I sleep with you, it's only because I want to fuck you out of my system."

The words hurt, but he wasn't going to stop. "And if I sleep with you, it's only because I love you and I want to imprint myself on you. We want to fuck you so hard, you'll never be rid of us. You'll always feel us deep inside you."

Burke took up the declaration. "You won't ever be

able to forget how it feels to be in between us, to be surrounded and loved. If we fuck you, it's because we need you. I love you, Jessa. I want to marry you and have more kids, build a real family with you. But if you need to call this sex, then I'll take that, too."

There were tears in her eyes. "I don't believe you. I'll never believe you. I hate you both."

Cole closed his eyes briefly. There was a part of himself that wondered if he should let her go and let her find someone who didn't come with baggage. She deserved a lifestyle that wouldn't isolate her. But he silenced that voice. She'd loved them once; she could do it again. Now that he knew she needed them, he couldn't walk away. No matter what the cost. He reached for her hand and swept her up into his arms, her weight reminding him of everything he'd missed for the last year. "Hate me all you like. We'll love you enough for all of us."

"This doesn't mean anything," she said, but she was already softening in his arms.

Cole scoffed. "Whatever. You remember your safe word?"

"Fuck you, Cole." She spat the words out. She'd apparently gotten comfortable with cussing. She'd likely cursed them every day they had been apart.

Cole didn't let it bother him. He knew the game now, and he intended to win. "Oh, we'll get to that. But you'd better spit out your safe word first, or we're going to stand here all afternoon and wait until you do."

"You bastard," she mumbled. "Resolution."

He smiled. "Good. Now I definitely think our little sub requires some discipline. Burke, we're going to need the clamps. All of them."

He tossed her on the bed. Her robe gaped open showing off the breasts he'd dreamed of every night since he'd met her. They were beautiful and a bit rounder after having their son, with skin so soft he'd never been able to forget the feel of it. Just like he'd thought, her nipples were hard little nubs. And for the first time, there was just a bit of fear in those green eyes.

Yeah, he liked that, too. His cock throbbed in his jeans when he considered all the nasty, explicit things he could do to her.

Every muscle in his body was on full alert. He'd dreamed of this, of having her again. Of sinking into her body and never leaving. "Pull the robe wide open. Let me see every fucking inch of you."

Her mouth firmed, and he watched as she undoubtedly decided whether or not to defy him. Her hands finally went to the tie of her robe, and she pulled it open quickly, without a hint of seduction.

If she thought that was going to deter him, she had another thing coming.

As Jessa revealed her body to him, Cole noted the differences. She carried a few more curves. She had a few stretch marks and a straight scar across her lower abdomen.

"I had a C-section. If it bothers you, I can get dressed." She started to pull the robe on again, but Cole pushed her hands away.

"You're beautiful." His whole body responded to her. Every cell inside him felt like it was coming to life after a long period of hibernation. He'd been surviving since the moment he'd walked away from her. Just existing. Now he felt alive again.

This woman in front of him was all that mattered. Jessa, his brother, and the son they had made together. If they were the only people in his world, he would be fine with that. He shoved aside everything else. No more guilt. No more doubt. No more hiding away. He had a new mission. To make Jessa love him again.

And Cole Lennox never failed a mission.

* * * *

Jessa held her breath. He'd said she was beautiful, but she knew she looked different than the last time he'd seen her naked. Her breasts weren't as perky. They had fed a child for nearly three months. She had scars from her surgery and stretch marks. She wasn't some perfect little virgin anymore. She was a woman, and she had the marks to prove it.

Was this a huge mistake? Probably, but it was hers to make. She wanted Cole and Burke. She wanted to remember what it felt like to be wanted one last time.

Oh, she wasn't going to take them back. She couldn't trust them. They could talk a good game, but she didn't dare open her heart up to them again. She just wanted tonight. Well, maybe a few nights. A few kisses and caresses and memories to keep her warm when they were gone again. That probably made her an idiot, but she'd never wanted anyone but them. They'd used her, and she still wanted them. This was her last chance to get over them.

"Baby, you're so fucking gorgeous." Cole stared down at her.

"Fuck. I didn't think I would get to see you this way

again." Burke breathed the words out. He stood beside his brother, his previous anger seemingly spent. Burke had been willing to fight. Cole hadn't. He'd closed in on himself. The walls he'd seemingly placed between them had enraged Jessa. But he'd still seen her, read her need. That was all that mattered now.

"I haven't lost all my baby weight." Now she was nervous. Without the anger raging through her system, she felt vulnerable, a little worried.

Cole's eyes went hard. "Not another disparaging word. You're beautiful, Jessa. I won't let anyone insult you, even yourself."

He was using *that* voice on her, the one that went to a deep, dark place when he took control. It was rich and oozed authority. Burke's rich tone was pure seduction, but when Cole started telling her what to do in that dark honeyed growl of his, she couldn't resist him.

"Put your hands over your head. It's been a long time, and I want to inspect you. I want to learn your body all over again."

Jessa winced. She just wanted to have sex, but he was going to drag this out, make it a lavish, prolonged affair. A glance into his resolute face told her that he wouldn't take no for an answer. She'd pushed, and now she had to take what he gave her. Oh, he would listen to her, but then he'd do exactly what he pleased. If she was going to get what she wanted, she'd have to play by Cole's rules. It rankled, but she also found an odd sense of security in it. He wouldn't let her fall, not in bed. He would take care of her. Burke would, too. They talked a good game, but it was still possible they'd walk away the instant Delgado no longer threatened her. But they would be utterly here with her now.

It was the only place she could trust them.

She let her hands drift up, threading her fingers together.

"Very good, baby. Now spread your legs. We want to see our pussy again."

She wanted to argue about the "our" part, but it was true. In the year since they had left, she hadn't even thought about another man. She'd met many attractive men, but not a one made her feel the way these two did. None had been as commanding as Cole or as smoothly seductive as Burke. Not one of those men had haunted her dreams or held a candle to their memories.

Her heart raced as she let her knees fall to the sides, and her legs opened to them, the cool air of the room sliding over her. She felt her nipples peak even tighter. Her skin came alive under their watchful gazes.

"Wider," Cole barked.

She stretched her legs out, putting her pussy on full display.

Burke breathed in, filling his lungs. "She smells delicious. Jesus…"

His voice wobbled, and he licked his lips. Jessa's pussy pulsed at the thought of his talented tongue on her, lashing her with pleasure until she couldn't see straight. Burke could feast on her for what felt like forever.

"Not yet, brother. She has to work her way up to that. That's too good a treat for a sub who's spent the last hour baiting her Masters." Cole held out his hand, and Burke placed something in it. It looked metallic and attached to a chain. "She manipulated us to get what she wanted without having to admit her desires, without having to promise or work anything out."

"Cole, don't push her," Burke practically begged.

"Oh, but she wants me to push her." Cole's smile turned slightly feral. "Tie her hands."

Her heart skipped a beat at his purred threat. God, she'd missed this side of Cole. When he used that smile on her, she was never sure if he was genuinely amused or just getting ready to do something really nasty that would get his cock hard and drive her wild.

Burke reached into Cole's brown leather bag and came back out with a length of thin rope. As he wound it around her wrists, binding them together over her head, she felt something in her relax. She sighed, having missed the feeling of truly giving over to these men, of not being alone. Even if it was just for a little while, she needed this fantasy. She wanted to linger because all too soon they would likely be gone again.

While Burke bound her hands together, Cole stripped. Jessa watched as that enormous, hard body was revealed inch by inch. She remembered what it felt like to run her hands across his smooth skin, to feel each hard, bulging muscle and know it was hers. Cole's hands went to the fly of his jeans, and he efficiently did away with them, tossing them over the chair. His cock stood out from his body, thick and long. She couldn't help but stare at it.

And then she saw that she wasn't the only one who had obtained a few scars in their time apart.

A nasty circular scar puckered up from the skin of his abdomen, just over his hip bone.

"What happened?" It looked angry, as though it wasn't finished doing its damage yet.

Cole touched it, his eyes going down as though he had to remind himself it was there. "Took a round outside of Medellin. It was no big deal. It was a through and through. Burke just stitched me up until we could see a doctor."

Burke hopped off the bed, seemingly happy with his knot now securing her. He pulled at his T-shirt, tossing it away. "We were lucky that time. We couldn't find a regular doctor for Cole, just a vet. There was my big, bad brother and twelve overindulged pussy cats."

"It's not funny. He could have died." Jessa's voice shook.

Cole could have died. He could have lost his life, and no one would have told her. She would have gone on, never knowing that he was gone.

"No, Jessa. This wasn't fatal. Show her, Burke."

Burke sighed, dropped his pants, and turned around. Jessa gasped. He had scars across his lower back that hadn't been there before.

"As we were fleeing with Alea, one of the brothel owner's brothers caught up with us. Burke took three in the back before I took the fucker down. This isn't the first time someone's family has come after us."

"I lost a good portion of my liver, but apparently it grows back. Lucky me." Burke turned back around. "Do you know what got me through?"

She shook her head. She didn't want to hear this. "Don't tell me."

Burke sent her a triumphant smile. "Too bad, because now that you're tied up, you're not going anywhere. As I lost consciousness, I thought about you. As I woke up, I thought about you. As I recovered, I thought about you."

"You did a lot of thinking, but not a lot of picking up the phone and calling."

Burke's eyes rolled. "Clamp her. Maybe it will make her more pleasant."

Cole let the metal object in his hand drop, holding on to a thin, silver chain that connected them. "These are clover clamps. They're for your nipples. Burke, I need those nipples hard and ready."

Burke climbed on the bed and brushed his fingers over her nipples, softly at first, then gripped them hard between his thumbs and forefingers. He squeezed, making her whole body pulse with anticipation. "Like this, brother?"

Cole's eyes never left her breasts. "Perfect."

He climbed on the bed, in between her legs, making the bed dip. Burke stayed at her side, holding her nipples for Cole.

"I think you're going to like these, baby. I know I will. The clamps go on comfortably. They'll grip your nipples and make them exquisitely sensitive, but they get tighter with every yank of the chain.

Moisture flooded her folds. She could feel herself getting wet, growing restless. Burke leaned over, his mouth hovering over one breast. A low growl of appreciation came out of his throat just before he set his mouth over the already impossibly tight nipple, twisting the other with his fingers. The suction jolted straight to her pussy, lighting her up and making her writhe.

"Yeah, baby, every time you do that, these clamps will tighten." Cole moved in the instant Burke lifted his head. Cole eased the silver clamp on to her nipple, ruthlessly placing it at the base, the bud plumping and reddening.

Burke put his mouth against her ear. "I know you feel that, sweetheart."

His whisper ran like wildfire across her skin. She felt the pressure on her nipple, but that was just the start. As she wriggled and writhed, the pressure began to build all over, like a bottle of champagne just waiting to be uncorked. So long. She'd needed this for so long. She needed this and so much more.

Burke leaned over her body, capturing the opposite nipple between his teeth and tugging, preparing it for the bite of the clamp. He pulled on the nub, abrading it with his teeth, prodding it with his tongue. With a little groan, Burke lifted his head. Cole slipped the clamp on. She whimpered, the pressure brushed the edge of pain, but she felt. She finally felt, and her men had given her this gift.

Cole sat back on his heels, his cock jutting out, but he seemed utterly in control. His dark brooding had transformed into sexual need. Jessa was shocked at just how much that excited her. She hadn't admitted how much seeing him shut down hurt her. Burke had been willing to fight, but she needed Cole, as well. And they seemed to need her, too.

"I can see her arousal from here. She's ridiculously wet," Cole said, his voice a deep groan as he palmed his cock.

Burke let his hand slide down her body, causing her to quiver. His fingers slipped over her clitoris. "Oh, she's a dirty girl. She likes her nipples pinched, clamped, and tortured."

"Those clamps look perfect on her, like jewels." Cole flicked at one.

Jessa shuddered, the sensation flaring. Her nipples were engorged with blood. Cole pulled lightly on the chain that draped across the valley of her breasts. Jessa moaned as the clamp bit into her flesh with ruthless pressure. She looked down and saw that her nipples were turning a deep red. The silver clamps were pretty against her flesh. She whimpered.

"That's right, baby," Cole said, nudging the chain again. "That sound goes straight to my cock."

"Mine, too," Burke chimed in, his fingers playing around her pussy. "I think our little Jessa wants the merciless Doms to hurt her a bit, take what we want from her."

"And we will," Cole promised. "But not until I have what I want."

She didn't like the sound of that. "I'm not going to promise you anything, Cole. If this is some power play to get me to do anything but have a little fun, then you should let me out now."

His eyes darkened. "I'll settle for you begging for some cock today, Jessa. But don't think for an instant that I won't get what I want. You and me and Burke forever. You can fool yourself, but I won't let you go. You had your chance."

She shook her head. "I just want the sex, Cole."

"Then you'll beg for it." He held out a hand. "I need the last clamp, Burke."

Burke's head came up. "You're serious?"

"Yes."

Jessa felt her eyes go wide. She shivered. She was

very aware of how vulnerable she was. They could do whatever they wanted. "I don't have any more nipples, Cole."

Cole stared down at her pussy, his fingers taking the place of Burke's. She whimpered as he teased her. She gasped when he took her clit between his thumb and forefinger and squeezed. "You have this. This belongs to us, the same way those nipples do. We want to decorate our prize. Give me the clamp."

Burke passed the little silver bauble to his brother, and Cole settled on his belly between her legs. This clamp also had a chain that Burke clipped to the chain on her nipples.

Cole pulled the petals of her labia apart, exposing her clitoris. He pulled the hood back. Jessa felt all of the blood in her body rush to that one tiny spot. Cole took a deep breath.

"You smell so good to me." He leaned down and touched her clit with his tongue. The chain that tied the clamps together was still in his hand, and it jerked when she moved, the pressure tightening ruthlessly on her nipples. The pain bit into her, heightening the pleasure of his tongue.

She squirmed as he slid the clamp over her sensitized clit. She needed him—touching her, inside of her. Both of them. This was what he'd meant. He meant to make her beg, and she was already on the verge. Her clit was throbbing, and when he leaned back down and swiped at it with his tongue, Jessa nearly came off the bed. Burke held her down, his hands molding to her curves.

"No, you stay still. You let him make you come."

He would do it. Oh, this wasn't what she'd planned.

She wanted him inside her, but he was going to do it his way. He was going to utterly undo her—on his terms.

Cole lashed at her clit, the pleasure stunning her into obedience. She wanted to tangle her hands in his hair. To force him to make her come. It was right there, just beyond her reach, but he kept his touch light and teasing, torturing her clit. She wanted to fight, to make him do what she needed, but he had her tied up and held down. She was spread for his pleasure, and all she could do was lay there, taking lash after lash of his tongue on her distended clit. Every press made her more sensitive. And the whole time Burke played with her nipples, making them flare with arousal, with need. She tried to wiggle away. It was overwhelming. Her heart felt like it would pound out of her chest. It was right there on the tip of her tongue to beg, exactly as he wanted.

Instead, she wiggled to make him stop. Cole slapped at her thigh and growled.

"No, fighting me. You can say your safe word or you can obey." His mouth came back. Little licks, long swipes all meant to keep her on the edge.

Jessa settled back, Burke's arms a loving cage around her.

"Give him what he wants, sweetheart. God, I'm going to die if I can't fuck you soon. I want you so badly."

She was going to die soon, too.

"Please, Cole. Please let me come." She couldn't hold out another second.

"Your wish, baby," Cole muttered before he sucked her clit into his mouth.

She hurtled over the edge, panting as the orgasm

overtook her. Every wiggle of her body tugged on the clamps biting her nipples and clit, sending aftershocks through her.

Burke held her, his body beside hers. She could feel the length of his erection against her hip. He moved restlessly against her, whispering in her ear. "That was fucking gorgeous. Do you know how long I've waited to see that?"

Yes, she knew. They had waited as long as she had. A year. Almost a solid year of longing and loneliness and anger, and now all she had to do was give over and she could pretend just for a little while that everything would be okay.

Cole looked up, leaving her pussy for a moment as she came down from the orgasm. She could see her arousal glistening on his lips. "Again."

"No! Cole, please." She wasn't sure she could take another one. Her body was humming, but she felt stripped and bare down to her soul.

"Again, Jessa. I told you. Not until you beg for cock." His mouth closed over her pussy in an all-encompassing kiss, and Jessa surrendered. There was nothing else to do. Burke continued to tell her how much they loved her while Cole drove her to orgasm over and over again. Each time she thought she was sated, the need would build again until she was breathless and begging to come.

She knew what Cole wanted. He wanted her complete surrender. He wanted her to let go of the aches and hurts of the past year and embrace what they might have together. Tears poured from her eyes as she peaked again. She felt so connected to them now, it frightened her. Somehow these two men completed her, and in return she made them whole. Burke told her that, too. She was the piece that had always been missing.

She shuddered as she came down again. Connected. Beyond any orgasm, this connection was what she had missed. Her heart was taking over, unable to hide in the face of their onslaught. The orgasms were amazing, but empty because they weren't with her, inside her. She could refuse to beg all night, and they would still give her this pleasure, but it wasn't what she'd really wanted when she'd started this fight. She wanted her arms around them, her skin against theirs, their scents mingling. She wanted to merge with them. The orgasm was secondary to the feeling of being one with them.

"Please, Cole. Please."

Cole's head came up. "That's not your safe word."

"Please. I'm begging you and Burke to make love to me. No safe words. Untie me. I want my hands on you." It was as plainly as she could put it. She held in the words that she wouldn't say. *I love you both. I love you so much.*

Cole hesitated, then got to his knees. Burke got up as well, leaning over to pepper her face with kisses as he reached for her hands.

"Sweetheart, I love you. God, I missed you. You can't imagine how much I missed you." His hands worked to undo hers. She breathed a sigh of relief as they came apart and she was able to touch Burke. She sank her hands into his hair and pulled him down for a kiss. She was hungry again, this time to please them. Burke kissed her, not holding back anything. His tongue surged in, playing with hers, as she felt Cole's hands on her body.

She gasped, nearly screaming into Burke's mouth as Cole unclamped her clit.

"It's all right." Burke petted her hair, keeping his arms around her, but giving Cole access to her breasts. "When the blood rushes back in, there's a little bite of pain."

But Cole was already soothing it. He kissed her clit, his tongue swirling around gently, making the blood flow again. Burke kissed his way down her neck to her breasts where he did the same thing there, unclamping each nipple and lavishing it with affection. The pain caused her eyes to water, but their tender care did strange things to her heart.

Burke finally lifted his head and reached over to the nightstand and the leather bag where Cole kept his toys. He pulled out two condoms. He passed one to Cole before ripping his open. Jessa watched him stroke that big hard cock with his hand before rolling the condom over it. "I want to get in your pussy, Jessa. Ride me."

He rolled with her on the big bed until she straddled him. She felt Cole's hands on her back, and her energy surged. Oh, yes, she wanted that. She wanted to feel the burn and know that she had both of them deep inside her body.

Burke gripped her hips and suddenly shoved up, his cock plundering her pussy in an instant. She was so soft from the orgasms they had forced on her that he managed to push his way inside with one long groan. Jessa let her head fall back. So full. She was so full, and it felt good. The orgasms had been sweet, but she'd wanted this fullness.

"Fuck, you feel so good. She's so tight, Cole. She's

so perfect."

"She's going to be so much tighter when I get in." Cole pulled her cheeks apart, and she felt the cool sensation of lube being dribbled on the rosette of her ass. "God, I love you, Jessa. I've never loved anyone the way I love you. I will die one day, and the best thing I will have done was to love you."

She gritted her teeth as she felt him line the head of his cock up to her ass. She groaned as he started to press in. So fucking good. He felt so good. The burn began, but she welcomed it because it meant she had them both.

"Push against me, baby. You're tight. So fucking tight. It's like you're a virgin again." Cole pulled at her hips, his voice rumbling.

She flattened her back, brushing her sensitive nipples against Burke's chest. Cole fucked her ass in short strokes, gaining ground with each pass. The burn made her hiss, but Burke's sweetness reminded her of all she had to gain. He kissed her, running his hands through her hair, tangling his tongue with hers.

Slowly, Cole worked his way in, inch by delicious inch.

"God, Cole. Give it to her. She's milking my cock. I won't last," Burke said on a moan.

"You'll last as long as we need. We don't go until we can do it together," Cole said, still taking his time.

"You're a fucking bastard," Burke said.

Cole laughed. She felt that chuckle all along her spine. "Takes one to know one, brother."

Burke's face showed the strain of waiting for his brother, but Cole didn't let up. He continued his slow advance and retreat.

"You are so fucking hot, baby. Do you have any idea how much I love to fuck this pretty ass? This ass is ours. Take us, Jessa. Take all of us."

She pushed back, feeling Burke deep inside her the whole time she adjusted to take Cole. She shivered as his cock breeched her ass, slipping behind the tight ring of her muscles and lighting her up. All the sensitive nerves sang out after such a long time left untended.

"Baby, you feel so good. I love you, Jessa. I won't let you go. I won't ever let you go. You might never believe me, but I'll never stop loving you. I'll never give up on us again." Cole pressed in until she could feel his balls tap just below the curve of her ass.

"We won't ever give up. We've learned our lesson. Never again, Jess," Burke promised.

She wanted to believe them, but it didn't matter. All that mattered was that they were all together in this moment. It was something she could hold on to later when she was lonely. She could remember how it felt to be loved, even if only for a moment. She would take a moment or two with them over a lifetime with anyone else. She might never trust them again, but she would go to her grave remembering what it felt like to be between them, their words, hands, and bodies caressing her.

Cole pulled out, almost all the way. She wiggled against him, not wanting to lose his cock. Just as Cole pulled away, Burke pressed up, hitting her G-spot. Jessa hadn't thought she could come again, but the need rode her hard now. She pressed back, seesawing between them, unwilling to give up either cock. She rode them both, every nerve in her body attuned to them. Back and forth she let her body be pulled, manipulated, as they shared her like a sweet sex toy. Desired. Wanted. Beloved.

Cole's hand came between them and plucked at her clit, the sensitive nub flaring to life. She came, the orgasm crashing into her, making her scream out their names. Cole stiffened behind her, gripping her hips, and he pulsed in her ass as he came. Cole's orgasm seemed to trigger Burke's. He pressed up, calling her name as he pumped into her and emptied himself into the thin latex barrier.

Jessa fell onto Burke's chest, her breath sawing in and out of her body. Cole pulled at her as he rolled to the side, bringing her in the middle, pressed between them. She was warm and happy. Fear and anxiety had no place in their bed right now.

"Jessa," Burke whispered against her ear, the words tickling her skin. "Talk to us. We still have hours. We want to talk to you, work this through. Tell us what happened while we were gone."

Why did he have to do that? She'd given him her body, but he looked for more. He wanted to know her damn soul.

"Talk to us," Cole cajoled, his hands caressing her. "Tell us, Jessa. Tell us about Caleb."

Her eyes watered. Caleb. Her only real and lasting connection to them. He reminded her so much of his dads. He might only have one as a biological father, but she saw them both in her boy. Caleb was a lovely combination of Burke's sunny charm and Cole's iron will. Her baby. "What do you want to know?"

It was the one thing she couldn't refuse them. Caleb was the gift they'd given her. Amid all the sadness, he had been her shining light. Even in her darkest hour, she'd known that she wanted that little spark of life that had begun that winter night.

"Everything," they said, their voices a stereo. They moved closer, invading every inch of her space. She knew she should protest, but their bodies warmed hers.

She choked back tears. She'd started this because she'd wanted a last moment with them. She'd wanted closure. But she'd made a deadly mistake. There was no closure. There could never be closure between them. What they had would never be over. She saw that now. She could walk away. She could allow the pain she'd felt to break them apart forever, but she wouldn't be complete. She would walk through life a ghost, remembering a time when she was whole. She belonged to them, and she always had. Even before she'd met them, she'd been theirs, a girl waiting for these two men, these halves of a whole, to walk into her life and complete her.

She took a deep breath and began to speak, telling her son's fathers everything they wanted to know, both loving and fearing the peace settling into her heart.

# Chapter Nine

Burke glanced over his shoulder at the clock, trying not to move the rest of his body. He didn't want to wake Jessa. The last thing he wanted to do was pull her from her safety and security, back out into this world they had dragged her into. She stirred beside him, but didn't wake, merely cuddled closer to Cole, who wrapped his arms around her.

The last two hours played back through his brain. He would go to his grave with the feeling of Jessa's pussy clamping around his cock, milking him, taking everything he had. It had been so much more than sex. It had been a merging of who he was with her. Love for her lodged in his chest. He was a better human being for loving her. He reached out and touched her hair. So soft. Like the woman.

With a sigh of regret, he sat up. If he had his way, he would never leave this damn bed. He would stay with her, only allowing her out to shower and eat. She would need her strength because he and Cole had a whole year of sex to make up for.

Nearly five o'clock. They would have to leave soon.

Burke preferred to travel deep in the night if he had to go by car. There were fewer people on the road late at night. It was far easier to tell if someone was following them. Once they got out of Dallas and into East Texas, the crowds would thin to nothing. He would be able to keep watch on anyone trying to sneak up on them.

Cole stared at him over Jessa's shoulder. His eyes widened, one brow rising up.

Burke knew what he was saying. They had discussed earlier that one of them needed to call Dex before they headed out for Louisiana. The James brothers had promised to spend the day working on the case, calling the DA and trying to find anyone in the FBI they could trust. If they'd gotten a reprieve from having to hole up in a swamp, Burke wanted to know.

Burke sighed. Why the hell did he have to get out of the warm comfy bed and make the call?

Cole smiled smugly and tightened his arms around her. *Because I have the prize, brother.*

*Fucking bastard,* Burke shot back, sending Cole a look he couldn't possibly mistake.

Cole simply grinned.

His brother was a bastard. It was only by chance that Jessa was in Cole's arms. They had passed her back and forth between them for hours, but Cole always seemed to have the best sense of timing. Burke sighed and rolled out of bed, grabbing his pants. Cold. It was fucking cold. He hoped it wasn't this cold in the swamp.

"Next time I get to hold her, asshole."

"There's not going to be a next time," Jessa said, but even as the words breathed from her mouth, she settled her head on Cole's chest and nuzzled him. "This was a one-time weakness on my part. Don't expect it again."

Burke froze. After all the intimacies and genuine need they'd shared tonight, she was pulling away again?

Cole huffed, gritting his teeth. "We'll see about that."

A deeply satisfied smile crossed her face. "Yes, we will."

Jessa didn't stand a chance. Cole had thrown down the gauntlet. She could play stubborn all she liked, but they wouldn't let her go. If they had to sleep on her doorstep, they would. But eventually, they would break down her resistance, and they would win. She'd shown them exactly how to win her back. Jessa craved their touch, but she couldn't submit just her body. When she gave her body to them, she also gave her heart and her soul. And when they dominated her sexually, she flowered open like a plant reaching for the sunlight. She unfurled, took from them, then gave everything back.

Burke intended to treat her like the precious gift she was. She was the only woman in the world for them, and he and Cole would prove that they were worthy of her. That they wouldn't let her down again. They couldn't.

Cursing the cold, he padded across the carpeted floor to the small desk where his laptop had been downloading files from the hard drives Dex had brought them.

He grabbed his phone and laptop, then retreated to the bathroom so Jessa and Cole would have a little peace and quiet while he made the call. They had made a tactical error with Jessa several months before in allowing their shock and misery at the news of her marriage to overcome their good sense. They should have left Colombia immediately, handed Alea over to Rafe and

Kade, and flown straight to New York. It was what they'd intended to do. The mission had taken far longer than expected. They'd gone to the office, meaning to have Hilary book tickets to New York, but she'd greeted them with that damn report. Jessa Wade had married. Jessa was happy with her new husband. She had moved from her aunt's hotel in New York to a fabulous property in Virginia. She had moved on without them.

He and Cole should have camped on her doorstep and demanded an explanation. They should have trusted that she'd keep her promise to wait. They should have been willing to fight.

Too many people in his life had left him, whether through disinterest, discontent, or death. He'd learned to let go, but he hadn't been able to let go of Jessa emotionally. Even after they had agreed to give Jessa the space to be happy with her husband, Burke had carried her in his heart.

It had known better than his brain. Never again would he let her go.

He winced as he tried to spread his equipment across the miniscule counter. God, he hoped the place they holed up in next had more space. Besides being tiny, the bathroom was cold.

He dialed Dex's number as he pulled up the files he sought. He wanted to do a bit more digging before they spent hours on the road. Once they got to Louisiana, he would have plenty of time to comb over everything, but he wanted to see the original reports from the PI, see if he could make heads or tails of how long it had taken Marco Delgado to corrupt their investigator.

"This is Dex James." Dex's voice was cautious, as

though he didn't want to give anything away.

"It's Burke."

There was a long breath from the other end of the line. "Thank god. We've been worried. We expected you to call hours ago."

Hours ago he'd been buried deep inside Jessa. He didn't feel bad about that in the least. "Something came up. We're all still fine. We're heading out in an hour or so. How's my boy doing?"

It felt good to ask about Caleb. His son. When this was over, he would never be apart from his son again. He would make up for all the lost time. He would convince Jessa to have another baby. A brother or sister for Caleb.

"He's good, Burke. He's a great kid. I can tell he's missing his momma, but he's enjoying playing with our kiddos. Hannah's feeding him dinner right now."

He remembered what Jessa had said earlier. Though he felt like an idiot, he asked the question. "Uhm, how's his poop?"

Dex's laugh made Burke pull the phone from his ear. "His bowels are fine, man. You tell Jessa that he's still on schedule. And get used to it. You're going to hear yourself saying things you've never before imagined would come out of your mouth. Your kids become your life. Don't worry. I'm a dad, too. I can tell you, though, that one of the joys in my life has been sharing this family with my brothers. Spread the pain, man. I don't know how couples do it. Kids are like little monkeys. They're everywhere and into everything. I swear, one of us has to save Eli at least twice a day, and I'm sure the same will be true of his sister when she starts walking."

Burke knew he should be horrified, but all he could

think about was how much he wanted to be there for Caleb and any other children he, Cole, and Jessa had in the future.

"Don't worry about us here," Dex continued. "We've hired extra security for the place. Round the clock. These guys are solid, man. There is no way Marco could get to them. I trust them with my family."

Burke breathed a sigh of relief. Marco had already proven he could get inside law enforcement. He'd even managed to pay off their private investigator. Burke was sure Marco knew about their ties to the James family. He had to trust Dex. The man and his brothers were putting their own kids in the line of fire to help Burke and Cole.

"Has anyone talked to the DA?" Burke asked. He didn't hold out much hope, but if the DA had anything on the younger Delgado, it might slow the fucker down.

"Slade has been on the phone with him for hours. God, Burke, next time this shit happens can you keep it in Texas? We would have this shut down here. We don't have the same pull in New York. Anyway, they're willing to offer you witness protection."

Fuck, no. "I'll pass."

"I wouldn't let you go," Dex admitted. "We know Marco Delgado has feds on the payroll. The DA seems solid, but I'm not going to turn you over to him. Even he didn't recommend going into witness protection. Off the record, of course. He's lost a witness in the last six months. She was connected to one of Delgado's distributors. Look, I think he's on the up and up, but he's only one man. The cops are going through what's left of Jessa's house. It's a mess. It's going to take time."

That was what Marco was counting on. "Did they

identify the body?"

Maybe the identity of the man Marco had sent to set those bombs would help.

"Not so easy in the charred remains. We're going to need dental records. He couldn't have been a higher-up in the organization. I don't think Marco intended for him to get out of that house alive. He knew when your plane was coming in. He had to. He was waiting there. The cops found what appears to be the trigger device about a quarter of a mile from Jessa's house. We think he was watching from the woods. With binoculars, he would have been able to see you coming."

"Yeah, we got that when he managed to call us just as we were fleeing the scene." Burke tried to juggle the phone and his laptop. "Did you manage to copy those files before you brought them to me?"

"Yes. That secretary of yours is a pit bull, by the way."

Hilary? She'd always been polite and spoken in soft Southern tones to him. She and Cole, had never gotten along, but he could be an ass, too. "Sorry if she gave you hell. I didn't think to call her first."

"She was pissed off. And damn but she thinks you walk on water. The whole time I was packing up hard drives, she was telling me how you would beat the crap out of me when you found out how I had treated her. You got something going with her?"

"God, no." He wouldn't touch her with a twelve-foot pole and a Hazmat suit. She was deeply competent, but the blonde did nothing for him physically. "I've never thought of her as anything but an office manager. Look, I don't know what's up with her, but she's just the woman who does my paperwork and books."

"I don't think she sees it that way."

With a grimace, Burke grabbed the CD he'd made earlier of files from Hilary's computer so he could transfer them to his and compare. He needed to keep searching, see what other weaknesses in their security he and Cole might have that Marco could exploit. He popped open the drive. "Seriously, man. She handles my travel and—"

Fuck. Lying there, small, black, deadly was a little tracking device. He knew what it was the instant he saw it. "Goddamn it."

"She knew when your plane was coming in, didn't she?"

"Yeah," he said, his mind racing. "We booked the flight from Medellin to Mexico City on our own, but she worked a miracle to get us on the flight to Dulles. It was full. I'm now wondering if Delgado helped her manage that." Maybe the PI hadn't been the only one on Marco's payroll.

Dex was quiet for a moment. "She was particularly upset that I took her hard drive, but by then she knew I wouldn't take no for an answer."

"You didn't insert a tracking device in my computer's DVD drive, did you?" Burke doubted it, but just in case...

"No. Why would I?"

"That's what I thought. Hang on."

He cursed as he raced to retrieve her computer. Quickly, he booted it up and retrieved her e-mails. She was meticulous. She kept everything. Every freaking e-mail. There were thousands. He typed the private investigator's name into the search function and finally had what he wanted. The original reports from the PI.

He cursed. "Fuck me, Dex. Hilary is our Judas. I gotta talk to my brother."

They were in way deeper shit than even he'd imagined.

\* \* \* \*

Cole sighed. He didn't want to get up, but the sun was just about to slip under the horizon for the day. Time to leave soon. Jessa lay on his chest, her soft breaths making a rhythm he found soothing. She was here in his arms. It was a fucking miracle.

"Baby," he whispered, his hands tracing her curves. Her skin was so damn soft. "We have to get ready to go. We have a long drive ahead of us."

She groaned, sounding drowsy and sleep-soft. "Don't want to. Cold outside."

He chuckled. She was so much easier to deal with after ten or so orgasms. He made a mental note. When Jessa got difficult, he would simply tie her down and make her come until she purred like a kitten and wrapped herself around him.

"I would do just about anything if we could stay right here." He meant it. He'd give anything for the danger to be over, for his worst problem to be figuring out how to change Caleb's diapers. He knew their son liked rice cereal, and that Jessa had just started him on mashed banana. She'd also told him that he liked to get both everywhere. The thought of their son made his heart twist.

Caleb was the expression of their love for Jessa. Cole

wouldn't take him back for anything. He would endure every minute of pain and isolation again for a single shot at knowing his boy and loving Jessa.

Jessa sat up in bed, the sheet coming down, and her breasts were on display for a moment. His cock hardened again. He wouldn't ever stop wanting her. All she had to do was be in the same room and he was hard and ready to mount her. His mate.

She rubbed at her eyes, then finally seemed to realize that she was naked. She pulled the sheet up. "Do you mind?"

She wanted to play modest now? *Ain't happening.* "Yeah, I mind that you covered them."

She shot him a look that was probably designed to kill, but he didn't let it affect him. "Cole, I'd like to get dressed."

"Then you should, I suppose. Baby, I'm not leaving the room. Nor will I turn away and pretend I didn't spend the last several hours with my cock inside your pretty ass."

"God, that was rude!"

He smiled, the very act lifting his spirits. "No, it was amazing. You have got the tightest little backside I've ever fucked."

Cool green eyes rolled. "Not exactly a compliment, Cole."

He shrugged. He'd thought it was. "Well, I wasn't going to put it on a bumper sticker or anything. Unless you want. Or a T-shirt. That might be nice."

Jessa shook her head, and her laughter was beautiful to Cole's ears. She hadn't laughed once since they'd pulled her from her big Victorian house. He could certainly see why she hadn't, but he wanted her to laugh now. He wanted to fill her life with it.

She turned, her hair covering half her face, making her look like a siren. "Burke would tell me how beautiful my eyes are. But not Cole. No. You discuss the elasticity of my anus. What the hell am I going to do with you?"

"Love me." The words were out of his mouth before he could stop them.

Jessa stopped, her laughter silenced, but Cole wouldn't take the words back. He was done being scared, being weak. How could he get what he wanted if he didn't ask for it? Maybe he wasn't good enough for her, but he could be. Loving Jessa had changed him already. He was better, and he would be the man she needed. If she didn't love him anymore, he'd work day and night until she fell for him again. He wasn't going to let his fucking uncle win for the rest of his life. He wasn't going to be the same sort of miserable prick Martin had been.

She sniffled and got out of bed. "Cole, I don't know if I can do that. I think the wounds run too deep." She reached for her bag and pulled on her underwear. "I'm not the same girl I was when you met me."

No. She was even more beautiful. Being a mother had made her stronger. "I'm not the same man."

She worked the hooks on her bra and started to put on the jeans Hannah had given her. "I think you are, Cole. I don't think a man like you changes. You need adventure. I can't give you that."

"You think I like getting shot at? Let me tell you something, baby. It sucks. It hurts, and I'm getting way too old for it. I would rather hang up my guns and spend the majority of my time playing Mr. Mom while you paint. But Jessa, there is one thing on this earth I am good at, and that's tracking down people. Burke and I are the best. We've used our expertise to track criminals and terrorists, but we found a calling in finding missing persons. I don't know if I can give that up, but I can promise that we'll stay in the States, and we'll always come home to you."

She smoothed the sweater down, her eyes still wary. "I don't..."

The door to the bathroom banged open. Burke rushed through, laptop in hand. He put it down on the desk and started shutting everything down. "Cole, get dressed. We have to get out of here. Hilary is in on this. She's in on everything. And she put a tracking device in my laptop."

Cole absorbed the information. It computed instantly. Fuck. Why hadn't he considered that Hilary was their leak? She was a cold bitch. He hadn't pegged her as the type to sell her beloved Burke out for money, but apparently he'd been wrong.

Jumping out of bed, Cole crammed his legs in his jeans, listening as Burke talked.

"The PI was on the up and up. I found his initial reports. There's nothing about her marriage. He simply states she came back from Scotland and adopted a cat named Angus. He gives updates on the progress of her pregnancy. He did a good job. And Hilary hid it all."

"Bitch. You know I never liked her." Cole had always felt her disdain for him.

"It's obvious from that one phone call I overheard that she wants Burke," Jessa said, rushing to get her meager belongings together. "So she made sure I was no longer 'available.' I'm sure when Delgado made his offer, she didn't hesitate. She wants Burke alive and me dead."

"Fucking bitch. I will deal with her," Burke promised, his face flushing a violent red.

"*We'll* deal with her," Cole replied, pulling his shirt on. "But right now, we're leaving. We have to dump the equipment. If she put a tracking device in your computer, she may have put one in something else we're carrying. And it's almost six o'clock. Our time is nearly up. We leave now with nothing but the clothes on our backs and the cash. Let's go."

He had to get Jessa out of here.

His hand was on the door when it blasted open. The door exploded inward, hitting him directly in the head, sending him reeling.

Then chaos ruled. The moment the door fell away to reveal a gaping hole to the winter, something flew in. Cole caught sight of it. A cylindrical black object. *Fuck.* Flashbang. Cole leapt for Jessa, trying to cover her with his body, but he couldn't quite reach her. She stood by the bed, her eyes wide with terror.

The stun grenade went off, deafening him. The sound shook the room, and his eyes shut to try to keep out the blinding flash of light. Heat and sound and fury all in one little package. Jessa screamed. He felt his brother beside him. Both tried to protect Jessa.

"Oh, Mr. Lennox, I don't think you need that gun." A smooth voice could barely be heard over the ringing in his ears. "Gentleman, take those two down."

Cole turned to the sound, trying to focus long enough to get off a shot. And then he lost all control as twin darts bit into his skin, sinking into his flesh and sending fifty thousand volts through his system.

Fucking Taser. Every muscle in Cole's body jerked and spasmed in a chorus of agony. He couldn't move. He couldn't scream. He couldn't do anything. He registered that his brother was beside him, body also jerking. In this, as in all things, they shared the pain.

The horrible cracking sound cut off, but Cole knew it wasn't over. Even his body couldn't take a military grade Taser and leap back into the fray. He tried to make his arms move. Nothing. Fucking nothing.

"Gentleman, this was far too easy." Marco Delgado came into view. He was dressed in an urbane suit, his hair perfectly cut, wearing a wicked little smile on his face. "I expected more. I suppose this means I win. I doubt you'll let it pass, but I want to remind you that I kept my word about the boy. I'm not a monster. Just a son looking for revenge. And now I have it."

He flicked a hand, and one of his goons walked forward, carrying Jessa's body. Fuck. She wasn't moving. His heart seized up. *No!* If she was dead, he wouldn't be far behind. Jessa. God, what had he done?

"Ah, there's the panic I wanted to see. I knew I was right about her when I bribed your secretary to send me the private investigator's files. I saw the adoration on your faces that day at the Waldorf. I knew for certain she was the proper instrument for my vengeance when I realized you were paying a fortune to keep tabs on her."

"Leeetttt heeerrr goooooo," Burke groaned, his arms jerking as though he wanted to get his hands around the man's throat.

Delgado scoffed. "No. And to answer the question in your brother's eyes, no, she's not dead." Delgado put a hand on her back, sliding it down her curves. "She's taking a little nap. In fact, I'm not going to kill her right away. That would be far too easy for all of you. You cost my father his life and the consortium I inherited, along with its good name in the business. I intend to get it all back, and your lovely lady will help me. Redheads are so hard to find, and they do so well in the more exotic places of the world. I'll sell her. Imagine that as you search for her. Imagine all the men who will enjoy her body and her pain against her will. I know I intend to. Good night, gentlemen. I expect the next phase of our game will be challenging for you."

And then it began again. Just as he managed to move his fingers with the slightest bit of purpose, the two men who stood over he and Burke, flicked the switch again. Fire lit through his system and he jerked. Angry tears he couldn't stop blurred his eyes. His head jerked, striking the floor over and over.

Finally, darkness took him.

# Chapter Ten

Burke came to in little stages. Flashes of reality. Flashes of horror. He blinked his eyes open, then slammed them shut when the lights were much too bright. Every muscle ached. Tired. He was so damn tired, as though he'd run a marathon. His muscles protested at any hint of use. His eyes drifted shut, and he wanted to let sleep take him, but something wicked played at the edge of his consciousness.

*Jessa.*

The events of the evening slammed back into his head with horrible clarity. Burke forced his eyes open. How long had she been gone? The tiny motel room shook. Thunder. A storm. God, Jessa was out in that storm, and he had no idea where, with a vengeful bastard determined to use and kill her. And where was his brother?

"Cole?"

"Fuck. I hate Tasers." Cole sat up, patting his chest. Tiny blood spots dotted his T-shirt where the darts had bitten into his flesh. Burke looked down and could see his own.

He struggled to his feet, his muscles shaking. "We have to go. We have to find her."

"Figure out where she is, yeah. What time is it? How long were we out?" Cole flexed his hand and stretched. His skin looked ashen, his eyes red rimmed.

"About twenty minutes." Long enough for Jessa to vanish. Long enough for her to be lost forever.

"We have to alert the police, have the airports shut down," Cole said. "Where's the phone? Fuck. They took the phones." He looked around the room. "They even took the goddamn landline. Fuck. Fuck. Fuck."

Burke took a deep breath, forcing the air into his lungs. "We have to stay calm and find a phone, call Dex." He darted for the door. There would be a phone in the lobby unless Delgado had murdered everyone in the motel and taken all their phones. Burke turned back to his brother. "Look around. See if they forgot anything."

He threw open the door and stopped in his tracks. A woman stood outside their room, the rain beating on her. She was turned away from him, her blonde hair wet and mangled against the back of her dark coat. Despite the darkness, he knew who stood there, and he was shocked that the bitch had the gall to ever stand in his presence again.

"Hilary."

Cole stomped to his side in an instant. "What the hell are you doing here?"

She turned slowly, as though forcing herself to make the movement. Mascara streaked down her face. Her blue eyes blinked in a vacant shock. Burke had never seen Hilary when she was anything less than perfect. Flawless makeup and hair. Designer clothes in the most flattering styles. Now Hilary was a wreck. She stood there, whole body shaking, and he knew she'd been through something terrible.

He didn't give a shit.

"Burke." His name fell from her trembling lips. She reached an entreating hand toward him. "I'm so glad you're okay."

"Is she fucking serious?" Cole growled low, his jaw tight as he grabbed her arm and jerked her inside, making Hilary cry out.

"Yep, and she's got balls of steel," Burke replied under his breath as he slammed the door shut. They needed answers from her. She was definitely the reason he and Cole had been parted from Jessa for the past year. She had to be in league with Delgado, but for some crazy reason she'd come here. Now, they had to use that to their advantage, get whatever information they could out of her that would help them locate Jessa. Scratch that; *he* had to. Cole would only try to intimidate and bully her. Burke knew how to handle Hilary, and she had a crush on him that he'd use to their advantage.

"Let me go, you animal. You're just like the men you chase down." Hilary fought Cole's hold, her legs kicking.

God, he was going to have to play this right. He didn't have time to torture her, though it would have pleased him greatly. But Jessa's life was on the line, so he had to work fast to gain Hilary's cooperation. Cole had to stand down.

Burke steeled himself for what he had to do, then turned a scolding look to his brother. "Cole, leave her alone. You're hurting her."

Cole turned, his eyes widening. His expression clearly asked *what the fuck is wrong with you?*

"You can't treat her that way. Let her go right now." He sent his brother a ferocious look.

Cole dropped Hilary like a poisonous snake. She wasn't ready for it and crumbled to the floor in a heap.

*Go with me.* He mouthed the words.

Cole's face fell. He gave a long-suffering sigh, clearly understanding. "Fine. I'll go to the lobby. Take care of your fucking girlfriend quickly, Burke. Why is she even here? We don't have time to deal with her…issues."

Hilary looked up, her face sheet white. "I knew Burke was in trouble. I put a tracking device in the drive when that awful Dex James walked in and started demanding things. He was not a gentleman. Burke, I was so worried about you. I did it so I could find you."

Was there any chance she'd just been concerned about him and hadn't actually been working with Delgado? Burke mentally raced through the facts. No. She might have doctored those reports initially to keep them from Jessa, but she'd used the information to completely eliminate the competition. After all, if she could get Delgado to do her dirty work for her…why not? He'd wondered where she'd suddenly gotten the money for a new Lexus. There was no way Delgado could have found them tonight without Hilary's help. Burke forced himself to remain calm. It was all he could do not to tear her apart. Had she felt even a moment's compunction about helping her employers' enemy and contributing to the potential death of an innocent woman?

Why the fuck hadn't he nipped this worship in the

bud earlier? Him not wanting to hurt her feelings unnecessarily and make waves in an otherwise smooth-running office may cost Jessa her life.

Cole gritted this teeth. "Be quick, Burke. We have to find *my* woman."

He'd put the emphasis on "my." Yes. His brother knew what he was going to have to do. Cole shot him a glance tinged with regret and apology before striding out into the storm, slamming the door in his wake.

Burke's stomach turned, but he forced himself to put his hands on her shoulders and help her to her feet. "Hilary? Are you all right?"

She raised her face to his, and her lips curled up slowly in a tremulous smile. "Better now that your brother is gone. He isn't kind and gentlemanly like you, Burke. You're...wonderful."

Yeah? When Burke had what he needed out of Hilary, he intended to prove to her once and for all that he wasn't a kind gentleman, either. He had to force back the urge to wrap his hands around her throat and squeeze until her eyes bulged for mercy—then keep squeezing. She'd kept him from his child, from the woman who should be his wife, all because Hilary, the fucking bitch, had some fantasy about him. He and Cole would have dropped everything the moment they knew Jessa was pregnant. Hilary was the reason they hadn't been there for Caleb's birth. She was the reason they hadn't held Jessa's hand and put together Caleb's crib and waited with blessed anticipation. She'd stolen a critical year from them.

And now he had to convince this bitch that he cared about her. Fuck.

"It's all right," he soothed. "I won't let Cole hurt you. Hilary, what's going on? You shouldn't be here. It's dangerous. You should be safe in a hotel suite."

He wasn't going to admit he knew anything. He had to draw out her admission to get any information that might help Jessa. He had to let Hilary hang herself.

She sniffled, then stumbled into him, her wet chest plastered all over his. It seemed like a calculated move to force him to hold her. With deep disgust, he wrapped his arms around her. She was soaking wet, cold rain clinging to her. He was only conscious of his revulsion and the time ticking away.

"Oh, Burke, some men broke into the office earlier today and tried to kill me."

Yeah, Delgado would want to tie up all the loose ends. "Hilary. I never meant to get you involved in this. How did you get away?"

Tears pooled in her eyes again. "Do you remember the woman who works in the accounting firm next door, the one who does our taxes? She was in the office so we could have a meeting. I had gotten up to get some coffee, and they just came in and…shot her. They killed her and thought she was me. She was sitting behind my desk. I don't know why she would do that. I think she was trying to get into some files she shouldn't have been looking at. You can't trust anyone these days."

A chill went through Burke. Hilary was playing the damsel in distress in fine fashion, and he wondered if she saw the irony in her statement at all.

The office had cameras. Hilary always had the security feed up and running on her monitor. But since Dex had taken all her computer equipment except that monitor, the only thing she'd have to do was watch that security feed. Hilary had to have seen the men coming in. What a stroke of luck that blonde, sweet Mary, the accountant from next door, just happened to be sitting there when Hilary left the room. Or had it been luck at all? Most likely, she'd set Mary up to take the fall. It was all Burke could do not to recoil back from the bitch. Hilary was willing to do anything to scheme her way into his love. Now Burke was going to use her desire against her.

"How terrible. I'm so sorry." He almost choked on the words. "I'll get you someplace safe. Then I have to help Cole go after Jessa."

Hilary's eyes flared at the mention of Jessa's name. "I-is she your girlfriend?"

Burke hoped he looked brutally confused. "No, she's Cole's girlfriend. And she had his baby. We just found out yesterday. That private investigator we hired was apparently on Delgado's payroll. Hilary, Cole has a son. I can't let my nephew's mother die."

"But I thought..." She flushed. "I heard a rumor that you and Cole...shared women." There was no mistaking the disgust in her eyes.

A little truth would help his lie. "We have in the past. But, Hilary, we never expected to live that way for the rest of our lives. I want a normal life with a nice, sweet wife who can stand beside me and be an asset to my business. Jessa is an artist, very Bohemian. She's nothing like what I imagine my wife would be. I want someone more...traditional."

Certainly, Hilary would see herself in that picture.

But Burke wanted Jessa desperately. He wanted to sit

and watch her work. She was so talented. He loved her open mind and her generous heart. Hilary, with her perfect manners, wouldn't know generosity if it bit her in the ass. Still, he could see that his ploy was working.

Hilary shook her wet, blonde head. "If she's Cole's, then let him handle it. He's capable. I'm just so worried about you. I don't want you to get hurt."

Burke pulled away, letting a tiny bit of his disdain show. "Cole is my brother. Where I come from, family doesn't let family down. I thought you felt the same way. I guess I was wrong."

She grasped his hand, her fingers like claws around him. "You're not wrong, Burke. Family is important. Even when they're not what we could have hoped for. Of course. You should call the police."

"I can't, darling." He shook his head, watching her eyes light up at the endearment. She was on the hook and buying into his act. "I'm sorry. I should be more professional."

"No." Her eyes practically begged him. "The feelings between us are more than professional. I think we both know it."

Clearly, she'd deluded herself into thinking he gave a shit. How? He'd barely spoke to her past giving her orders and asking for updates. He'd never done more than shaken her hand before tonight. But she'd invented a whole bunch of crap about them in her head and convinced herself it was true. He could seal the deal by flirting. It was definitely in his skill set.

"You're right, darling. We should stop pretending. The whole idea of you being shot at…god, I can't imagine it. But, my worries must wait, Hilary. I can't let my brother down. We're going after this terrible man who tried to kill you. I won't stop until we find him. Then I'll come back to you and…" Burke forced a smile and a sigh, his hand to caress her waist. Bile rose in his throat.

"I heard them," she blurted.

Now that she thought he was on her side, she was going to talk. He forced patience. "What do you mean?"

"When the two gunmen came, I hid. I didn't know what else to do. One shot Mary, then they talked. The other made a phone call from the office phone. I overheard the conversation. They called some private airfield. They talked about getting everything ready for a flight. I'm sure the number is still on our phone. We could go back to the office and get the number, then Cole can go after her."

Delgado was taking Jessa to a private airfield. Of course. It had to be private. He couldn't exactly haul a drugged woman through security at DFW. A private airfield would allow him to simply drive into the hangar he'd rented and load the plane, far from prying eyes.

The door opened, and Cole walked in. Burke pushed Hilary away. He'd gotten everything he needed, and he'd fucking cut his hands off before he'd ever touched her again.

"He's taken her to a private airfield," Burke said. "How fast do you think Dex or Slade can get to our office and check the outgoing calls? Idiots called from there to make the last of their plans. They probably didn't think about leaving behind evidence."

"Or they were taunting us with the information, thinking that by the time we figured it out, they'd be long gone. We need that number."

"Is that all the information she had?" Cole asked, his cold eyes raking her.

He grimaced. "It's all I'm willing to touch her to get."

"What are you talking about?" Hilary eased closer to Burke as Cole stalked her way. She turned her head from one brother to the other. "Burke, we should get out of here. Your brother can find the artist now. You'll take care of me, won't you? I...I think I might need to go to the hospital. I might be in shock. And I have to deal with the police about poor Mary's murder." She gripped his shoulders. "I need you, Burke. I need you."

Cole held up a cell phone, utterly ignoring their former secretary. "The owner gave me her cell. If he's taking Jessa to a private air field, I think it's a safe bet that, at some point, he's planning to take her out of the States. The woman in the lobby says there's an airstrip about twenty minutes away. She's always suspected that criminals use it. She's a paranoid crazy. On the plus side, she's armed to the teeth." He held up a pair of Glocks. "But we have to pay cash. I also had to promise not to sue. She saw the whole thing, but she doesn't want to call the cops. I suspect she has a record."

"Good work," Burke praised his brother.

"I'll call Dex and get his help." Cole stepped away, punching buttons on the phone.

"Burke?" Hilary called for his attention, starting to cry and cling again. "Burke. I love you. I've always loved you. I'm so glad you've realized that we're supposed to be together. I know you want me."

Burke only wanted to save Jessa. He jerked away from her and turned a face full of disdain on her. "The only thing I want now is to kill you. But I would never be able to explain that to my soft-hearted fiancée. You're lucky. If it were up to me...you'd be six feet under."

Her head shook violently. "Fiancée? You aren't going to marry that tramp. You can't."

"I am. In my heart, she's already our wife. And we have a son."

Cole punched a button to end the call, then approached again, his eyes narrowed on Hilary. "We've got to go, start heading for that airfield and hope it's the right one. Dex will call to confirm and to get the police out there. What about her?"

Hilary backed up. "No. No. This isn't right. Burke, you and I are meant to be together. You don't want that slut from New York City."

Burke looked to his brother, his partner, his other half. "Did they leave us some rope?"

Cole nodded, a slow smile spreading. "And my best ball gag."

"Then work quickly. We have to rescue our girl."

Hilary screamed, but it didn't take Cole long to shut that up. Burke spared only the merest glance at the woman who had become obsessed with him. In minutes, she was tied to a chair and gagged, her eyes angry and wide. Then they shut the door behind them, Burke satisfied Hilary couldn't cause any more trouble.

They were already in the car, racing through the night toward the nearby airstrip when the phone rang again. Dex had their answer, and they were heading to the right place. Now he just had to hope they weren't too late to rescue Jessa.

\* \* \* \*

Cole drove through the driving rain, his stomach in knots. The windshield wipers thudded, making a rhythm that did nothing to cut through the tension in the car.

"Do you see the turn off?" Cole asked.

Burke hadn't said a damn word since they had tied up Hilary and gotten the call from Dex confirming the location of the airstrip and vowing to call in the police. After that, Burke had shut down.

"It shouldn't be more than a half a mile. Do you think she's already in the air?" Burke's voice was a flat monotone.

"If they're in as small a plane as I believe, they would be insane to take off in this storm. And Marco isn't crazy. Evil, but very intelligent. She's still here." As Cole slowed the SUV, he hoped he wasn't giving his brother false hope, but it was pouring, the rain lashing at the vehicle in straight lines. "Besides, he thinks Hilary is dead. From his perspective, we would have no way of knowing which airport they were at. This one isn't even listed. It's a miracle we had a number."

It *was* a miracle. And a clue that they would get her back. Cole felt it deep in his soul. She was out there waiting for them. He knew he was the one who usually took the pessimistic view of life, but with his brother sitting beside him, guilt eating away at him, Cole had to bring the balance. That's the way it had been all of their lives.

And they'd felt complete because they had found Jessa. He'd given up on her once. He wouldn't do it again.

He caught sight of a line of flashing white lights

blinking in the distance. He moved cautiously. "Get the binoculars."

Either Marco hadn't been sure of which car was theirs, or he'd been smug that they couldn't catch up. Either way, the binoculars were right where he'd left them in the SUV.

Cole stopped the car. Burke peered through the lenses and turned on the night vision.

"I see a hangar. There's only one. Nothing on the tarmac. If they're still here, they have to be inside the hangar, waiting out the storm," Burke said. "We're going to have to walk."

They couldn't take the chance of tipping off Delgado. The element of surprise might be their only possible advantage. They didn't even know how many men were in the hangar, between them and Jessa. Everyone would be armed, for sure. They didn't know exactly where Jessa was being held. Inside the plane? Deep in the hangar? Did she have a gun to her head? Was she tied up? Had Delgado already assaulted her?

Every one of those thoughts terrified him, but he couldn't give in to panic. Rushing in wouldn't save Jessa, just get them all killed. And Burke didn't have his head on straight.

"It wasn't your fault," Cole assured him. "We don't have time to go into freaking therapy over this, but you have to know that. Hilary was living out some fantasy in her head. That is not your fault."

Burke's face turned down. "I knew she thought of me as more than a boss. I should have found some way to gently squelch her feelings long ago."

Cole groaned. He knew what his brother was

thinking, but Burke had to let it go. "I knew she had a crush on you, too. But neither of us ever imagined she would go to such lengths. You can't go after Jessa with your head all fucked up. Put the guilt and shit out of your mind for now. You have to go in there confident in one thing."

His brother finally looked at him. Cole could see the guilt weighing him down. "What is that?"

"That we have the right to protect her, to love her. She belongs to us, and we're going to save her. No more mistakes. No more letting things come between us." Cole had been right where Burke was. In many ways, he still struggled not to fall into that dark place in his soul. But he refused to let guilt and doubt cost him another minute with Jessa. She might never forgive them, but by god she would have to deal with them. She would have to see them because he wasn't going to let his son grow up without a father. And he wasn't going to let her be alone again. Even if he had to protect her from afar, he would.

Burke took a deep breath. "I love her."

"And she loves us. We just have to remind her."

Cole felt a deep sense of relief as Burke's eyes hardened and his hand curled around the Glock on his lap. "We're going to kill him."

Cole understood what his brother meant. No matter what happened, Marco Delgado was going to die. They wouldn't hold him for the police. They wouldn't make a case against him and hope that the justice system worked. Marco Delgado's trial was over. He was guilty, and his punishment would be swift.

"We're going to kill him," Cole agreed.

They took a moment to discuss strategy, making a

few assumptions based on what they knew of Delgado, combining tactical experience. They threw in a few prayers for good measure.

"Then let's go." Burke tucked his gun under his coat and took off in the pouring rain.

Cole followed. There was no other person he would want watching his back than the man who shared half of his soul. And he knew one thing for sure. Somehow, someway, they would win.

\* \* \* \*

Jessa shivered. She tried to hold it in, but she'd gotten drenched in the rain, and now the cool air of the hangar in which Delgado held her prisoner mingled in her blood with shock. She couldn't stop shaking.

"There's no use pretending, Miss Wade. I know you're awake."

His voice filled her with dread. She'd come back to consciousness as they were carting her into the hangar. She'd listened to him scream about the weather and threaten to kill the pilot, who had simply told him that taking a small plane into straight-line winds was the same thing as putting a bullet in his brain, and the bullet was faster.

Marco had backed off, but he hadn't been happy about it.

There was a long sigh. "Keeping your eyes closed will not solve the problem, Miss Wade. And you'll continue to be cold. If you give up the game, you'll find I've provided you with a blanket."

There was a tense atmosphere pervading the hangar, but Delgado seemed to have calmed down. Having little choice, Jessa opened her eyes. She would have preferred to play possum for a while longer, but she was freezing. And the drugs they had given her made her head ache.

She sat up, a dizzy feeling taking over. She was inside the plane, but she could see the lights in the hangar from the small windows. Delgado sat across from her, a glass of amber liquid in his hand. He seemed perfectly comfortable. Just a businessman about to go on a trip in style.

God, if she didn't do something, this was the end. She wouldn't see her baby again. He would grow up, and he would forget her face. She would be a ghostly vision in photographs, a simple image who wouldn't mean anything to him. He would have another mother figure. Tears squeezed from her eyes. Her baby. She would give anything to hold him one last time, to feel his hands patting her cheeks, to rub her nose against his.

She had to trust and pray that if Cole and Burke were still alive, they'd take care of her son. Oh, she wasn't giving up. Jessa intended to fight until the bitter end. But at the moment, the odds for an escape tonight weren't looking good. And if Cole and Burke weren't alive... God, that thought was too painful.

"Are they alive?" She had to ask.

The last thing she could remember was the world lighting up around her and thunder cracking through the room. Cole and Burke had tried to get to her, protect her. She'd reached for them, but her ears had been ringing and her vision had been blurred. And then she'd felt the sharp stab of the needle entering her flesh. Nothing after that.

Delgado took a long sip of his drink. "Yes. Though I doubt they're happy about it right now. I can only imagine the terror they feel. It is horrible to know that your loved one is in danger when you know where to find them. I imagine the terror is a million times worse when you do not know where your loved one is."

He smiled, seemingly satisfied with the pain he was causing. Jessa breathed a sigh of relief. Burke and Cole weren't dead. They would look for her. She might not trust them with her heart, but they wouldn't let her down in this. They were heroes. They would never stop until they found her.

Delgado's plan chilled her to the bone. She'd heard him talking to his guards while she'd pretended unconsciousness. She would be sold, used. Something she'd only done in a loving fashion would be forced on her by men she didn't know. After hearing what Alea had gone through, terror filled her. But she would survive somehow. She vowed to stay alive until they found her.

Then she'd see her son again. No matter how long it took. No matter what she had to endure.

And she wasn't taking shit from this asshole.

"You know a lot about causing pain. The women you sell into slavery have families, you know."

He stopped in the act of drinking, his hand freezing in midair. It tightened around the glass, and then he set it back down. "You have a very narrow view of the world, Miss Wade. This is the way it works. The strong use the weak. You can be a predator or you can become prey. My father taught me that. You are a lovely woman. Your only mistake was choosing weaker men. The Lennox brothers think they can change the world, but I'm going to show them that the world does not wish to change. The world has worked as I have explained it since man first walked upright. It will work this way long after I am gone."

Delgado clearly believed it. It made her sick. "I'm not interested in your lecture. I'm sure you have a hundred intellectual reasons to excuse your bad behavior, but I don't care. I'm not buying your crap. The world isn't always that way. There are some people who genuinely care and want to help others. Those people would be appalled and horrified by you."

"They are nothing to me. I don't care." His perfectly coiffed head shook. "You are so naïve. No one cares."

"Burke and Cole do." They had fought against this man. The fight might have taken them away from her, but they had saved women and put families back together. They had done good. How much more could they have done if they'd had more help? A whole team and a huge pool of resources? What could a foundation do? They were soldiers. They wouldn't think about things like that. But Jessa had grown up in a world where money made a difference.

What if her money, her connections, could help bring women out of their dark prison and back home?

"I'm going to take you down, you know." Tears blurred her eyes, making the world seem watery, but she found an odd strength. She was here. The worst was yet to come, and yet she felt strong, powerful. He could do what he liked to her, and she would still fight. Her cause was just, and she wasn't some woman who lightly accepted what fate handed down. She rolled with life, made changes as necessary. She had walked away from wealth because the cost was too high. She'd given birth to a son alone. Some people in her life loved her. She was worthy, and no one could convince her otherwise. And she wasn't going down without a fight.

Delgado threw back his head and laughed. "I love the spirited ones. You're like beautiful horses, you know. I love to ride. My father spent many hours teaching me. He believed that the stubborn horses made for the best ride. I will teach you, too. I will break you."

"You will try." It wouldn't work. She would close her eyes and dream of Burke and Cole. She vowed it. When someone touched her, she would divorce from her body and reach for them in her mind. She would shut out the pain and be with them. She would survive.

He leaned forward, his eyes narrowing. "I will win."

She pulled the blanket around her and glanced around the plane. It was small, with only six seats in the body. Gavin James's plane had been larger, but the layout similar. The door at the back was open. An armed man, leaning against the wall with eyes half closed, blocked the staircase leading down. She could see the inside of the hangar by looking out of the three small windows. They made a mural of the world outside, but not a whole picture. How many men lay between her and freedom?

Delgado sat across the aisle, beside her. She could see the gun on his belt. Besides the guard at the door, she could also see two others walking outside the plane and the pilot in a folding chair, reading a magazine. The guards patrolled the area, but there was a relaxed feel to the operation. One sort of shuffled along, and the other stood just inside the hangar door, smoking a cigarette. They believed they'd already won.

She watched, wondering if they would all be on the plane when it took off or if some would stay behind. She hoped for the latter. She was studying the man smoking just inside the hangar when the door opened slightly, just a foot or so, and the smoking man disappeared into the night.

Not as if he'd walked into it, but like he'd been taken.

She sat up straight, felt her eyes going wide. What had just happened? The man had disappeared...and no one seemed to notice. The pilot appeared absorbed by the magazine in his hands. The man in the doorway of the plane stared at his feet and yawned as though the sound of the rain was making him sleepy. No one seemed to have noticed that one of the guards had just—poof!— disappeared.

"What?" Delgado asked, turning and looking out the window.

Jessa scrambled. "I was just wondering where we're going. The pilot doesn't seem very friendly. Does he have any experience? I don't like to fly."

Anything to turn his attention away from that window.

Delgado turned back, taking another sip of his drink. "Wilcox? He's been in my family's employ for years. It's the only reason he isn't dead now."

But he *was* dead. Jessa watched as Burke stalked the man, coming from behind. In one swift move, he grasped the man's head and twisted. The pilot's neck turned far past the point where he could live. Burke let the man slip out of his grasp and caught his magazine. The pilot slumped over in his chair, and Burke set the magazine on the concrete as Cole stalked into the hangar, sans the smoking guard.

They were here. They'd come for her.

"I don't like to fly. I don't want to fly." Jessa let her voice rise high, putting a little hysteria behind it. Any distraction could give Burke and Cole the advantage they needed.

The guard hovering at the plane's stairway came awake, but he fixed his stare firmly on her. His eyes rolled as though he'd expected her to be difficult.

Oh, she could absolutely be difficult.

Delgado laughed. "I'm taking her to a brothel where she will be raped multiple times a day in ways she can't even conceive of, and the stupid bitch is complaining about the flight?"

He and the guard exchanged a look. Jessa took those seconds to watch as Cole, his hair plastered to his face, soaked to the skin, moved like a wraith toward the guard pacing the hangar. He moved so fast for a big man, his feet lighter than she could imagine. The guard didn't stand a chance. Cole had an arm around his neck before he could move.

"I hate flying. I won't go. You can't make me!" Jessa screeched. "No one will let you take off with a woman screaming inside the plane." She knew her arguments were stupid, but they were doing the trick. The only two men remaining between her and freedom were staring at her like she'd gone slightly crazy.

In seconds, Cole had pinned the guard to the ground, denying him air until his legs finally stopped kicking. Burke stood in the shadows, his gun out, his eyes on the plane. Cole stood, and they both began coming closer. The guard at the top of the stairs would see and hear them coming a mile away. He'd have plenty of time to draw his gun and shoot them both—unless she distracted the guard.

"I won't go." She stood up and stamped a foot like a toddler in need of a nap. Anything to bring their focus on her and not the men moving to the plane. She let it go, throwing a fit to end all temper tantrums.

"Shut up," Delgado growled.

"No!" she screamed, tossing the blanket in Marco's face. His eyes widened before they disappeared under the scrap of black felt. He batted at it, the glass slipping out of his hand and spilling.

The guard rushed forward, grabbing at the blanket.

"Sit down, bitch," Delgado said, baring his teeth as he swiped at the Scotch on his slacks. "No, wait. Don't sit yet. Michael, teach her a lesson first."

The hulking guard near the door stalked closer and lifted his hand. Jessa braced herself, but she still lost her balance from the vicious slap that smacked her head back. She fell against the chair, her skin burning and stinging. But she couldn't give in. The doorway was tight. Both men would have to come through there first. They'd be in deep danger. She couldn't stand either one being hurt. She forced herself back to her feet and shoved at the guard using every bit of strength she had. She screamed as she pushed at him to let Burke and Cole know that she was in the plane.

"Two! Two! Two!" Jessa screamed. If they heard her, they would know that there were two people on the plane with her. They would know they had two men to kill.

"She's gone crazy," Delgado said, reaching out to grab her hair. His fingers tangled brutally against her scalp, forcing her head back. "We can start your training now, bitch. Michael, get the duct tape. I don't want to hear her scream when I use her ass."

There was a loud crack, and Michael stopped, his enormous body frozen for a single moment. There was a neat hole where a bullet had exited his forehead, blood blooming around the circle.

Cole entered the plane behind the falling guard, his gun ready once more. Burke was right behind him.

Delgado pulled her against his body. She felt the sting of his hand pulling at her hair and the hard press of metal against her flesh. "Get back. Both of you."

Cole's gun went down. He let it fall to the floor. "Let her go and you can do anything you want to me."

"Or I could just blow a hole in her side and you two can watch as she slips away," Delgado shot back. "Your brother will put his gun down, and you will both allow us to leave this plane or I'll kill her right here."

That wasn't happening. If Burke dropped his gun, Delgado would simply shoot them all. She understood their hesitation, but she had to take a chance if she was going to save them. "Cole, Burke, I trust you. I trust you."

The minute the words were out of her mouth, she let her body go completely lax. She fell toward the floor. The only thing holding her up was the hold Delgado had on her hair. But it was enough. He couldn't balance and hold on to her.

Another shot rang out, the sound ricocheting through the plane. She hit her knees as the hand in her hair let go. Cole caught her before she hit the ground, his arms pulling her away.

Burke stood over Delgado's prone body. He kicked

the gun away. In the distance, Jessa could hear the roar of sirens coming their way. Cole held her close, but all she could see were dead bodies.

"Baby. Baby, are you all right?" Cole's hands were everywhere, looking for damage. "Did someone hit you? Did they hurt you?"

Burke was at her back, crowding her. "Sweetheart, he's dead. They're all dead. They can't hurt you again."

Yes. They were all dead, and she was alive. Her hands shook as she pulled away. So much had happened. She felt herself shake again, the shock setting in. Her knees threatened to crumble beneath her. Delgado was lying dead feet from her. She knew that in her head...but destructive thoughts crept through her mind. What if he'd somehow gotten to Caleb? After all, why should she trust a criminal to keep his word to leave her baby unharmed?

She looked at Burke and Cole with stark terror and begged, "Take me to Caleb. Please. I need to see my son."

# Chapter Eleven

Jessa stared at the door that separated her from Caleb. She'd thought about sleeping on the floor beside his crib, but decided that simply leaving the door open between their rooms would work. When they'd arrived at the James' condo, she'd spent over two hours holding him, cradling his little body, but he'd been sleeping fitfully, waking with an occasional cry. She'd known that if she didn't let him be, he would be one cranky boy in the morning. And in the morning she had to decide what to do with her life.

She sat up in bed, knowing that sleep wasn't coming soon. She'd made it through the police interview and the paramedics examining her. She'd held herself together through it all, but now that the distractions were gone and she was all alone, the tears fell.

Why couldn't she just take what Burke and Cole were offering and so willing to give her? Tonight, they had hovered over her, telling her again and again how much they loved her. And she kept pulling away, almost afraid to believe that it was true. Trembling at the thought they might leave her again—this time for good. Maybe

she was exhausted and not being terribly rational.
But…broken trust was hard to repair. She wanted to try,
but being so utterly alone this past year as she'd tried to
live without Burke and Cole had been torture. Some
days—and nights—she'd thought that if she had to spend
another minute without them, she'd go insane.

She frowned. She still loved them. That wasn't ever
going to change. Something in her was wired for them.
So why couldn't she cling to them now? Why was she
holding herself back?

Fear.

Jessa rolled out of bed, her feet sinking into the
luxurious carpet. She was wearing one of Hannah's silk
nightgowns, the material soft on her skin, but all she
could think about was her men's strong hands caressing
her, their arms surrounding her.

What was she doing? What was she going to do?

She walked to the windows and opened the blinds.
The soft lights of the Dallas skyline played across the
room. Marco Delgado was dead. She could leave
tomorrow, and the Lennox brothers couldn't stop her if
she really wanted to go. She could pack Caleb up and
find a new home. She could go on with her life.

Jessa sniffled. It sounded a bit mean and petty to
move Caleb away from their fathers. To punish them by
leaving just because they'd left her. In fact, it sounded
terrible. So what the hell was she to do?

Tired. She was so tired and she felt a little empty.
They were in another room. Doors, a hallway, and
distance lay between them because she hadn't been brave
enough to approach them last night, tell them how much
she needed the sense of safety and love they gave her so

freely. She'd been too afraid to try with them again.

"Come on." The low whisper came out of nowhere.

Jessa turned toward the door to the nursery with a start. Someone was in there. She frowned, her heart beating out a rapid rhythm as she padded across the floor and grabbed a heavy, decorative candlestick as silently as possible and drew it up over her head. Since she'd left the door open to be closer to Caleb in the night, she easily heard the masculine voice that whispered in the air.

"God, you're a baby hog. I want to hold him."

She closed her eyes and had to grin a little. The sweet grumble of Burke's voice pierced her heart. They were here. She'd turned away from them, but they had snuck into the nursery to be with their son. The miracle they'd created with her.

She peeked through the crack in the door.

There were two rockers in the nursery. Hannah had explained that this was the east wing bedroom, for times when one of her babies was sick. It must be nice to be wildly wealthy. Jessa would have to settle for a lovely home with only one nursery. It would have been enough if Burke and Cole hadn't come back in her life. Now it seemed like…settling. They'd come back into her life and made her want more—a house with a bedroom big enough for the three of them, along with more love to fill it. No, she'd always wanted more, and now she knew they wanted to give it to her.

She had to make a choice.

Burke and Cole sat in the rockers. Cole had his shirt off and cradled Caleb against his chest. Her son, who never seemed to sleep when she held him, was like a limp noodle in his father's strong arms.

"I can't help it. Look at him. He's so fucking beautiful." Cole smiled down at the baby.

Burke kicked at his shin. "Don't cuss around the baby. Do you want his first word to be fuck?"

"Shit." Cole winced. "Sorry. I hadn't thought of that. No."

"Then watch your language. We have to do things differently now. We have a son."

Cole rocked back and forth, cuddling Caleb. Burke leaned over, his fingers stroking Caleb's hair. "We might have to move. If Jessa goes back to Virginia, we'll follow her. She might not want us now, but I'm not giving up. And I can't let him go."

Jessa felt tears prick her eyes. Cole's voice, his strong, deep voice, had hitched when he'd said she didn't want them.

Burke took a deep breath. "I thought if we found her in time and eliminated Delgado, that she'd want to be with us, would see…" He shook his head. "I'm not willing to give up, either."

"I love her. I need her."

"We both need and love her." Burke sat back, his head resting against the chair. "She's the one, but we can't force her to love us back. We can only be there. We can only prove that her hardheadedness can't drive us away. We made some horrible mistakes, but we won't make them again."

Cole sighed, his lips cracking into a sad smile. "I'm glad you feel that way. I was worried that all the bullshit with Hilary would turn you into me."

"No. There's only room for one brooding butthead in our lives." He chuckled. "You took that role on long ago.

I'm going to be the happy dad. And you're right. He's so fucking beautiful. He's the best thing we ever did. Do you think he'll love us? Or do you think he'll be angry that we couldn't love his mother separately? Do you think he'll be ashamed?"

The tears coursed down her face. She'd hurt them, made them worry about their relationship with their son. Made them doubt what they needed. God, she hadn't meant to.

"We can only try, Burke. We're going to love him. We're going to be the best fathers we can, and that starts with cutting back on work. We can't risk ourselves anymore. He needs us. Even if Jessa doesn't want us around, we have to be here for him. I love Jessa, but I owe this child."

They wouldn't leave Caleb—or her—again. Deep down she'd known it all along. She'd known that they would be good fathers, but she was still afraid that the only reason they would settle down would be for Caleb's sake, and she wanted to mean more to them than a successful breeder. Her fear and insecurity was roaring in her head. And a single quiet voice spoke below it. A little whisper.

*You are more than that.*

She'd let her grief and fear lead her. She was allowing her need to protect herself to keep her from them.

But she wasn't the girl who was going to let fear trump happiness. She was a woman who knew what she wanted. She'd been brave enough a year ago to take them on, and damn the consequences, because she knew that it was better to try than to regret. She'd turned away privilege and money because they came at too high a cost. She'd been braver in the past. She'd been a woman two men could fall in love with. She'd been enough for them.

If she'd dig for a little courage, she could be enough for them again. She had to dig for it. She didn't want to give them up, either.

Cole finally passed Caleb to Burke, whose arms curled around his tiny body. His lips curled up in a smile.

"Hey, buddy. We're your dads. You're lucky. You got two. We're not very smart, but we're tenacious. We won't let you down." Burke kissed his forehead.

"And we won't give up on your momma. We're going to be patient. We're going to show her. We'll move. We'll buy a house close to you. We'll build another business, one that won't take us away from you."

Jessa pressed on the door, pushing it completely open with a little smile. She was done with fear and doubt. She was done with pessimism. She was going to live her life the way she wanted, with hope in her heart. She was going to be the mother Caleb deserved—a brave woman who followed her heart and didn't regret. If it all went wrong, then at least she'd know that she tried. She would open her heart to love because that was the only way to find it.

"Jessa?"

She moved to the doorway, revealing herself. "Hi."

"Hi yourself, sweetheart."

God, they were so beautiful it hurt. Her two men had traveled a hard road, too, looking for so long for a woman who could accept them as they were. They had never compromised. They had held fast, looking for what they needed.

They'd decided what they needed was her. Jessa's heart skipped. She was taking a leap. They could decide tomorrow that they'd rather return to their dangerous lives. They could decide they didn't really want her, after all. The world could end. Any number of things could happen, but she only had control over what she did. At the end of her life, she would only be able to look back on what she had done and find some modicum of pride. She would be damn proud that she'd stepped out of her shell and tried to be brave. She would be proud that she'd loved with her whole heart. She would love them until she took her last breath. Then she would love them more.

"Come to bed."

The rocking stopped.

"Jessa?" Cole froze, stared.

It was funny that other people couldn't tell them apart. It was so obvious to her. "Are you going to make love to me or are you just going to rock our son and say my name?"

"You didn't want us earlier." Cole stood.

Burke remained rocking, as though he wasn't sure what to do about the baby in his arms. "We should talk about this."

"I still don't want to talk. I want to make love. I want to lose myself in your arms." She grinned, the love she felt for them suddenly light and buoyant. It was crazy, but jumping off the edge of her cliff of fear felt…good.

"I love you both," she murmured. "I want us to be a family, and I won't force you to move. I can handle it here in Texas. I can two-step and eat steaks." There was one thing she was immovable on. "But you're finding a new secretary."

Cole nodded, easing closer. "Fuck, yeah. We kind of left her tied up and gagged. I'm sure someone is going to find her tomorrow. They have a maid staff at the motel, right?"

"You left her tied up in our motel room?" Jessa stared, stunned.

Burke flushed. "Yeah. I wasn't sure what else to do. Maybe we should call someone."

Maybe they should stop what they were doing and call someone to help out the woman who had kept them apart and tried to have her killed and attempted to steal one of her men? Hilary could rot...until the police came for her. "Put Caleb to bed, Burke. His parents need to be together."

Burke stood, his movements slow and steady. He would get more sure of himself, of that she had no doubt, but she would always remember this time when he treated Caleb like a precious, fragile gift.

Cole pulled a blanket over the sleeping baby's body, then both men turned to her. She backed up, drawing them into her room.

Her nipples tightened. They had gone from loving fathers to dominant lovers in a heartbeat. Both men stared at her before looking at each other, their conversation going silent.

"I get so nervous when you do that 'silent twin mind-meld' thing. What did you two just decide?"

Burke's lips curved up in a sexy smile as he tugged his shirt off and revealed his magnificent chest. "How we're going to make love to you."

"Shouldn't I have a say in that?" She sent them a

saucy grin.

"Never," Cole replied. "We're the Masters in the bedroom. You're the queen outside, but here we want our precious submissive who takes us every way we want her."

Cole shoved his jeans off, his cock bobbing up, begging for attention. Beside him, Burke stood naked as well, his body ready for whatever they had silently agreed upon.

She stared for a moment at her men, loving the identical tats on their biceps and the way their movements mirrored each other. She loved everything about them, including the way they mastered her in the bedroom. When she pushed the straps of her gown off her shoulders, it pooled at her feet. Jessa stepped out and dropped to her knees in front of them, pushing her knees out, straightening her spine. She was offering herself to them—her pussy, and her breasts, her heart and her soul.

"Beautiful," Cole said, placing a hand on her head. "You are the most beautiful woman I've ever seen."

With them, she felt beautiful. No amount of makeup or designer clothes could recreate the way she felt when her men told her she was lovely.

"Jessa Wade, we're getting married in three days," Burke proclaimed, taking her hand and lifting her to her feet. He hauled her into his arms, cradling her close, then looked down, his eyes shining. "That's how long it takes to get a license and fill out the paperwork. None of this 'living together' crap. We have a son. We have to be respectable."

She smiled as he climbed on the bed, placing her in the center. "We will be as respectable as one woman and two men can possibly be."

"I'm not going to be respectable at all tonight, baby. So you should be ready for that." Cole opened the drawer of the nightstand. He sighed as he pulled out a tube of lubricant. "I can always count on the James gang. I don't see any condoms though. I'll go get my bag."

She shook her head. "I don't want them. I want another baby, one we all watch grow together. I want Caleb to have a brother or a sister."

Burke's hands tightened around her. "Sweetheart, we want that, too. We want that so badly. Are you sure you're ready now?"

She'd barely finished nodding when Burke kissed her, his mouth covering hers, tongue seeking. She wrapped her arms around him and let her tongue slide against his. He cupped her breasts in his warm hands, his legs tangling with hers. Burke rolled on top of her, pressing her into the mattress. He kissed her until they were both breathless.

And then it was Cole kissing her as Burke moved down her body. Burke started suckling her nipples as Cole dominated her mouth. She had a brother on each side, surrounding her, enveloping her. Loving her. Their hands were everywhere. Their mouths caressed her, lavishing attention on her. They whispered to her, telling her how beautiful she was, how much they loved her. They wrapped her in desire and passion and love.

Jessa clung to them, allowing them access to her body and soul. She opened herself completely, not letting fear or worry or the past between them. With every touch, she could tell they'd put it behind them, too. For once, she was the canvas, and they painted her with kisses and caresses. They adorned her with devotion.

"I love you." Jessa didn't hold back. She never would again. She would build her life with these men, not regretting anything. They'd struggled and suffered, but their love was stronger for having survived the hurt.

"I love you, Jessa," Cole said.

"I love you, our beautiful bride." Burke pulled her back into his arms, fusing their mouths together, rolling them over. "Ride me."

He maneuvered her until she was astride his hips, his big cock thrusting up toward her. She was slick and ready for him.

"Take me, sweetheart." Burke pressed up, pushing his thick cock deep inside in a single strong thrust.

She gasped as he filled her. Her cunt was already clamping down on him, but they weren't done yet. Cole pressed a hand to her back, lightly pushing her against Burke's broad chest. Her nipples brushed his fevered skin, making her shiver all over again.

"You feel so fucking good, sweetheart. I missed you so much." His hands gripped her hips, holding her still while Cole began to prepare her. She shivered as he coated her with lube and began pressing his finger in to open her wide for his pleasure.

"We were lost without you," Cole murmured, pulling his finger out and pressing something far larger against the rosette of her ass.

She'd been lost, too. She grasped at Burke, forcing herself to hold still as Cole fucked her ass in short, smooth thrusts. He gained ground with each pass until finally he slid his hot length deep inside her. Tears pricked her eyes at the sublime feeling of completeness and joy that infused her. It didn't matter that her house had been destroyed. It didn't matter where they lived at all. Right now, with them, oh, this was home. Finally.

They took her, their movements a bit slow and rough, but perfectly timed. Burke thrust up as Cole retreated, his cock dragging over the nerves of her ass, making her moan. Her breath merged with Burke's as pleasure washed through her. Cole nipped a tender chain of kisses across her shoulder as he thrust deep. Burke pulled on her hips, grinding on her clitoris as he hit that perfect spot that sent her soaring. Jessa gave up. She let the orgasm take her and rode the powerful explosion of ecstasy, rocking back and forth between her men with a keening cry. Cole shouted out behind her, and Burke thrust up, his body tensing, shaking. She was filled with them, each giving her his come in a hot wash that started another wave of pure joy. Jessa's body was wracked with it, her every muscle suffused with a delicious tension, followed by a happy lethargy as she fell forward, and her head found Burke's chest. He cuddled her for a moment, catching his breath.

Cole slipped from her body, rolling off and pulling her with him. She was in the middle, their big bodies surrounding her, nestling her. Warm and safe and loved—that's exactly how she felt. Happy tears burned her eyes. This was what she'd missed, fulfillment, peace, adoration.

"Oh, baby, we love you. We won't ever leave you again," Cole said, his voice thick with emotion. "We promise."

"Not ever again, Jessa." Burke's hand caressed her cheek, brushing away her tears. "You won't regret giving us another chance. We're in this for life."

"Forever," Cole vowed.

Forever just might be long enough for her.

With a little smile of contentment, Jessa fell asleep between them. Her world was finally complete.

\* \* \* \*

Read on for excerpts from Shayla Black, Lexi Blake, and Eliza Gayle.

# Their Virgin Concubine
## Masters of Ménage, Book 3
### Now Available!

*The country of Bezakistan—renowned for its wealth and the beauty of its deserts*

Piper Glen is thrilled when Rafe and Kade al Mussad ask her to visit their country on a business trip. Madly attracted to both, the virginal secretary knows that neither of her intensely handsome bosses desires her. But every night she dreams of having them both in her bed, fulfilling her every need.

Rafe and Kade have finally found the perfect woman in Piper. Sweet and funny. Intelligent and strong. Before they can reveal their feelings, the brothers must fulfill an ancient tradition. Every sheikh must steal his bride and share her with his brothers. They have thirty days to convince Piper to love them all forever.

*The country of Bezakistan—notorious for its danger…*

Sheikh Talib al Mussad knows his villainous cousin seeks to take his throne. If Talib and his brothers fail to convince the beautiful Piper to love them, all will be lost. After meeting Piper, he knows he would risk everything to possess her heart.

Khalil al Bashir has long coveted his cousin's rule. Without a bride to seal their birthright, his every wish will come true. If Piper falls for them, he will lose everything but Piper can't love them if she's dead…

* * * *

Piper stared boldly at the sheikh. He was a gorgeous predator, every line of his body hard but graceful. And he was definitely interested in her. If she'd been worried he was just going along for his brothers' sake, his erection put that idea out of her mind. His cock stood straight up, thick and long, reaching almost to his navel.

"I hope you like what you see. My brothers are right. This is for you." He wrapped his hand around his cock, stroking from base to bulb. Tal's cock swelled, growing thicker and longer right before her eyes. "Now show me what belongs to me and mine."

She started a bit as she felt a hand on her zipper.

Kade steadied her or she would have fallen. He righted her, holding her hand. "Don't be afraid. Let us show him. This is tradition."

"You traditionally show off naked women to your brother?" She sometimes didn't understand this place. And she wondered just how much stuff they made up to get her to do things she otherwise never would.

Kade slowly dragged the zipper of her dress down, every inch a big step toward that moment when he and Rafe would unveil her. "Yes, we do. When brothers take a concubine, the younger ones present her to the eldest. She is a gift to be shared."

"Concubine." She knew the word. Mistress. Lover. It seemed so much heavier than girlfriend or momentary hookup.

"Yes, for now," Rafe said. "Relax and let us show

246

you off. We think you are beyond beautiful, Piper. Let us share this lovely view with Talib."

The straps of her dress slipped over her shoulders as Kade finished unzipping the garment. She was suddenly grateful for all the spa treatments. Earlier in the day, they had buffed her skin to a dewy glow and taken care of those pesky extra hairs on her brow line. They'd also rid her of every single strand of hair below her neck. Sure, she'd screamed at the time, but now she could stand there with some small amount of confidence.

Her hands shook as the bodice of the dress was lowered.

"You selected her clothes, Rafe?" Tal's voice was deeper than before, his eyes on her. His hand continued to move up and down his cock in a slow, sexy rhythm.

"The dress is Marchesa. I love how the white makes her skin luminous. She did not care for the deep V-neck at first, but it shows off her lovely breasts."

He'd known she'd been worried about the dress? It was so much sexier than anything she'd ever worn.

"She looked stunning. But every man in the room was staring at her breasts." Tal frowned, sitting up, his eyes accusatory.

Rafe chuckled, kissing the curve of her shoulder. "Perhaps, but they did not touch. They can look at our beautiful concubine all they like and merely wish they were the ones in her bed."

"But the minute they touch, well, we have traditions for that as well," Kade promised.

Piper was pretty sure she wouldn't like those traditions. They likely involved blood.

"Show me the corset," Tal commanded.

The lines of the dress hadn't allowed for a traditional bra. She'd squeezed into a white satin and silk corset that forced her breasts up like ripe melons being displayed for sale.

"I strove for perfection on the lingerie." Rafe pushed the dress off her hips, and Kade whisked it away. "La Perla. I think you can agree she looks exceedingly lovely."

She looked half naked. More than half, actually. She was left in her corset and a tiny white thong, along with stark white stilettos that elongated her legs.

She gasped as Rafe's hand cupped her backside, his fingers snapping the thong.

Tal stood, staring down at her. "She glows like a pearl. You have an eye for dressing her, brother. But I need to see more. Show me her breasts."

She felt caught. Trapped by Rafe and Kade's hands. Captive to the dirty promise in Talib's dark eyes.

Cool air caressed her skin, causing her nipples to tighten even before Kade and Rafe went to work on the corset. In mere seconds, they were lifting it away from her, and she was left in nothing but a tiny thong and her shoes. She bit her bottom lip, forcing herself not to cover her breasts with her hands.

Tal simply stared, his eyes on her nipples. He didn't move toward her, just stroked his hard cock and looked. "They are beautiful. Like the woman herself. Lift them for me."

Kade sighed from behind her, his arms sliding around her torso. His big hands cupped her breasts, lifting them up. His thumbs flicked her nipples, making her shake in his arms. Piper held her breath to trap in her moan.

"She has the loveliest breasts in the world, and they're so sensitive." Kade demonstrated by pinching them lightly and watching them bead tighter. "See. She responds beautifully."

Tal sat up and leaned closer, his fingers lightly touching her nipples. "Tell me something, beautiful girl. Have my brothers played with your breasts?"

"Yes." The word came out on a breathy moan. She had two sets of hands on her. While Kade's lifted her breasts, Tal's fingers continued to toy with her so-sensitive nipples. He stroked lightly at first and then caught them between his thumbs and forefingers, twisting just a bit.

"Did you like it? Did you like it when my brothers licked and sucked your nipples?"

She was shaking, a dizzying ache coursing through her. Embarrassment rapidly drowned in a sea of want. Being put on display should make her angry, but nothing about this felt wrong. In fact, the hunger in Talib's eyes made everything about this feel good and right. "I loved it when they touched me."

Rafe stood behind Tal, watching with a smile on his face. "Our pretty concubine has trouble with dirty words, brother."

His fingers tightened, making her moan again. "Does she now? Tell me what they did to your breasts, Piper. And your pussy. I want to see that, too. I think, perhaps, my brothers made a meal of you. I might need a taste."

Kade immediately pushed the thong off her hips as Tal stepped back, the loss of his touch making her cold. Kade held her hand as she stepped out of the thong, and

Tal took in a long breath, his smile dangerous and predatory. Then she wasn't cold anymore. The raging heat in his stare made her shiver and swelter with need.

"Rafe, you've been at work here, too. That is a lovely pussy. Spread your legs, Piper. I can already see those lips are wet. I want to see them as you tell me the tale."

They expected her to talk? She was lucky to be standing.

Tal edged closer and loomed over her, a patient expression on his face. "I need to make something clear. When we are in the bedroom, you follow my rules. I won't hurt you, but I will spank that gorgeous ass if you don't obey. Indulge me. I love to give a good spanking."

"He does," Kade affirmed. His hand slipped to her backside, cupping a single cheek. "He would love to get this ass a sweet pink. And he'll make you love it. Before we're done with you, you'll love many things you can only dream of now. We'll have you bound and blindfolded so all you can concentrate on is the sensation of our tongues and our cocks. And we're going to make you love it when we're all inside you. But not tonight. Tonight should be gentle. Don't tempt Tal's beast tonight. Give him what he wants. Tell him about our night together."

Spankings and bondage? She couldn't say she was completely terrified by the thought, but daunted at the moment, yes. She just needed to get through her first time. Right now, Tal wanted words.

"It will be all right." Rafe's soft tone soothed her. He winked at her as he dispensed with his shirt before working his way out of his slacks. "I'll help you. We were in the plane, and Piper kissed me. I love the way you kiss."

Nervous laughter bubbled up. "I didn't think I was very good at it."

Rafe strode over to her. "Well, let me remind you."

# Theirs To Cherish
## Wicked Lovers, Book 8
### By Shayla Black
### Now Available!

*The perfect place for a woman on the run to disappear...*

Accused of a horrific murder she didn't commit, former heiress Callie Ward has been a fugitive since she was sixteen—until she found the perfect hideout, Club Dominion. The only problem is she's fallen for the club's Master, Mitchell Thorpe, who keeps her at arm's length. Little does she know that his reasons for not getting involved have everything to do with his wounded heart...and his consuming desire for her.

*To live out her wildest fantasies...*

Enter Sean Kirkpatrick, a Dom who's recently come to Dominion and taken a pointed interest in Callie. Hoping to make Thorpe jealous, she submits to Sean one shuddering sigh at a time. It isn't long before she realizes she's falling for him too. But the tender lover who's slowly seducing her body and earning her trust isn't who he claims...

*And to fall in love.*

When emotions collide and truths are exposed, Sean is willing to risk all to keep Callie from slipping through his fingers. But he's not the only man looking to stake a claim. Now Callie is torn between Sean and Thorpe, and though she's unsure whom she can trust, she'll have to surrender her body and soul to both—if she wants to elude a killer...

\* \* \* \*

Callie trembled as she lay back on the padded table and Sean Kirkpatrick's strong fingers wrapped around her cuffed wrist, guiding it back to the bindings above her head.

"I don't know if I can do this," she murmured.

He paused, then drew in a breath as if he sought patience. "Breathe, lovely."

That gentle, deep brogue of his native Scotland brought her peace. His voice both aroused and soothed her, and she tried to let those feelings wash through her. "Can you do that for me?" he asked.

His fingers uncurled from her wrist, and he grazed the inside of her outstretched arm with his knuckles. As always, his touch was full of quiet strength. He made her ache. She shivered again, this time for an entirely different reason.

"I'll try."

Sean shook his head, his deep blue eyes seeming to see everything she tried to hide inside. That penetrating stare scared the hell out of her. What did he see when he looked at her? How much about the real her had he pieced together?

The thought made her panic. No one could know her secret. No one. She'd kept it from everyone, even Thorpe, during her four years at Dominion. She'd finally found a place where she felt safe, comfortable. Of course she'd have to give it up someday, probably soon. She always did. But please, not yet.

Deep breath. Don't panic. Sean wants your submission, not your secrets.

"You'll need to do better than try. You've been 'trying' for over six months," he reminded her gently. "Do you think I'd truly hurt you?"

No. Sean didn't seem to have a violent bone in his body. He wasn't a sadist. He never gripped her harshly. He never even raised his voice. She'd jokingly thought of him as the sub whisperer because he pushed her boundaries with a gentleness she found both irresistible and insidious. Certainly, he'd dragged far more out of her than any other man had. Tirelessly, he'd worked to earn her trust. Callie felt terrible that she could never give it, not when doing so could be fatal.

Guilt battered her. She should stop wasting his time.

"I know you wouldn't," she assured, blinking up at him, willing him to understand.

"Of course not." He pressed his chest over hers, leaning closer to delve into her eyes.

Callie couldn't resist lowering her lids, shutting out the rest of the world. Even knowing she shouldn't, she sank into the soft reassurance of his kiss. Each brush of his lips over hers soothed and aroused. Every time he touched her, her heart raced. Her skin grew tight. Her nipples hardened. Her pussy moistened and swelled. Her heart ached. Sean Kirkpatrick would be so easy to love.

As his fingers filtered into her hair, cradling her scalp, she exhaled and melted into his kiss—just for a sweet moment. It was the only one she could afford.

A fierce yearning filled her. She longed for him to

peel off his clothes, kiss her with that determination she oft en saw stamped into his eyes, and take her with the single-minded fervor she knew he was capable of. But in the months since he'd collared her, he'd done nothing more than stroke her body, tease her, and grant her orgasms when he thought she'd earned them. She hadn't let him fully restrain her. And he hadn't yet taken her to bed.

Not knowing the feel of him deep inside her, of waiting and wanting until her body throbbed relentlessly, was making her buckets full of crazy.

After another skillful brush of his lips, Sean ended the kiss and lifted his head, breathing hard. She clung, not ready to let him go. How had he gotten under her skin so quickly? His tenderness filled her veins like a drug. The way he had addicted Callie terrified her.

"I want you. Sean, please . . ." She damn near wept.

With a broad hand, he swept the stray hair from her face. Regret softened his blue eyes before he ever said a word. "If you're not ready to trust me as your Dom, do you think you're ready for me as a lover? I want you completely open to me before we take that step. All you have to do is trust me, lovely."

Callie slammed her eyes shut. This was so fucking pointless. She wanted to trust Sean, yearned to give him everything—devotion, honesty, faith. Her past ensured that she'd never give any of those to anyone. But he had feelings for her. About that, she had no doubt. They'd grown just as hers had, unexpectedly, over time, a fledgling limb morphing into a sturdy vine that eventually created a bud just waiting to blossom . . . or die.

She knew which. They could never have more than

this faltering Dom/sub relationship, destined to perish in a premature winter.

She should never have accepted his collar, not when she should be trying to keep her distance from everyone. The responsible choice now would be to call her safe word, walk out, quit him. Release them both from this hell. Never look back.

For the first time in nearly a decade, Callie worried that she might not have the strength to say good-bye.

What was wrong with her tonight? She was too emotional. She needed to pull up her big-girl panties and snap on her bratty attitude, pretend that nothing mattered. It was how she'd coped for years. But she couldn't seem to manage that with Sean.

"You're up in your head, instead of here with me," he gently rebuked her.

Another dose of guilt blistered her. "Sorry, Sir."

Sean sighed heavily, stood straight, then held out his hand to her. "Come with me."

Callie winced. If he intended to stop the scene, that could only mean he wanted to talk. These sessions where he tried to dig through her psyche became more painful than the sexless nights she spent in unfulfilled longing under his sensual torture.

Swallowing down her frustration, she dredged up her courage, then put her hand in his.

Holding her in a steady grip, Sean led her to the far side of Dominion's dungeon, to a bench in a shadowed corner. As soon as she could see the rest of the room, Callie felt eyes on her, searing her skin. With a nonchalant glance, she looked at the others scening around them, but they seemed lost in their own world of pleasure, pain, groans, sweat, and need. A lingering sweep of the room revealed another sight that had the power to drop her to her knees. Thorpe in the shadows. Staring. At her with Sean. His expression wasn't one of disapproval exactly . . . but he wasn't pleased.

# Dungeon Royale
## Masters and Mercenaries, Book 6
### By Lexi Blake
### Now Available!

*An agent broken*

MI6 agent Damon Knight prided himself on always being in control. His missions were executed with cold, calculating precision. His club, The Garden, was run with an equally ordered and detached decadence. But his perfect world was shattered by one bullet, fired from the gun of his former partner. That betrayal almost cost him his life and ruined his career. His handlers want him to retire, threatening to revoke his license to kill if he doesn't drop his obsession with a shadowy organization called The Collective. To earn their trust, he has to prove himself on a unique assignment with an equally unusual partner.

*A woman tempted*

Penelope Cash has spent her whole life wanting more. More passion. More adventure. But duty has forced her to live a quiet life. Her only excitement is watching the agents of MI6 as they save England and the world. Despite her training, she's only an analyst. The closest she is allowed to danger and intrigue is in her dreams, which are often filled with one Damon Knight. But everything changes when the woman assigned to pose as Damon's submissive on his latest mission is incapacitated. Penny is suddenly faced with a decision. Stay in her safe little world or risk her life, and her heart, for Queen and country.

*An enemy revealed*

With the McKay-Taggart team at their side, Damon and Penny hunt an international terrorist across the great cities of Northern Europe. Playing the part of her Master, Damon begins to learn that under Penny's mousy exterior is a passionate submissive, one who just might lay claim to his cold heart. But when Damon's true enemy is brought out of the shadows, it might be Penny who pays the ultimate price.

\* \* \* \*

"I'm going to kiss you now, Penelope."

"What?"

"You seem to have an enormously hard time understanding me today. We're going to have to work on our communication skills." Damon moved right between her legs, spreading her knees and making a place for himself there. One minute she was utterly gobsmacked by the chaos he'd brought into her life in a couple of hours' time, and the next, she couldn't manage to breathe. He invaded her space, looming over her. Despite the fact that she was sitting on the counter, he still looked down at her. "You said yes. That means you're mine, Penelope. You're my partner and my submissive. I take care of what's mine."

She swallowed, forcing herself to look into those stormy eyes of his. He was so close, she could smell the scent of his aftershave, feel the heat his big body gave off. "For the mission."

"I don't know about that," he returned, his voice deepening. "If this goes well, I get to go back out in the field. It's always good to have a cover. Men are less threatening when they have a woman with them. If you like fieldwork, there's no reason you can't come with me. Especially if you're properly trained. Tell me how much your siblings know."

She shook her head before finally realizing what he was asking. His fingers worked their way into her hair, smoothing it back, forcing her to keep eye contact with him. "Oh, about work, you mean. Everyone in my family thinks I work for Reeding Corporation in their publishing arm. They think I translate books."

The Reeding Corporation was one of several companies that fronted for SIS. When she'd hired on, she'd signed documentation that stated she would never expose who she truly worked for.

"Excellent. If they research me, they'll discover I'm an executive at Reeding. We've been having an affair for the last three months. You were worried about your position at the company and the fact that I'm your superior, but I transferred to another department and now we're free to be open about our relationship."

"I don't know that they'll believe we're lovers."

"Of course, they will. I'm very persuasive, love. Now, I'm going to kiss you and I'm going to put my hand in your knickers. You are wearing knickers, aren't you?"

"Of course."

He shuddered. "Not anymore. Knickers are strictly forbidden. I told you I would likely get into your knickers, but what I really meant was I can't tolerate them and you're not to wear them at all anymore. I've done you the enormous service of making it easy on you and tossing out the ones you had in the house."

His right hand brushed against her breast. The nipple responded by peaking immediately, as if it were a magnet drawn to Damon's skin.

"You can't toss my knickers out, Damon. And you can't put your hand there. We're in the ladies' room for heaven's sake."

"Here's the first rule, love. Don't tell me what I can't do." His mouth closed over hers, heat flashing through her system.

His mouth was sweet on hers, not an outright assault at first. This was persuasion. Seduction. His lips teased at hers, playing and coaxing.

And his hand made its way down, skimming across her waist to her thigh.

"Let me in, Penelope." He whispered the words against her mouth.

Drugged. This was what it felt like to be drugged. She'd been tipsy before, but no wine had ever made her feel as out of control as Damon's kiss.

Out of control and yet oddly safe. Safe enough to take a chance.

On his next pass, she opened for him, allowing him in, and the kiss morphed in a heartbeat from sweet to overpowering.

She could practically feel the change in him. He surged in, a marauder gaining territory. His tongue commanded hers, sliding over and around, his left hand tangling in her hair and getting her at the angle he wanted. Captured. She felt the moment he turned from seduction to Dominance, and now she understood completely why they capitalized the word. Damon didn't merely kiss her. She'd been kissed before, little brushes of lips to hers, fumblings that ended in embarrassment, long attempts at bringing up desire. This wasn't a kiss. This was possession.

He'd said she belonged to him for the course of the mission, and now she understood what he meant. He meant to invade every inch of her life, putting his stamp on her. If she proceeded, he would take over. He would run her life and she would be forced to fight him for every inch of freedom she might have.

"That's right, love. You touch me. I want you to touch me. If you belong to me, then my body is yours, too."

She hadn't realized her hands were moving. She'd cupped his bum even as his fingers slid along the band of her knickers, under and over, sliding along her female flesh.

He'd said exactly the right thing. He hadn't made her self-conscious. He'd told her he would give as good as he got. It wasn't some declaration of love, but she'd had that before and it proved false. Damon Knight was offering her something different. He was offering her the chance to explore without shame.

# Tucker's Fall
## Purgatory Masters
### By Eliza Gayle
### Now Available!

Scandalized professor Maggie Cisco returns to her hometown to lick her wounds and reconsider her future. Her years of personal and professional research into the BDSM lifestyle has landed her in jail, in divorce court and now in the headlines of more newspapers than she cares to count. The worst of all? The entire debacle is being blamed on a bestselling book she hasn't even read!

Just when she thinks her only solution is a tell all memoir, a snowstorm puts her in the path of stunningly handsome, insanely rich and equally intense, Tucker Lewis.

Tucker remembers Maggie well. They once shared a mind-numbing kiss at the annual St. Mary's carnival when her boyfriend wasn't looking. No stranger to scandal, he looks past public opinion to the submissive craving a master's touch and decides then and there what he wants. He's going after Maggie and her heart's kinkiest desires.

Unfortunately, no amount of money can change the sins of the past and when they're certain they know everything there is to know about each other, one discovers a secret they aren't prepared for.

\* \* \* \*

Tucker Lewis stared into the crowd and wondered when it would all end. He tightened his grip on the shot of Jamieson and brought the glass to his lips. Across the bar and generous play space, fake smoke, dancers in chains, and throngs of half naked partiers filled the club. The intense edge of the Lords of Acid music pulsed in rhythm with his heartbeat and the occasional scream of a submissive from the far side of the room fit right in with his dark mood. For better or worse this was the place he'd needed to be tonight.

Purgatory had come to be in a different life and the longer he sat here watching the scene around him; the less he believed he belonged. Of course his self-imposed exile hadn't helped much. He'd been riding high on life on borrowed time and didn't even know it. All it took was a simple house fire to bring his world crashing down.

"Wow, as I live and breath. Is that you, Tuck?"

Yanked from his mournful thoughts, Tucker focused on the man standing in front of him. Tall and imposing he wore black leather that emphasized a gleaming bald head that drew women of all ages. It didn't surprise him his old friend from better days and one of the best damn rope riggers on the planet, stood there with a smug grin.

"Fuck you, Leo."

"C'mon, Tucker. You know I'm not your type. But maybe this one is." Leo tugged on a leash he'd been holding and a very pretty redhead cautiously stepped out from behind him. Even with her eyes cast down, it didn't take much for Tucker to recognize her nervousness. Her hands intertwined with each other repeatedly as she shifted her weight from foot to foot.

Long, thick hair brushed the tops of ample breasts

that were barely hidden by a thin, black nightie that stopped before her thighs began. But it was the thick leather collar at her neck, branded with two names that stood out to him.

"I see things have changed for you since I last visited."

"Tends to happen when you disappear from the face of the earth." Leo clapped his shoulder and took a seat on the bench next to him and his lovely submissive went to her knees on the floor at Leo's feet.

Tucker tried to ignore the slight pang inside him. It had been a long time since a submissive had caught his eye but that didn't mean the desire to have one of his own had completely disappeared.

"Will you introduce me to your lovely?"

Leo beamed. "Katie, say hello to Master Tucker. He's an old friend of mine."

With what looked like some reluctance, the little subbie lifted her head and met his gaze. "Hello, Master Tucker. It is nice to meet you." Immediately her eyes lowered back to the floor.

"You'll have to excuse Katie this evening. She's had a tough time with her commitments lately so Quinn and I have decided to devote this entire week to her correction." Leo stroked his pet's hair and brushed her cheek when she turned toward him.

The pang inside him clamored louder. The affection between Master and submissive was so obvious it was difficult for Tucker not to experience some degree of jealousy. Although settling down had never been in his previous plans. "No need to excuse her. I completely understand." Maybe it was time to get back into the scene. He could meet a willing submissive here at the club and work out some of the kinks that had plagued his art this week.

"You thinking about rejoining us? Maybe some play tonight?"

Tucker shrugged, amazed Leo had read his mind. Tucker's body warred with his mind for control. Part of him definitely needed to move on, but the other—well, he wasn't so sure.

"I'd be happy to offer Katie for service tonight. I think it would do her some good. She needs to get her head in the right place for everything she will be put through this week. What do you say?"

Tucker considered the offer while staring at the top of the pretty sub's head. She'd not uttered a word or made a move except for the tiny shudder he'd detected along her shoulder line when Leo offered her services. She impressed him and that wasn't an easy thing to do these days.

He stood from his seat and positioned himself, legs apart, in front of Katie. Leaning down he cupped her chin and tilted her head back until her gaze met his. "I have a feeling I would enjoy your service very much."

She swallowed before a small smile bowed her lips. Whatever trouble she'd been having it was obvious how much she needed whatever Leo wanted to give her.

"It would be my pleasure, Sir."

A part of him very much wanted to enjoy Katie. To take part in her discipline and let go of some of the stress he'd endured lately. His self-imposed exile needed to come to an end.

Tucker suppressed a smile. "You're such a good

girl."

Unfortunately, his body had a mind of its own and wouldn't cooperate like he wanted it to. Flashes of another lovely lady filled his head. A woman he'd not actually laid eyes on in over fifteen years. Maggie Cisco. Professor. A former wife. Closeted submissive.

While he couldn't actually confirm the submissive part yet, his gut told him the truth. She'd been studying BDSM for so long there was no doubt in his mind there was a hidden ache behind her research. And he refused to entertain the alternative of her being a top. That didn't match the Maggie he knew from high school at all. Sure people changed. He certainly had. But the fundamental core of who you are and what you need on a cellular level doesn't change in adulthood.

He'd bet every last dollar that Maggie possessed the heart of a true submissive longing to take her place at her Master's side and he'd waited her out long enough. Her reappearance eight weeks ago had sparked more than gossip. Something inside him akin to hunger had unfurled and dug in and refused to let go. His recovery had taken a very long time. Too long. Now he needed to rejoin the world, engage in a healthy if somewhat temporary relationship and he'd chosen Maggie to do it with. She didn't know it yet, but he was coming for her.

For more information, visit http://www.elizagayle.net/.

# About Shayla Black

Shayla Black (aka Shelley Bradley) is the New York Times and USA Today bestselling author of over 40 sizzling contemporary, erotic, paranormal, and historical romances produced via traditional, small press, independent, and audio publishing. She lives in Texas with her husband, munchkin, and one very spoiled cat. In her "free" time, she enjoys reality TV, reading and listening to an eclectic blend of music.

Shayla's books have been translated in about a dozen languages. RT Bookclub has nominated her for a Career Achievement award in erotic romance, twice nominated her for Best Erotic Romance of the year, as well as awarded her several Top Picks, and a KISS Hero Award. She has also received or been nominated for The Passionate Plume, The Holt Medallion, Colorado Romance Writers Award of Excellence, and the National Reader's Choice Awards.

A writing risk-taker, Shayla enjoys tackling writing challenges with every new book.

Connect with Shayla online:

Facebook: www.facebook.com/ShaylaBlackAuthor
Twitter: www.twitter.com/@shayla_black
Website: www.shaylablack.com

# About Lexi Blake

Lexi Blake lives in North Texas with her husband, three kids, and the laziest rescue dog in the world. She began writing at a young age, concentrating on plays and journalism. It wasn't until she started writing romance that she found success. She likes to find humor in the strangest places. Lexi believes in happy endings no matter how odd the couple, threesome or foursome may seem. She also writes contemporary Western ménage as Sophie Oak.

Connect with Lexi online:

Facebook: Lexi Blake
Twitter: twitter.com/authorlexiblake
Website: www.LexiBlake.net

Sign up for Lexi's free newsletter at www.LexiBlake.net

# Also from Shayla Black and Lexi Blake

## MASTERS OF MÉNAGE
Their Virgin Captive
Their Virgin's Secret
Their Virgin Concubine
Their Virgin Princess
Their Virgin Hostage
Their Virgin Secretary, Coming April 15, 2014

# Also from Shayla Black/Shelley Bradley

EROTIC ROMANCE

THE WICKED LOVERS
Wicked Ties
Decadent
Delicious
Surrender To Me
Belong To Me
"Wicked to Love" (e-novella)
Mine To Hold
"Wicked All The Way" (e-novella)
Ours To Love
Wicked and Dangerous
Forever Wicked
Theirs To Cherish

SEXY CAPERS
Bound And Determined
Strip Search
"Arresting Desire" – Hot In Handcuffs Anthology

DOMS OF HER LIFE
One Dom To Love
The Young And The Submissive

STAND ALONE
Naughty Little Secret (as Shelley Bradley)
"Watch Me" – Sneak Peek Anthology (as Shelley
Bradley)
Dangerous Boys And Their Toy
"Her Fantasy Men" – Four Play Anthology

# PARANORMAL ROMANCE

## THE DOOMSDAY BRETHREN
Tempt Me With Darkness
"Fated" (e-novella)
Seduce Me In Shadow
Possess Me At Midnight
"Mated" – Haunted By Your Touch Anthology
Entice Me At Twilight
Embrace Me At Dawn

## HISTORICAL ROMANCE (as Shelley Bradley)
The Lady And The Dragon
One Wicked Night
Strictly Seduction
Strictly Forbidden

## CONTEMPORARY ROMANCE (as Shelley Bradley)
A Perfect Match

# Also from Lexi Blake

## EROTIC ROMANCE

### Masters And Mercenaries
The Dom Who Loved Me
The Men With The Golden Cuffs
A Dom Is Forever
On Her Master's Secret Service
Sanctum: A Masters and Mercenaries Novella
Love and Let Die
Unconditional: A Masters and Mercenaries Novella
Dungeon Royale
Dungeon Games: A Masters and Mercenaries Novella,
*Coming May 13, 2014*
A View to a Thrill, *Coming August 19, 2014*

## CONTEMPORARY WESTERN ROMANCE

### Wild Western Nights
Leaving Camelot, *Coming Soon*

## URBAN FANTASY

### Thieves
Steal the Light
Steal the Day
Steal the Moon
Steal the Sun
Steal the Night, *Coming June 10, 2014*

Made in the USA
San Bernardino, CA
16 April 2014